BLOWFISH

Also by Kyung-Ran Jo

The French Optical Shop
Searching for the Elephant
Time for Baking Bread
Family Matter
Tongue

BLOWFISH

Kyung-Ran Jo

Translated from the Korean by
Chi-Young Kim

ASTRA HOUSE
NEW YORK

Copyright © 2010 by Kyung-Ran Jo

Translation copyright © 2025 by Chi-Young Kim

Originally published in 2010 by Munhakdongne as *Bokeo* in the Korean language

This book is published with the support of the Literature Translation Institute of Korea (LTI Korea).

All rights reserved. Copying or digitizing this book for storage, display, or distribution in any other medium is strictly prohibited.

For information about permission to reproduce selections from this book, please contact permissions@astrahouse.com.

This is a work of fiction. Names, characters, places, and incidents are products of the author's imagination or are used fictitiously. Any resemblance to actual events, locales, or persons, living or dead, is entirely coincidental.

Astra House

A Division of Astra Publishing House

astrahouse.com

Printed in the United States of America

Library of Congress Cataloging-in-Publication Data
Names: Cho, Kyŏng-nan, 1969- author. | Kim, Chi-Young, translator.
Title: Blowfish / Kyung-Ran Jo ; translated from the Korean by Chi-Young Kim.
Other titles: Pogŏ. English
Description: New York : Astra House, 2025. | Summary: "For readers of Han Kang and Sheila Heti, an atmospheric, melancholic novel about a successful sculptor who decides to commit suicide by artfully preparing and deliberately eating a lethal dish of blowfish"-- Provided by publisher.
Identifiers: LCCN 2025010207 (print) | LCCN 2025010208 (ebook) | ISBN 9781662601781 (hardback) | ISBN 9781662601798 (ebook)
Subjects: LCGFT: Novels.
Classification: LCC PL992.17.K96 P6413 2025 (print) | LCC PL992.17.K96 (ebook) | DDC 895.7/35--dc23/eng/20250314
LC record available at https://lccn.loc.gov/2025010207
LC ebook record available at https://lccn.loc.gov/2025010208

First edition

10 9 8 7 6 5 4 3 2 1

Design by Alissa Theodor

The text is set in Sabon MTPro.

The titles are set in Alegreya Sans.

I have wrestled with death. It is the most unexciting contest you can imagine. It takes place in an impalpable greyness, with nothing underfoot, with nothing around, without spectators, without clamor, without glory, without the great desire of victory, without the great fear of defeat, in a sickly atmosphere of tepid skepticism, without much belief in your own right, and still less in that of your adversary.

—Joseph Conrad, *Heart of Darkness*

Part One

1

IF SHE HAD TO LEAVE
A COLOR BEHIND

The city was the color of oxidized blood. She was standing before the sliding doors, which opened and closed, closed and opened. She didn't step outside, nor did she retreat back inside. It was almost sunset. She thought she'd heard something.

A faint purple-navy streak across the sky. A blackbird was flying by; maybe that was what had drawn her outside. The bird was an especially vivid black, flapping its wings with majestic conviction. She looked up as it glided away. It was four thirty in the afternoon, a Thursday. The breeze was coming from the west. In the high-rise across the way, lights turned on, one after another. The curved pale-gray wall around Gyeongbokgung Palace darkened. The city would glow brighter as the night grew darker. That was what a city was—a place so blinding that nobody could see you cry. She knew more about these things than most.

The gallery was so bright that her eyes burned. The light didn't shine down so much as it splintered coldly, like radium. People in their finest gathered under those lights. She didn't like coming to galleries. Often a gallery was filled with exaggerations, with falsities. This time she was hoping for something different. She wanted to fill the space with objects that were closer to the truth. With things that were true but couldn't be readily seen or felt, like silence. For all she knew, this was a quality impossible to capture in sculpture. It was time to do something she'd never done before. Before it was too late. The more challenging the better.

It was the opening of her exhibition.

The gallery was a rectangle. On the table in the middle of the room were silicone peels reminiscent of cast-off snakeskin. She had made the peels, which were seventy-nine by twenty-eight by twenty-four inches, by molding silicone to different parts of her body. She'd laid the pieces in the form of a person in repose and stitched some of the parts together with thread. When the small, bright overhead light was turned on, shadows appeared where the silicone overlapped, accentuating the contours. Skin left behind after someone had wriggled out. A needle sparkled in a sharp sliver of a line between the torn knee and thigh. For a moment she recalled the times she'd spent in her cold studio, repeatedly pasting and removing silicone from her body. She had called this work *Sew Me*. She had thought it would be more powerful to display the work on a regular table instead of in a display case. Some might see this table strewn with the remnants of a person and think it was a desk, while others could see it as a dining table. A display case would simply and inevitably bring a coffin to mind. She hadn't wanted it to be so obvious at first glance.

At the press preview, she had been asked about her invitation to exhibit at Tokyo's Mori Art Museum. An art collector in Tokyo expressed interest in purchasing one of her works at the conclusion of this show. It would be her biggest sale since last year's biennial. During the press preview, she felt calmer than she had ever been. Some journalists might write that her career had taken off or that she was becoming internationally known. It wouldn't matter if someone judged her exhibition a failure. *Only I can judge this show*, she thought. She had accomplished something difficult, something beyond her own expectations. When judging yourself, you are more accurate the more detached you are. She was unflappable, though she did feel a tad on edge all afternoon, worried that someone would ask her what she was working on next.

She didn't have the courage now to step back into the gallery. Wineglasses and champagne bottles glittering like crystals, subdued praises and smiles, lights shining down. The only thing missing was her.

The curator came up to ask if she was waiting for someone. She shook her head and said she was fine. The curator held out the master key for the elevator that led to the gallery director's top-floor office. The curator suggested she take a moment for herself in Director Hyeon's office and have a cup of tea. Director Hyeon's office was filled with art, a small gallery in itself. She liked sitting at the walnut George Nakashima dining table and looking out at the gentle slope of Inwangsan. She nodded at Director Hyeon, who was inside the gallery greeting guests. She wanted to stay where she was even though it was cold. Right now she wanted to stand here, just outside the doors. Or was it just inside the doors?

A gust of wind. Tears fell from her eyes, surprising her. She swiped them away with her palm. It was odd to cry at a happy moment. Her emotions flared; she was tense. She thought about it again. "I'm ready now," she murmured. "I'm done thinking. Thinking isn't acting. Right now should be the beginning of the best, most beautiful story. A story so short that it might end as soon as it begins." Her tears grew hotter, then stopped. Director

Hyeon was beckoning her over. She smoothed her clothes. She wasn't often the star of the show, but today would be the most spectacular of such times. She had made the right choice to wear a fitted white shirt without any jewelry. Her white shirt would gleam like chrome under the metallic lights. The most beautiful of all colors, if she had to leave a color behind.

2

YOU COULDN'T LEAVE CERTAIN OPENINGS YOU ENTERED

The window was closed tight. Even the curtains were drawn shut. What did people see the moment they opened their eyes in the morning? Was it good or bad that what he saw upon first waking was the window? Was it right or wrong? His mother knew that air came in through that window. And that heat went out through there. In fact, she might have known more about windows than he had. Every night she crept in while he was asleep to close it, though she knew he could not fall asleep without it open.

He would wait for her in the dark, feigning sleep. Sometimes he would actually fall asleep. Once he had opened his eyes to see her standing in the middle of his room in her baggy cotton pajamas and almost screamed. Not that she would have heard him. She would not have noticed, not even if he had grabbed her by her emaciated arms and shaken her. His mother stood marooned in a deep stillness. All she knew was that she was in her son's room and that he was still alive. The room brimmed with the faint rasp of his mother's breathing, his own breath quiet, as subdued as a crumpled sheet of paper unfurling on its own. It wasn't pleasant to suddenly see his mother's face in the middle of the night.

At one time he'd found windows alluring.

Some years ago he and Abe Kengo, who'd since become the CEO of the architecture firm, had accompanied the assistant director of TV Asahi to Konstantin Melnikov's house in Russia. It was for a documentary called *The History of World Architecture*. The house, which was in the heart of Moscow, resembled two white cylinders standing side by side. Melnikov was a key practitioner of Russian avant-garde architecture. The house was renowned for its orderly pattern of diamond-shaped windows. Even though sunlight was sparse in that northern country, light poured in from the third-floor windows. He'd had to lift a hand to shade his eyes. As with darkness, one needed time to get used to light. The dozens of hexagonal windows glittered like diamonds. They looked like doors through which wind and light and birds could come and go freely. They were what taught him about the beauty of architecture, not exteriors or large spaces or furniture or gardens. Later he would remember those windows. They'd gone to Melnikov's house in the fall of 2005. Everything changed the following March.

The icy January wind, the sunlight, the second-floor verandas on the building across the way, the black plastic bags that sometimes flew in by accident, the baby crows, the scent of incense. Their neighborhood was home to Tokyo's largest cemetery, as well as more than seventy temples of various sizes. The smell of incense wafted in at all times of the day. So many things entered and exited through his window. His mother would not acknowledge that light was one of the things that could. He wanted to visit Melnikov's house with her, holding her frail hand in his. His mother never went anywhere. When she finally left his room, he would get up, open the window again, and fall asleep.

He braced himself against the windowsill, his toes curled. He gazed down at the children wearing backpacks, walking in a neat row, and at the bicycles whizzing down narrow alleys. The morning rush. He had to hurry if he didn't want to be late. What would people think if they saw him right now? In his pajamas and his face dark with stubble, hands gripping the windowsill, lips pressed into a thin line. He could see himself as if in a mirror. He'd stopped trying to convince his mother long ago—he couldn't refute the fact that this narrow rectangular window was an opening through which a man's life could leave. If one could enter an opening, one could leave through it, too. But not always—sometimes you couldn't leave certain openings you entered, and then you would live there forever.

His neck was stiff. He could stand there all day long. He felt a chill, almost as if something small with veins and seeds, like a leaf or an apple, had lightly, cautiously grazed his forehead. He needed to figure out what it was, this restlessness that skittered through him. It was eight. He had a meeting at Tokyo University of the Arts at nine thirty. He gripped the air to make a fist, then let go.

3

The many things Baek had given her

She didn't have all that much to prepare. She went over the list in her mind, but it was very short. She didn't have to notify or see anyone. She didn't have a cat or a dog or even a goldfish. Given how long she'd thought and gone back and forth about it, she was embarrassed by how ridiculously simple it had been in the end to make the decision. The opening was over, and there was nothing more she had to do for the show. She did have a magazine interview scheduled this afternoon at the gallery. She brewed a cup of coffee and headed outside, up the stairs. She probably spent most of her time on the roof instead of in her half-basement studio.

She had been shivering under her thick coat the first time Baek had shown her this place. The temperature had dropped below freezing. Baek had driven them past Tongin Market and climbed a winding alley so narrow that it barely fit a single car. Looking out the window, she figured it would be hard to find her way up here again, even in daylight. They seemed to be going up a tall, never-ending mountain. They stopped in an empty lot; it looked like a puddle in the dark. Baek turned off the car. She hadn't wanted to get out. She hated the cold. Baek got out first. They weren't in an empty lot, actually, but a church parking lot at the top of the hill. Just down from the church was a house; they could see its roof covered in green waterproof paint. She spotted a wooden swing on the roof and thought maybe kids lived there. She watched Baek unlock the front gates of the house. Baek had shown her a lot of things. She figured this would be one of them. At the time she didn't know the house would become hers. And until that night, she had never accepted anything Baek had wanted to give her. That was the only thing about their relationship she was proud of.

His hands in his pockets, Baek had walked up to her. She could see the brightly lit N Seoul Tower to the southwest, and the highrise in Naesu-dong where they'd just had dinner, and the logo on the newspaper headquarters in Gwanghwamun where Baek worked. She was looking out at Seoul's nightscape from the highest, most secluded spot. An inexplicable anticipation filled her heart. Her face burned. She shivered.

"There's a half-basement space that should be pretty useful," Baek had said, his breath visible.

She had wondered what he had meant.

Even though it was partially underground, the space received plenty of natural light, and it was at least twice the size of the Sangsu-dong studio she had, up until then, been sharing with two painters. She had realized she'd already decided to live here when she found herself thinking that, by taking this space, she'd have to end her relationship with Baek.

Now her coffee was cold and bitter. She sat on the swing and pushed her heels against the ground. The rusted links squeaked as the swing swayed slowly, back and forth. Coffee spilled on her thighs. In Naesu-dong, the alleys and houses were clustered together as if leaning on one another's shoulders. When work wasn't going well, she came on this roof and wondered about all the strangers living in these houses, stacked together like a beehive. When she felt lonely, too. From here she could see all the way to Hongeun-dong, where her father and her aunt ran their businesses. If she couldn't, maybe she would visit them more.

    This house was the most practical of the many things Baek had given her. This house, where Baek had grown up, where she now made things with clay and silicone, then destroyed and remade them. She shook her head. Emotions blurred judgment. She would inevitably leave traces of herself in this house, the most significant being her body. She might need to see Baek one last time. Should she tell him what she needed to do in this house? Did she want her words to sound like an apology? She remembered why her gaze had been drawn to him at their first meeting, this man who had been standing off by himself, apart from the crowd. A man who was more pessimistic than optimistic, a man who wouldn't be shocked even if something bad, something terrible, happened. That had been her first impression of him. Her legs were damp; the coffee stains looked like footprints left hastily behind.

The Seoul Art Foundation called as she arrived at the gallery.

    After hanging up, she realized that her plans may need to be delayed, which meant she might not need to apologize to Baek after all. She was standing still, suspended between the panels of the revolving doors. "Is this sudden change of plans the right thing?" she asked the air. Behind her, someone pushed the revolving doors, causing them to move. The glass panels turned, and she stepped out, as resolutely as she did whenever she made up her mind about something.

4

MEETING HER FOR THE FIRST TIME

It was a snowless, windless January; the temperature rarely dipped below zero. Everything seemed suspended in a pale, achromatic color. At this time of year, expressionless faces looked even more rigid. With the dawn of the new year, he automatically began anticipating the advent of spring. Looking at flowers, even for a brief moment, brought him peace. In that moment it felt entirely normal that people enjoyed the cherry blossoms in the cemetery in his neighborhood. When he was admiring the flowers, he could take in the sky and the trees all at once. That sliver of peace suggested the possibility of a freedom of sorts. That was why he liked to gaze at flowers, though he knew they wouldn't bring a lasting peace. He also knew these were feelings invisible to everyone else. Waiting for flowers to bloom after a brutal winter was better when it happened gradually, like so many things in this world. There were still two months to go before the beginning of spring.

Nanae, on the lead design team, was molding a clay model, the sleeves of her tartan shirt rolled up. When the design for a building was completed, they would translate it into another model, made of poster board, fiberglass-reinforced plastic, Styrofoam, and regular plastic in order to better understand the project. Nanae had majored in sculpture rather than architecture, and she approached the intricate clay models as if she were making art. Last year she had given him a birthday present, quickly making a clay model of his face right in front of him and handing it over. It had been quite good. But Nanae had failed to consider one thing—that clay tended to dry out and crack as the day grew hotter.

Now he watched the building's shape change under Nanae's hands. She seemed entirely different when she was focused, at odds with the way she was while yawning in meetings or sitting alone in the empty office at lunch, absentmindedly eating onigiri. Now she looked as if—as if it would be impossible to take the clay away from her.

Some people couldn't properly express themselves without something in their hands. He remembered a woman like that.

It had been around the first week of December. He'd attended a dinner hosted by Park, the CEO of Korea Architecture Company, which had offices in Tokyo and Seoul. KAC's Seoul office doubled as a branch of Abe Kengo's firm. Park was a talented man known for his long list of acquaintances. That evening various people from all walks of life had gathered in Park's Shibuya living room. There had been several actors working in both Korea and Japan, painters, sculptors, chefs, wine importers, and a few who hadn't revealed their occupations. The woman in question had been sitting at the end of the table, visibly at a remove. Someone had clearly dragged her there. It hadn't been her looks or her outfit that had caught his interest but the way she had played with an eraser-sized ball of clay all night. Had he been sitting beside her, it would have annoyed him, like being stuck next to someone jiggling a leg or tapping a table with a pen.

He had been sitting diagonally from her, his chair pushed away from the table. Her movements had been cautious and secretive but persistent enough to draw his attention. He could tell she was the type to wear her feelings on her sleeve. He had watched as she had sculpted a giraffe before crushing it, then the head of the person next to her, then a beast resembling a fox or a leopard before twisting its neck and pressing it into a ball. Next she had made a tiny hand, which had such intricate and delicate knuckles and nails that it had looked like the real thing. Their eyes had met once, maybe? He could have talked to her. Nobody had introduced her to anyone else or asked what she was making. The only person she had spoken with all night was the balding middle-aged man seated next to her.

Bored, he had sniffed the heavy aroma of cigars perfuming the air and emptied his glass. He had taken in the night view of Shibuya through the window behind her. When he came to attention again, she was exchanging business cards with the balding man. He stood up. He wanted some fresh air. He was in a high-rise for the first time in a long while, and cold sweat was trickling down the back of his neck. She wasn't in her seat when he returned. Only after a good ten minutes passed did he realize she had left.

Now he got himself a fist-sized ball of clay from Nanae and returned to his desk. The clay was sticky and warm and hard, like a smooth, sun-warmed pebble. He leaned against his desk. He couldn't believe he was still thinking about that stranger with a bell-shaped bob.

When he encountered the woman again, he realized, to his surprise, that he remembered more about her than he'd expected to. Her clothing, her appearance, the glint in her eye—all of it. Perhaps this was the kind of thing he would remember for the rest of his life.

5

Are you even coming back?

She thought about everything she knew about Baek. He didn't like to be questioned, he didn't like fuzzy fruit, he didn't like the opera. He could keep his anger in check for a long time, but when he did lose his temper, he was unable to conceal it, no matter where he was. Same with his sadness. He had lost his mother at a young age and had been raised by a much older sister. He had a discreet side to him, evident in the fact that his wife did not know he owned this house. He'd been forty-six or forty-seven when she had first met him three years ago. Even if she didn't tally it all up, she knew this didn't amount to much. If Baek were a six-sided die, she might have only seen one side so far. She had never been unhappy about that, and she hadn't ever tried to see more. Could it just be the nature of their relationship? He was fifty years old. She felt deflated. He was the kind of person who decided what they would do, where they would go. He would go a month or two without calling, then show up in the middle of the night, smelling like petroleum. Theirs was a relationship that didn't require any promises or demands. By the time it had occurred to her that this kind of relationship might have been what Baek had wanted from the beginning, she had already gotten used to its rhythm. Three years. So much had happened in that time. She hadn't needed anyone else. She had to admit they'd had good times, too. Now she wanted to return the keys to his house.

She waited until Baek sat up straight, then said, "I think I'm going to be moving out."

Baek pushed the blanket off his knees. "Are you going somewhere?"

"Yes."

It was the kind of night when you could nod in agreement to anything. Sincerely to some things, not to others. But now insincerity would no longer create any issues between them.

"Where are you going?"

"Tokyo."

"Not far."

"No, not far."

"How long will you be there?"

She would be there for a three-month residency. After she had been invited to exhibit at the Mori Art Museum last fall, she'd applied to a residency program cosponsored by the Tokyo Art Center and the Seoul Art Foundation. She'd planned to stay a while in Tokyo while the show was up.

Now she was in a different headspace from when she'd applied, but she thought a change in scenery might not be bad. Most importantly she would avoid leaving Baek with a burden. And Tokyo wasn't entirely unfamiliar to her.

She placed her keys on the table. The brass clacked against the glass top. Several more copies were scattered inside various drawers; Baek was perennially forgetful. She was handing over only one set of many. But formalities were needed in times like these. Baek stared at her as her hand shrank away. She regretted not having asked about Renate first. She was curious but felt she couldn't ask. If she said another word, Baek might catch on and try to stop her. Or he might just observe her plans dispassionately, his eyes cold and serious to the end. Neither was what she wanted from Baek. What she wanted was a quiet dinner, a quiet farewell. She didn't want to see Baek with his sorrow undammed.

Renate was a German reporter Baek had been close with back when he had been the Berlin correspondent. Her husband had attempted suicide with a gun, but the bullet had merely severed his optic nerve, rendering him blind. When Baek had told her that story, she had decided that had to be the worst possible scenario, more awful than dying. Renate could have divorced her husband and left him for good, but surprisingly she had left Berlin to be with her newly blind husband. Privately she was disappointed that Baek thought highly of Renate's actions. Maybe Baek considered Renate's choice to be a noble one. The Baek she knew would have dissuaded Renate, as hers was not a rational nor realistic choice. They seemed to be in occasional touch these days. Last she'd heard, Renate and her husband had moved to Irvine, California, a city near the coast blessed with good weather. Renate moving with her old blind husband to the coast—was that an expression of pity or compassion or understanding or love?

"Just keep them," he said.

"Even if I come back, I won't be coming back here."

"Why not?"

"I just get that feeling."

"You're being ridiculous today." He sounded annoyed.

"Thanks for everything."

"Are you coming back?"

"I'm pretty much all packed. You can get rid of whatever else is left."

"Are you saying we shouldn't see each other anymore?"
"Something like that."
"Is everyone your age like this?"
"Like what?"
"It's always all about you."
She was silent.
"Answer me. Are you even coming back?"

She couldn't breathe, as though she were wearing an unbearably tight outfit. Even if this was the end, she couldn't answer his question. A damp wind drifted in through the living room window.

"This is the first time you're telling me where you're going before you go," Baek said. "Isn't it?"

6

You with white stones and your opponent with black stones

He looked at the number floating on his cellphone screen. The call had come in ten minutes ago. He had used to dial that number half asleep, with his eyes closed. Now it was unfamiliar, a series of numbers his eyes happened to light upon by chance. Ten minutes ago. What had he been doing? He'd watched his phone ring and waited patiently until it stopped. He should have picked up. Maybe Sinae was just calling to complain like she used to, her voice sleepy: "I want to be alone, but the cat needs to be fed, and it's so windy that the windows are rattling." Questioning it, ending it—these were the hardest things about love. Both good judgment and courage were required. Precisely the qualities he lacked. He should have come up with at least one decent reason for his decision. "You're a coward," she had said, crying, and slapped him across the face. "A coward." *Right*, he'd thought, *I am a coward.*

He walked out of Omotesando Station and headed down the narrow street by Benetton. The street was now famous for the Omotesando Hills shopping mall, designed by Tadao Ando, which had replaced old, shabby apartment buildings. But before the mall had been built, it had been known for its many trees, perfect for a nice walk. Behind Omotesando Hills were a warren of alleys and a bevy of unique shops and restaurants without signs. Sinae had liked this neighborhood even before Omotesando Hills had been built.

He pushed open the door to Desert, an old, deserted bar in a basement off the alley behind Tojukan Gallery. Not an establishment anyone would expect in a residential area. Mun, who owned the bar, threw him a welcoming look. Only one other customer was present, sitting before a Go board in a corner and reading the paper, likely one of Mun's Japanese friends, who were the majority of those congregating at Desert. He would never have known Mun was Korean had Mun not gone out of his way to make that known; Mun's demeanor and accent were entirely Japanese.

He perched on a barstool. The lights were too dim. Images flashed by on the TV hanging from the ceiling, casting ever-changing shadows and smudges across his face. Sinae used to stare at him as they sat there, giggling. He shouldn't have come here.

Mun handed him a glass of vodka garnished with a slice of lime.

Once he stopped bringing Sinae to Desert, Mun had said to him, "Look, don't sit there looking all depressed, like something terrible has happened. Love is like sitting across a Go board with someone. Did you know that a Go board isn't actually a perfect square? It's sixteen-and-a-half inches wide, but it's longer by about an inch. So the board is deceptive. It's a rectangle. You know why? It's so that you can keep your distance from the person you're playing against. A psychological distance. Love is about maintaining that distance, building your own house on your own side. You with white stones and your opponent with black stones. And they can't ever be mixed together. When you start to understand how many variables there are in the world, you'll realize that you aren't going through anything special."

He'd grimaced at that. Despite Mun's speech, he knew as well as any of Desert's regulars that Mun had lost his first love and spent the ensuing twenty years alone. It was because of that bit of personal history that Sinae trusted Mun implicitly. Mun was stubborn, physically imposing, and drank a lot, but he also understood things innately and was a vault when it came to secrets. After they broke up, he and Sinae had starting coming to the bar separately.

A majestic German requiem was playing. He was glad the volume was low. Mun dried his hands on a towel and glanced over at him to see if he needed anything else. He shook his head in response. Maybe wanting to be alone was a silly excuse. Every time the door opened behind him, he hoped Sinae was walking in. As if by coincidence. But it went without saying that a chance encounter like that would only make things worse. The ice in his glass was melting. He quickly downed his drink. His relationship with Sinae had been left ambiguous. *What would you do, Hyeong?* he silently addressed his brother, looking down into his empty glass. *How can I explain that you're the reason I can't see her anymore?*

Mun approached with a bottle.

He continued gazing into the bottom of his glass. He wanted to know what else it could hold.

7

Legacy

There were so many things to do before moving out. As she walked around the house, small but important tasks kept popping up. She had to make phone call after phone call. She dealt with the utilities, and canceled her newspaper and magazine subscriptions, and stopped the deliveries of water and the yogurt that had soothed her sensitive stomach. She emptied the bins throughout the house and the studio, and cleaned out the fridge and rice jar. She threw out or left on the street anything that might go bad or grow mold. She felt overwhelmed when she opened the closet. Clothes and bags didn't rot or get moldy. Neither did shoes. She left everything other than what she would take to Tokyo. Everyone left things behind when they died, even if they didn't want to. The best thing about self-immolation was the ability to burn everything you cherished, along with yourself. But that wasn't the way she wanted to go. She would choose a dispassionate death, and nothing that could be mistaken as an accident. She closed the closet doors. Clothes, bags, and shoes would not hold any significance for the people she would leave behind.

There was one more thing to do. But it felt daunting to go see her father. If she saw him, their last time together could remain a huge, searing regret for him. It would be better to avoid what she could at this point. The best thing she could do for him was to avoid him.

As she got out of the taxi, Aunt Sukhui, who had been watching from inside the restaurant, came out to greet her. Her aunt used to run an antique store in Itaewon, long before the row of antique shops settled there. The store had smelled like burning dried mugwort, and ever since she was little, she had thought of that scent as her aunt's. After her youngest uncle vanished, however, her aunt closed the antique store and moved next to her father's woodworking shop to open this tofu restaurant.

She watched Aunt Sukhui boil water in an electric kettle. These days her aunt didn't smell like anything. She had given up so much of her own life in order to be there for her father. Sukhui was the second eldest of her three aunts and now the youngest of all the siblings. Once her father had said about his little sister: "She's the kind of person who shrinks away before you even approach her." Even though the two siblings exchanged few words, drinking silently whenever they got together, they were the closest among all their siblings. They were always headed in the same way even if they were looking in different directions, as if pedaling on a tandem bicycle.

So coming to see her aunt was the same thing as visiting her father, she reasoned, accepting a cup of tea from her aunt.

In college she had grown close to a girl she'd met in painting class called Saim, who had epilepsy. Saim would suddenly tumble to the ground like a branch breaking in half, during lectures and in the studio, in the bathroom and in the cafeteria, anywhere on campus. "This is my family's legacy," Saim had told her with a smile, her voice bitter and self-mocking. She hadn't been able to bring herself to tell Saim that she knew of a family whose legacy was suicide. Would it be better if her own family legacy was characterized by collapsing on campus, or falling asleep in inappropriate places, or pathological drinking, or depression, or falling in love too easily, or not being able to eat fish, or running away from home?

Her youngest uncle had been diagnosed with a mysterious, unidentifiable illness about a month after they buried her youngest aunt, who, before jumping into the ocean one night, had practically been his twin. Her father's siblings and half-siblings had gathered to discuss next steps. Though her eldest aunt and her father disagreed, the consensus was to admit her youngest uncle into a psychiatric ward. The siblings argued over the decision, but it seemed to be the only option. To end the bickering, her father had broken a bottle and rammed a shard of glass straight into his left hand. Her father, the carpenter. Blood soaked his pants and the floor. The blood quieted the siblings, who finally came to their senses. But the night before he was to be committed, her youngest uncle left home, a knapsack on his back.

Legacy. For her there was always something following her around, making her think about death. Persistently, the way emotions tended to burst out the more you tried to suppress them. A wall that incrementally but insistently closed in on you with the sole purpose of crushing you, obliterating you.

She had been mixing plaster in her studio when she had first been made aware of its force. This was a few days after her youngest uncle had left home. As she worked, a single light beamed down onto her worktable. She didn't want to get distracted. But heavy air brushed damply across her face and neck like numerous feelers. She whirled around. Someone was sitting in the red wooden chair placed against the wall. She forced her eyes wide open and straightened up. She had to keep some part of her body alert so she wouldn't lose touch with reality. She was tense. A heavy silence. That was when she saw with her own eyes the very thing she had been desperately avoiding. *Who—who are you?* she asked silently. The presence, clad in a long, dark cloak, sat in the hard chair, watching her life tick by. She felt herself beginning to hyperventilate. Water that had begun lapping at her shoes was rising to her chest. If she opened her mouth, she would swallow water. She would be unable to do anything once the water reached her heart. She shuddered and flapped her hands wildly in the air. She was actually more terrified of plaster hardening on her hands than of the presence of something in the room. Death sat still for a long time, observing her actions.

When she next encountered that presence, she wasn't taken aback. By then she had realized that she, like her father and his siblings, had grown tired of plodding forward in an attempt to avoid death. Her decision had required a lot of effort, but in the end it hadn't been a difficult one. All she had done was move herself from this side to that. She had merely chosen a different world.

Seated across from Sukhui, she told her aunt that she was headed to Tokyo. Her aunt didn't look at her at all, keeping her head bowed, watching the dried chrysanthemum bud blooming in her teacup. Aunt Sukhui, who, among all her aunts and uncles, always had a soft spot for her, who had become a mother figure after the death of her own mother. If she were to summarize in one word the feeling she got when she thought of her aunt, it would be *wonder*. That her aunt was still alive. If their family legacy was what she thought it was, her aunt should have died a long time ago. One night Sukhui's husband, a sexual deviant, had gotten drunk and attacked his wife, biting off one of her nipples. Her aunt had climbed onto a window ledge in their thirteenth-floor apartment but had eventually descended, shaken, looking like she had seen something more terrible than death. Then her eldest uncle, who had been the one to help Aunt Sukhui off the ledge, was suddenly diagnosed with terminal liver cancer and died three months later. Her aunt had sat still during the entirety of the mourning period, biting her lip, her face crumpled into a frown. Everyone in the family grew used to that expression of hers, like a part of her lip and one eye had been scrubbed away.

No one else entered the restaurant. Dust and steam curled faintly up through the manhole cover out front. She couldn't hear anything from the kitchen. Silence flowed between them. Then Aunt Sukhui said, "I have something for you."

8

HOW TO SELECT A HOME

It was Saturday afternoon. After a late lunch, he washed the dishes. His father went back up to his room while his mother made a call to his father's close friend and psychiatrist, Dr. Suzuki. His mother refused to acknowledge that some types of anxiety and pain could be treated with medication. His father, on the other hand, believed otherwise. After all, his father was the one who insisted on continuing treatment.

He placed his father's medication and water on a tray.

His mother tied a wool scarf around her neck. He reflexively glanced at the clock: three in the afternoon. Three in the afternoon was when his mother went out for her walk, whether it was snowing or raining or freezing cold. For an hour nobody could disturb her, not even his father, who couldn't so much as drink a glass of water without her assistance. His mother had developed her habit of taking afternoon walks when they had moved into this place two years ago. The apartment they had lived in before had been small but had a garden. The neighborhood also had a spacious park. While their new neighborhood did have green space, it was the front lawn of a cemetery, not a park. This was the only neighborhood that had managed to escape intact from both the great earthquake of 1923 and World War II bombings. The snaking alleys still retained the character of old Tokyo before modernization. His father felt safe here, a quiet, idyllic place in the middle of the city. His father had wanted to move here because Dr. Suzuki lived nearby. But their small house had no natural beauty or soil, as his mother would say. Their front door was a few steps from the gate, the narrow, unused space in between barely a yard. They had hastily decided to move here without paying much attention to the details, and his father's illness had taken a turn for the worse before they could move again.

"I'll come with you, Eomeoni," he offered.

"Why?"

"You're getting groceries, aren't you?"

"I can do it myself."

"Eomeoni."

"It's fine."

"I'll just walk behind you."

"You have to look after your father."

"He's about to take his medication."

His mother looked back at him, peeved. After taking his medication, his father would sleep for a few hours. He knew she was seeking time alone, not necessarily exercise. But he pulled his sneakers on. Anxiety tailed him like a white string destined to be attached to him forever. Pulling her rickety bicycle along, his mother passed Yanaka Cemetery and went north toward Nippori Station. He had to walk briskly to keep up with his spry sixty-year-old mother.

Even at this age, he hadn't forgotten the things he'd learned as a child from her. How to fold a paper airplane, how to make a kite, how laundry had to be taken off the line before sunset, how to neatly fold his father's shirts. Perhaps she had considered her second son not a son but a daughter. She hadn't taught her eldest son any of these things. But she had taught him, her second son, so much more—how to tie his shoelaces, what to do with his underwear after a wet dream, how to behave on a first date. How to select a home.

In her youth his mother had lived in Ogin-dong in northern Seoul. It was a middle-class neighborhood populated by families that had worked in the palace during the Joseon dynasty. She hadn't strayed too far from the area, even after marriage. Only once had his parents not lived together. For five years, when his father was finishing his degree at Tokyo's Waseda University. Every day after his brother went off to elementary school, it would be just him and his mother. She would dress nicely, take him by the hand. She usually went to viewings organized by the neighborhood realty office. But she knew that real estate agents had a cache of houses they didn't show to people who appeared ordinary. From the age of five he went with his mother to view those hidden houses in Seongbuk-dong and Jeongneung. He never knew if she was really looking for a house to move into. She would merely sit for a moment in someone else's living room or in a chair in the garden, then come back out. With a single glance, she could discern the pros and cons of any house. A house would be disqualified at once if the hills weren't visible from it or if the yard didn't have a single decent tree. If there was a yard, she would squat and feel the dirt with her hands. She said stag beetles and other insects could not inhabit dirt that wasn't dark and lustrous. It was her belief that the resident of a house that couldn't sustain life would never be able to relax; without nature, they would become vulgar. From that young age he understood that his mother wished to live in a place surrounded by nature. Like some kind of imprinting phenomenon, his mind was engraved with that idea. He and his mother continued to roam and view houses until his father returned to Seoul. That was how his mother had made it through the years her husband had been away.

His mother suddenly stopped and turned to look at him.

"What is it?" he asked.

"Stop following me."

"Let's go together, Eomeoni."

"I want to be alone."

He didn't answer.

"I said, I want to be alone."

"All right."

"I'll be home soon."

"It's icy in the shade. Be careful."

He caught her eyes darkening with bitterness and resignation. A damp breeze rolled in like fog. She was someone who could look despondent even while looking at beautiful flowers. "Yeobo, please smile, even if it's just once a day," she often pleaded with his father, who had stopped talking after what had happened to their eldest son. A smile was the one thing he wanted from his mother, too. Before all this had happened, his mother had crafted sentences with a few concise words and had been more sensitive than anyone to the changing seasons. It was excruciating to watch her day after day. Hers was a sorrow that made his blood run cold. He wanted to look away every time he encountered it.

His mother walked up the old, rickety footbridge in front of the tofu restaurant Sasanoyuki. She didn't ask for his help carrying her bike up the stairs. He stood hesitantly behind her and looked across the street at Negishi Elementary School, which featured a wall relief of a pine tree and a flock of birds taking flight. His mother lifted the bicycle down but pitched forward, having missed a step. He rushed toward her and grabbed her by the elbow. He felt her flinch in resistance. Her wavy bob danced in the wind. A few strands of hair stuck to her cheek like lines drawn in error. Her eyes were panicked, as if she had been caught in the nude, clutching clothes she couldn't put on without assistance. Her light brown eyes sparkled faintly, turning wet. He avoided them. How would she make it through the years without his brother?

There was one more thing his mother had taught him. That one's bedroom should be warm. What she needed wasn't a walk but restful sleep in a warm room. A deep, peaceful sleep from which she could not be roused.

9

SHE, DEPARTING TO TOKYO

On the afternoon of Monday, January fifth, she was flying across the East Sea. Her hands with their black nail polish looked alien to her. After she had finished packing that morning, she'd had some time to spare. She'd strolled around the neighborhood, then gone into a nail salon near the Gyeongbokgung Palace Station. The shop had dozens of colors. When she departed this place for the new city, she would wear a thick black turtleneck sweater and black jeans. She wanted her polish to go with her outfit and so had chosen a hue that vacillated between jet-black and dark gray depending on the light. She'd watched as her cracked and bruised fingernails were painted black. She could never paint her nails while she was working on a sculpture. But she could do something new with hands like these. They felt like someone else's hands, hands she wanted to clasp together forcefully. Now her pearly black nails shined subtly every time they caught the light. They looked as sensual as the shade of a blooming tree; if she stared at her nails for a long time, everything around her might sway in a dreamy black. Black. Everything was converging into one. Stories popped into her head. Stories that were sad but beautiful, stories that were neither sad nor beautiful but plainly tragic, stories that ended in catastrophe. There were so many stories; she was glad every story had an ending. She stroked the back of her hand. It felt as if all along she had been struggling to write stories with her right hand while her left hand had gripped it tightly, rendering the right hand immobile. She thought about Seneca, the philosopher. Seneca had said that people had the right to choose how they left the world, just as they had the right to choose the house they wanted to live in. He and his wife, Paulina, had slashed several veins in their arms. But he was so old that the blood did not leave his body quickly enough. Dismayed, Seneca had gone to another room and severed the veins in his calves and the backs of his knees.

She followed the instructions relayed to her by the Tokyo Art Center employee and took the monorail from Haneda Airport to Hamamatsuchō Station. She was to take the JR Yamanote Line to Nippori Station; while Uguisudani Station was closer to where she was staying, that station didn't have an escalator. But she'd only brought a small suitcase.

The apartment building was a plain, ten-story structure. Two trees were planted on the narrow sidewalk in front, looking like commemorative milestones. She would be staying on the sixth floor. She got off the elevator lined with gray noise-reduction blankets and turned right; number 605 was down the hall. The kitchen sink and counter faced the living room, and a toilet and shower were on either side of the hallway that led to the living room. She'd heard that her predecessor had been an Israeli artist invited by the Japanese government. When she sat on the toilet, a world map greeted her from the back of the door. The unit had two rooms and was furnished with all the basics, including a bed and a desk. The long apartment was much too small for her to work in but the perfect size for one person to live in. "It's cold," she muttered. A chill encircled her, making it impossible to consider taking off her sweater, let alone wash up, even as the day grew late. Turning on all the lights and heating this unfamiliar apartment felt like the most important task ahead of her. She found an electric blanket in the closet, spread it out on the living-room floor, and pressed the button on the wall to turn up the heat. The vent started to whir. Stale dust rose as a gentle breeze grazed the top of her head. She opened the sliding door and stepped onto the veranda. Across the way were more apartment buildings, topped with pointy roofs that looked like triangular straw huts from the Bronze Age. Faint shadows blurred past in the windows. Right across the street were a yogurt factory and a facility of some sort piled with old tires.

A crow cawed, loud and forceful. Here darkness would descend exactly thirty minutes before it did in Seoul.

Seneca's story taught her that death did not come easy. If you wanted to end your life instantly, perfectly, you needed practice and preparation. What Renate's husband had lacked. It was essential for her to fully understand her surroundings; the environment around you could affect your death in important, decisive ways. People started falling to their deaths after 1969, once the construction of high-rise buildings became more prevalent. In places where you could obtain a firearm, like in California, more people killed themselves with guns. In a city of forests, people hanged themselves from trees. Understanding her environment would give her an idea of how to approach the end. Holding on to the windowsill, she looked down, her eyes serious. The sixth floor was too high. Falling to your death wasn't an ideal method. She didn't want to be eviscerated. She didn't want to leave behind any misunderstanding. She needed to find a purposeful, flawless method. She thought about Baek's house. The house where she'd prepared and planned everything. That would have been the way to end it, sitting with dignity. Now that she was here, she would have to come up with something else. The westward sky became deeply saturated with color, as if a condensed ball of light had burst open. She felt a wrenching pain tear through her body whenever she looked up at the sunset. "There aren't that many sunsets left," she whispered to the deathly presence embracing her shoulders with a hot, powerful force.

Number 605, 3-5-19, Negishi, Taitō-ku, Tokyo.

Her final address on this planet.

10

HE, AT MARRONIER PARK

His suit tightened around him each time he took a deep breath. It was a black suit with a two-button jacket, a simple garment with clean lines, one that radiated alertness even as it hung limp in his closet. Every time he went to Seoul for work, his mother would place a matching shirt, tie, and trench coat on a hanger. Of course, she selected a suit before picking out these other components. Her styling was always impeccable. A few years ago, he would go on business trips wearing a baggy jacket, cotton pants, and beige sneakers. He went into meetings like that and sometimes hopped in a rental car afterward to go sightsee at Buseoksa Temple or Gyeongju before returning to Tokyo. But nowadays his mother wanted him to go to Seoul wearing nice clothes. He didn't want to know what that signified.

If he were to build a house, he would design one that privileged comfort over style. If he were a clothing designer, he would make garments that became more beautiful and comfortable when worn. He loosened his tie. His next meeting at KAC was in the morning. He was staying in the guest quarters on the fifth floor of the KAC offices in Nonhyeon-dong. Park was hosting dinner there for the project team working on the remodeling of W Bank's corporate headquarters and the photographer documenting the work. These types of evening gatherings happened frequently, with Park cooking for everyone. He had to return to Nonhyeon-dong by seven. He usually stayed in the guest quarters when he came to Seoul for KAC business. Park boasted that Daniel Libeskind, who designed the World Trade Center buildings in New York after September 11, had stayed there when visiting Seoul. But when his brother had lived in Seoul, he had stayed with his brother. Work trips were at most a week, more often a few days. Sometimes he would arrive on a morning flight and take the last flight out at nine, but he always tried to find some time for himself, even if it was only thirty minutes. It was astounding to him that he no longer knew anyone in Seoul. Now he wouldn't have anyone to see or anywhere to go even with three or four hours of free time.

Pigeons pecked the park grounds, making *kukuku* noises. Dappled light filtered through thin, overlapping sycamore branches. Four college-aged women sat on a curved bench and took pictures of one another, and an old woman in a woolen sack-like outfit sat on a slide, talking incessantly to herself, a fake red flower tucked behind her ear. Sanitation workers came by regularly to clear away trash, people walked by with briefcases or guitars slung over their shoulders, and women in short skirts passed through. The ground was littered with bits of crushed food and cigarette butts and flyers. *Most city parks would look like this in the afternoon*, he thought. It wasn't too cold. He stuffed his hands in his trench coat pockets. He needed to kill some time. Ten minutes from here was the university that had employed his brother. If he had enough time he could even go down to Andong to see the gentle curves of the pavilions at Byeongsan Seowon. He recalled the slice of the Nakdong River visible beyond the pavilions of the Confucian academy. His brother had visited that place often after moving to Seoul. It had been the perfect place for his brother. Spiritual and austere at the same time.

He began walking toward ARKO Art Center. A stranger might think he was an ascetic because of his stiff expression. Suddenly light poured down in front of him. A red glow seemed to be seeping toward him in an almost tactile way. He shaded his eyes and raised his head. The red bricks that protruded from the facade of the art gallery created dark shadows in the sunlight, resembling ivy snaking up a building. Vibrant light moved against shadow as if alive and ablaze. He was gazing at a redbrick building in the sun, standing within immense beauty. Using brick to build was different from using glass or steel or concrete. With those other materials it was hard to feel you were building something with your hands, layer upon layer, one at a time, creating shallow lines of space between the bricks. To him bricks were the most humanistic material to build with. Not many materials gave off warmth and solidity and majesty and trust all at the same time. Brick didn't reflect or absorb sunlight but rather highlighted shadows. As the angle of sunlight shifted, so too did the ratio of light to shadow.

If he were to build a house to live in for the rest of his life, he would use red bricks. A house that would be beautiful to look at *and* comfortable to live in. If he were to move back to Seoul, it might be to build a brick house. You couldn't use brick in San Francisco or Tokyo, in earthquake-prone cities. An outer wall couldn't be finished with broken glass or marred cement—but with bricks, such a thing was possible. Forget about perfectly straight red bricks; when morning light fell on buildings built with warped or damaged bricks, it was almost overwhelming to witness their powerful beauty and dynamic character.

A house whose bent, cracked, missing, twisted, and protruding parts looked all the more striking and glorious in the sun. Standing there in his brother's suit, he stacked red bricks in his mind, one by one.

11

WHY DID THE DROWNED MAN HAVE BALLED FISTS?

A dark object bobbed in the river. The object was not an object but a drowned man in his forties. The news anchor reported that the man had been found with his hands balled into fists. She changed the channel to something that wasn't the news. She managed to fall asleep, thinking all the while about the drowned man. She didn't want to know whether it was a suicide, or a murder disguised as a suicide, or even a simple accident. After all, the result was the same regardless of how it had happened. A man was dead. She was curious about one thing and one thing only. Why did the drowned man have balled fists?

She bolted up in bed. She was soaked in sweat, as was her bedding. Her own hands were balled into fists. She flapped her hands in the air, shaking off the ominous feeling. Her nails had dug into her palms and left four deep red marks on each. Death in and of itself didn't terrify her. But dying in her sleep, without being aware of it, did. Dying without any preparation, dying without leaving behind a will. The bloodred nail marks on her palms gradually returned to a pinkish color.

She slipped on a heavy windbreaker that came down to her knees and a pair of rectangular sunglasses. There were a few routes to Ueno Park from the apartment. She could take the Hibiya Line from Minowa Station and get off at the second stop, Ueno Station, or she could pass Uguisudani Station and walk up the hill, or she could take the JR Yamanote Line from Ueno Station and get off after one stop. The quickest route would be to take the Hibiya Line from Minowa Station. The park was twenty minutes away by bike and forty minutes on foot. She headed southwest toward Nippori Station. Today she would walk all the way to the park instead of riding her bicycle. She wouldn't be able to take the chair if she biked. The only option was to walk. A few more practice runs might be necessary; after all, she might encounter unexpected obstacles. Cool sunlight cascaded over everything. Water-filled plastic bottles stationed in doorways to shoo away feral cats reflected the sunlight and glowed like squat silvery fences.

This neighborhood had a remarkable number of facilities processing discarded goods. Recyclable papers, plastics and cans, and black tires were piled in tall mounds before her eyes. The stacks of hard, round black tires looked like enormous, sturdy balls on the verge of collapse, as though they would careen wildly through the narrow streets. She was standing in the exact place she should be. Isolated; nobody knew where she was, and nobody would unless she reached out first. She liked that she was staying near Ueno Park, which was her favorite place to visit whenever she was in Tokyo. If she was bored, she could look out the window and watch how old tires and recyclable papers were broken down. Ten minutes northeast from the apartment was a large, traditional market, and if she went over the hill by Nippori Station, she found herself in a neighborhood rich with temples and cemeteries. She and Saim had once stayed in that area for Saim's show at a gallery in a renovated bathhouse called SCAI The Bathhouse. Some of the streets were so narrow that they didn't seem habitable. As she walked, she swung her arms, the rustling against her windbreaker sounding upbeat. People were out exercising. Stick-skinny young men whose sole purpose seemed to be walking from dawn to dusk stalked by. She wasn't walking meditatively; rather, she had a clear purpose for walking, and she was headed toward that purpose.

Whenever she had to make a decision or felt confused, she split herself in two. Now she asked herself, *Why should you choose death? Or why shouldn't you choose death?* Though these two questions seemed to be at odds with each other, death was a given. That the question had solidified into conviction meant death was a given. Humans rationalized their own convictions rather skillfully, even if they were wrong. Nobody had told her that an ingrained desire for death was wrong, this conviction that tugged at her. Even if she realized it was wrong, she wouldn't have given up on it. After all, a conviction had to be rationalized. She had restrained her other self so many times—when a relationship went awry, when she was in a lethargic slump, when her artistic pride was injured, when nobody acknowledged her, when she lost all confidence in her work, when she felt stuck in her art practice. She told her other self it wasn't the right time, that dying in a state of failure, dying without ever having accomplished anything, was an act of discarding life, not actively choosing death. She wanted to be someone who didn't throw life away but voluntarily opted for death. So she had continued to work. Desperately, with a whisper of hope that if she could achieve something in her art, she would be able to extricate herself from the ups and downs. But happiness—this was a door forever closed to an artist. She would never be able to transcend her limits. A repetitive life, a life that would continue forever if she didn't give up. She was exhausted to the bone.

She was relieved that her most recent show had been a success. Now was the time to sever whatever chains tethered her to this world; now was the ideal time. She and her other self agreed on that point. Now only death remained. Death she chose herself, which meant she wouldn't be on the receiving end of anyone's sympathy, anyone's tears or words of consolation, none of which she wanted. Embarrassment, however, might remain to the end. The embarrassment that came from opting to lean in to her conviction. People didn't kill themselves for no reason. An emotion existed beneath every death, whether it was hate or rage or sorrow or resentment or shame or love. Embarrassment—this was hers, and sometimes this emotion made her feel a stabbing pain. But everyone died within their own particular pain.

The hill sloped up once she passed the footbridge. At three or four in the afternoon, middle school students in shorts ran practice races. Dozens of them in white gym uniforms ran in formation, brimming with vitality and energy. At night the street became deserted, other than a handful of people biking home. She started feeling more settled once she realized that her favorite park in Tokyo was nearby. The Tokyo Metropolitan Art Museum, Ueno Royal Museum, the National Museum of Western Art, Tokyo National Museum, University Art Museum at Tokyo University of the Arts, Shinobazu Pond, and the Ueno Zoo were all in or near the park. Lugging a wooden chair felt like she was carrying an armful of books. It wasn't too heavy, nor was it too cumbersome to hold it by its back and walk along with it. After her trial run, she planned to walk all the way to Ueno Park with the chair. She would pass the zoo and turn right at the fountain to head into the forest. Where cherry trees would be in full bloom in two months' time.

She spotted wide-open greenery; she was getting close to the park. She took a seat on the first floor of Café Pronto, below the Keisei Line overpass. From here she had a clear vantage of the stairs to the park entrance. Though obscured by the door, the crosswalk was just to the right of the café. Pedestrians, hunched against the cold, crossed the street and went up the stairs into the park. She ordered toast and coffee. The café was ridiculously tiny. Upstairs was the smoking section. The tables and chairs vibrated every time the Keisei Line rumbled by. She took a pencil and piece of paper out of her pocket. She started drawing a map, then stopped. She had sketched straight lines and ovals, direct and curved, lines that were simple but purposeful and contained meaning. Lines that could convince and bring understanding. She remembered the many nighttime hours she had spent drawing lines like these. Times she could never return to.

12

ALL THE THINGS THAT COULD HAPPEN

He was walking along Kitajuken Street, by the canal. Earlier he had gone straight from Haneda Airport to a restaurant in Asakusa; over dinner he'd filled Abe Kengo and Director Yun in about the meeting with KAC. In Korea his headache had persisted, and unpleasant smells had dogged him. Now he felt as though he were standing, hands and feet tied, in front of a huge arch whose headstone was starting to wobble. *Am I nervous?* he asked himself. *Am I feeling unsafe? Why am I feeling this way?* He needed to figure it out; otherwise, he was liable to be pulled by some uncontrollable, mysterious force in a direction he didn't particularly want to go in. "You have to stay alert," his mother always told him. But nothing was sounding alarm bells at the moment. Maybe he was being oversensitive. If he emptied his mind, he would be able to placidly walk along, feeling the not-cold-but-slightly-damp night breeze, familiar, like the breath of a woman he knew intimately. He strode along the narrow, winding canal, which linked with Sumida River. Maybe he was asking himself the wrong questions. *Am I sad?*

Construction netting blocked passage by the canal. He stopped in his tracks. A new transmission tower was being built; it was expected to be completed in 2011. A two-thousand-eighty-foot-tall tower. Once completed it would be the tallest broadcasting tower in the world. The formwork for the new tower had risen about thirty feet off the ground. Like with most towers, the base was triangular for stability. Then, the higher it went, the more rectangular it became, before turning into a sphere near the top. Forming a sphere by shaving the edges off the rectangular shape would concentrate the load toward the core. The key would be ensuring an even load distribution while arriving at the golden ratio. In other words, cross sections of the new tower would result in a triangle, a rectangle, and a circle at different junctures. The tower was designed to resemble a long, sleek, curved nihondo—the Japanese knife. It had taken some time to conceive a design that would be earthquake-resistant. He had been the one to come up with an idea borrowed from a five-story stone pagoda. It had been well-received.

At its full height, the tower would appear to reach all the way up to where the crescent moon appeared to him presently. Of course it wouldn't be that tall, but the tower suggested that possibility. The crescent moon hung in the night sky like someone had pressed their fingernail into it.

His brother had been interested in the blueprints. So he had shown him the tower's elevation drawing and section drawing, along with an animated 3D rendering of the completed structure. At the time he had been surprised by his brother's interest in his work. He'd felt both buoyed and flustered by his questions. That was right after his brother had suddenly quit his university job and returned home to Tokyo, had stopped going out or wanting to see anyone. But his brother had seemed less intrigued by the design of the tower and more by the beauty of the illuminated tower at night.

"What if someone fell off this tower?" his brother had asked.

"What kind of question is that?"

"Just curious," his brother had replied. "I'm just thinking of all the things that could happen at this tower."

He could have continued working on the new tower. He could have also gone for a walk somewhere else.

On the afternoon of Wednesday, March 29, 2006, his brother had jumped to his death from his apartment window on the fifth floor. When he ran over after receiving the call, his brother was lying in the street, one cheek pressed to the ground, limbs sprawled. It took some time to recognize that he was looking at his brother, at the body of a human being. His brother's neck and limbs twisted in strange angles. His brother's ruptured intestines spilled out, blood gushing from his temple. It had only been from the fifth floor.

"If you really wanted to fall to your death, you could do it from the third floor." He had said this to his brother carelessly. "You wouldn't have to go up that high." That was what he had said.

2011, the year the tower would be completed, felt far away, never to arrive. Tokyo Skytree. *Will I be able to watch this tower's lights turn on?* He wanted that to be the last question of the day. He was afraid of going home. The tower's steel frame looked like an enormous structure rushing toward dreams yet unaccomplished. He heard running water, faintly. He gripped the sides of his head as though his ears were throbbing.

13

THE TIME SHE SPENT EATING DESSERTS

She got off at Roppongi Station. She walked around the Japanese lacquer exhibition at the Suntory Museum of Art, on the top floor of Tokyo Midtown. She took the elevator down one flight and poked around a shop selling kitchenwares and a store stocked exclusively with clothes made of pleated fabric. She didn't bother going into the shoe and bag stores; looking in the windows was enough. Especially if the displays were nicely designed. At a store selling essential oils, she weighed whether to buy a bottle of bergamot oil to squeeze a drop or two onto her pillow every night. Apparently it helped you fall asleep. She wasn't used to feeling the need to buy something; it made her uncomfortable. A bamboo cutting board, a tea set, leather shoes and a bag, a dinosaur robot with sensors, a hefty notebook she picked up and put down several times, a feather pen. An object's initial power was in the way it drew out possessiveness. A feeling that began with ordinary desire. She had been thinking about the power inherent in objects, and a part of her thoughts had been devoted to the special objects at the center of her work. "Not now," she murmured, then realized that everything was hurtling toward the end, despite what she told herself. At this specific moment in her life, what she said to herself was more significant and meaningful than what she said to other people. "One day," she said to herself. "Just one more day." There was still an hour to go before the sun would begin to set. She took the escalator down to B1.

Dark navy, clear blue, bright yellow-green, fresh purple, greenish tan, pure yellow, pale neon green. Colorful macarons were displayed in a clear glass case like expensive accessories. Looking down at the display case, she pronounced each of the colors. It felt like an eternity ago that she'd mixed such vibrant colors and used them with abandon. She spotted a hazy yellow macaron with the name Sakura. She ordered a double espresso, a neutral gray macaron, and a white macaron that reminded her of scallion blooms. Macarons went well with tea. But drinking hot black coffee brought out their sweetness. She toyed with the two macarons delivered to her on a silver tray, then plopped the white one, whole, in her mouth. An intense sweetness overtook her, practically numbing the tip of her tongue. Sweetness spread in an instant, blasting her taste buds. It tasted of sorrow. Memories flashed by— of anxious nights, nights she had thought about the end, lonely nights, all of those countless nights eating sweets. Macarons, cream-smothered mille-feuilles, cakes, cream puffs, mousse, dark chocolate. Maybe what allowed her to keep her anxiety at bay wasn't the time she spent consumed by work. Maybe it was the time she spent eating desserts all alone, late at night, in despair. For a moment the remaining gray macaron appeared to take on a metallic sheen. She marveled that she could detect this sheen, this achromatic color, through her tears. Even if it was an illusion, she wanted to remember that sparkle. Because it lasted only a split second.

She exited Tokyo Midtown and headed toward the intersection. She could see Roppongi Hills ahead of her. The Mori Art Museum was on the fifty-third floor of the Roppongi Hills Mori Tower. Her work *Childhood* was on display. She had made it in 2002, when she had first been entranced by silicone as a medium. She had been younger, grappling with even more anxiety and inner conflict than now. If she closed her eyes, she could still remember making that sculpture, feeling as though she were being pushed to the edge of a cliff. And how she felt at peace only when she was working, everything suspended in place. Maybe she should go visit *Childhood*. But maybe that would make her feel like she was reading something about herself that had been written long ago. She turned instead toward the Hibiya Line. The past could no longer be a source of strength.

She took Exit 1 out of Kamiyacho Station. She wanted to watch the sunset. From somewhere high up, somewhere so crowded that nobody would give her a second glance. She turned left across from the Russian embassy. Tokyo was a city with many corners; she had to pay attention so that she didn't get lost. Tokyo Tower appeared in front of her, glowing orange, like an enormous signpost. A tree holding up the sky, bathed in light. The lights on the tower were starting to turn on. She began walking quickly. Once it was completely dark, she would only be able to see her face reflected in the glass. She wanted to see the world before it was too late, to see the city turn gradually darker from the outer edges and the lights blink on, one by one. She wanted to see the harmony of light and shadow, something she had always wanted to express in her art but had never succeeded in doing.

14

SHE WAS STANDING TO THE WEST

It was cold and overcast. Thick gray clouds had settled over everything. It wasn't ideal weather in which to look out at the city. In the high-speed elevator, hurtling up to the observation deck, he checked the time. 6:03 p.m. He was meeting Jun Lee at six thirty. They'd become friends when they'd studied architecture together at the University of Chicago. This time Jun was on his way back to New York after attending the International Skyscraper Forum in Seoul. Jun, born to a Korean father and a Vietnamese mother, knew hardly anything about Korea. When they were roommates, he had taught Jun a few words of Korean. Jun stopped in Seoul on every business trip to Asia and always dropped by Tokyo to see him, even if only for a few hours. "I have two hours," Jun had exclaimed over the phone before leaving Seoul. "We can hang out for two whole hours." They hadn't seen each other in two years.

He bought a few T-shirts for Jun at the gift shop on the main observation deck, then went down a flight of stairs and settled in at Cafe333. From his seat he could see the panorama of the south. He could have seen the peak of Mount Fuji if the weather had been good. People began gathering around the stage inside the café. Indie bands played on Wednesday and Thursday nights, the busiest nights for the café. He'd completely forgotten about that. He was sitting too close to the stage; it would be too loud to carry on a conversation. He picked up his coffee and got up, looking around.

She was standing to the west.

He spotted her from behind. Her profile was reflected faintly on the glass of the observation deck. Without thinking, he sat down at a random table. He had somehow picked the most secluded spot in the café, half hidden by the protruding metal staircase to the main observation deck. He placed his coffee down. His ears burned. She was staring out, lost in thought, so close to the glass that she might have been pressing her forehead against it. His eyes followed her gaze. She was looking out toward Roppongi Hills and Shibuya, where you could normally see all the way to the snowcapped summit of Mount Fuji, spreading out on the horizon. Now only its outline was faintly visible. If you didn't know it was Mount Fuji, you might not even realize a mountain was there. Concertgoers settled near him. A man circled the observation deck, holding his elderly mother's elbow. Several middle-aged women clacked by in their geta.

She looked up at the sky painted with big gray clouds and crossed her arms. Her profile cut a sharp line, perhaps because her mouth was closed, and a shadow was cast on the glass. Still, there was something about her that looked deflated, like she was a rag doll with a stitch undone. As if she knew something was leaking out of her body but wasn't doing anything to stop it.

His last sight of her: that night at the gathering, her blank face and her indifferent eyes sweeping over him. He had just stood up from his seat. It must have been the lighting that turned her eyebrows so dark. It had only been the first week of December, but Park had wanted things to feel festive. Candles inside cubes of recycled paper lined the middle of the table. Pine cones were strewn around the candles. Certainly a wintry scene, but the flickering light warped and distorted everyone's faces. He pushed his chair back, away from the table, wanting to get some fresh air. The candlelight trembled every time someone laughed. She was sitting diagonally from him. Her face appeared mottled, as though streaked with long-dried tears. When he returned to the table, she was nowhere to be seen. Behind her now-empty seat were the living room windows, blinds thrown open. Seated there, she could have looked down ten stories over the night streets of Shibuya. But she had sat with her back to the windows. He had sensed that she was conscious of the location of the doors, sitting in a way that allowed her to observe whoever was approaching. Protected from at least one side. That was the year he turned thirty-five, when he was often dizzy and felt clammy, even when the blankets pulled over his head were crisp and dry.

Now she was looking out the glass on the observation deck. Her cheeks turned white and then orange, as if penetrated by light. Jun should be arriving at any moment. He was about to turn his head toward the entrance when she glanced back. The lights of the metro snaked slowly between the buildings behind her, writing out the kanji for *big* in red. Their eyes met, and she cocked her head slightly. She didn't seem to recognize him. She seemed not to know where she was, as if she were preoccupied by a single thought. That face. Her vacant face. He'd seen that expression before. The expression worn by someone who had voluntarily let go of something, something they had long been struggling against. Hyeong.

Something sparked in his head. He sprang from his seat and took a step toward her.

15

THAT MEANS, FROM NOW ON, YOU'RE FREE TO DO ANYTHING YOU WANT

She had not expected the man to recognize her voice. Only after she hung up did she realize that it wasn't surprise she was feeling. What she was feeling was the sensation of being locked in a predetermined course.

Last winter, before her solo show, she had briefly visited Tokyo to take part in an exhibition at the Tokyo Metropolitan Art Museum. Along with her gallerist and a few other artists, she had attended a gathering at the apartment of the head of an architecture firm, who was also an art collector. That was where she'd met this man. An average, middle-aged man, ordinary in every way. She usually didn't know most of the people at these types of gatherings and often found herself bored. She wouldn't have been able to stand it for even an hour if she hadn't been playing with a ball of oil-based clay. Seated next to her, this man had studied her as she had made objects in miniature. She molded the man's unremarkable features, transforming the clay into a face with a balding head and a rounded nose and wearing oval glasses. She showed it to him.

The man laughed lightly at the coin-sized birthmark on the clay cheek beneath the clay glasses, his expression natural and relaxed. He seemed to be the kind of person who could complete any and all tasks discreetly, like a shadow. She spoke to him to stave off boredom. When she took his business card, she thought she misunderstood his occupation, which was printed in Japanese next to his name. For a moment she kept her head bowed. "You must be well-versed in this line of work," she said. "I guess you could say that," the man replied offhandedly. "I've been doing it for a while." She slid his business card into her pocket and left once the room became a little livelier.

That had been a few months ago. Somehow the man remembered her. It was seven in the morning; through the phone she heard the clattering of the subway. She invited him to her place the following morning. He asked her what was going on. She didn't answer but instead told him her address, quickly, in case he declined. She couldn't tell if he was writing it down.

"I'll leave your fee on the table," she said.

"Wait," he said.

"Yes, go ahead."

"So, is it a suicide?" the man asked courteously.

She didn't respond. She hung up after about ten seconds. There wasn't much she would leave behind, anyway. But she would still need someone to clean the apartment and remove the traces of her brief stay, which was what the man did for a living. The man was a death cleaner.

Ten hours later, she brushed her hair and pulled a padded vest with pockets over her windbreaker. She coiled her leather belt and slipped it into the topmost pocket. She tucked in a handkerchief in case she drooled at the very end. The night before, she had slid her passport into the top pocket to aid in identification. As she did that, her thoughts had flitted briefly to Saim. Saim always wore a pendant with her name and contact information around her neck so passersby wouldn't rummage through her bag when she collapsed in public. Saim would never forgive her for this. Saim wouldn't even try to understand her decision.

She left the apartment, chair in hand. She locked the door behind her and slipped the key into one of her bulging pockets. Forty minutes by foot to Ueno Park. The sun would set gradually as she walked. She headed toward Uguisudani Station. Would the death cleaner come closer to the evening? Maybe he wouldn't come at all. No, she was certain he would. He might be relieved that there wouldn't be much to handle. He would call the residency program director at the Seoul Art Foundation and then her Aunt Sukhui, following the directions she had written out. Not that it mattered in what order he made the phone calls. She had already emptied the fridge and the garbage and the drawers. She might not have needed to call the man. She shook off that thought. Her chosen spot in the park wasn't an obvious one. She had to be discovered no later than three or four hours after drawing her last breath. Even five minutes after death, the body, formed of trillions of cells, would slowly—but then terribly quickly—start to decompose. It would disintegrate from the innermost part, turning her into a mass of mush. She shuddered. She couldn't forget what the death cleaner had said to her at the party. "Do you know what a body looks like at the very end?" Quietly, avoiding her eyes: "It turns into liquid. A terrible, stinky, sticky liquid." At the very least, she wanted to be discovered before the branch broke and dumped her body onto the ground. At the party, people had enjoyed the French wine specially brought out by the host. Bing Crosby was crooning "White Christmas" in the background. She remembered the lyrics. The man had glanced at her tense face. And then said with finality, "Actually, liquid is not the final state. It eventually becomes vapor."

She hurried along. She was hungry. All she'd had was coffee and the two macarons at Tokyo Midtown the day before, as well as a few sips of water. There had been so many things to work out once she'd decided to hang herself from a tree. She had to figure out how to get up the tree, what kind of strap to use, how she would position herself, the timing, and a plan for what to do if her resolve faltered at the last minute. You had to weigh your pockets down with stones or tie heavy rocks around your waist and wade into a river like Virginia Woolf. If she was too heavy, the branch wouldn't be able to support her weight, and she might tumble to the ground before she was dead. She had emptied her body for a week as if emptying and cleaning a glass bottle. There were dozens of ways to position your body when hanging yourself, depending on the location and what you were using—placing your feet on the ground, kneeling, lying down, sitting on a chair, squatting. But there was only one way if you hanged yourself from a tree: jumping to your death.

The street rose uphill. She was out of breath. The chair legs banged against her shins. She could see the dark green clump of forest ahead. Goodbye to the nights she kneaded clay, quaking with suffocating anxiety and fear; goodbye to tears, to erupting belly laughs, to love that made her feel like she was stabbing and being stabbed with sticks; goodbye to nights spent trembling in the basement, burying her face in her arms as if attempting to avoid falling rocks; goodbye to her father, to everything. It was time to bid farewell to everything that had ever caused her to feel unsettled. She looked up at the dark trees and squeaked, "Goodbye."

She looked around. People were heading toward the exits, and she spotted a few unhoused people hauling sacks and boxes for shelter. She didn't want to piss herself. She left the chair in front of the women's restroom and headed in. There was a sheen of sweat coating her back. There was hardly any pee in her bladder. She scrubbed her hands clean. She kept her head bowed to avoid seeing her reflection. Water splashed the mirror.

Outside she found a little girl in a lacy hat sitting on the wooden chair, swinging her legs. Was she waiting for her mom to come out of the restroom? Feeling chased by time, she frowned at the girl and said, "This isn't a chair you can sit on." Maybe she should have said, "This isn't a chair." Her armpits got damp. *Don't get anxious*, she told herself. *Maybe she doesn't understand my Japanese.* The girl was gazing silently up at her with innocent eyes, but she didn't get up. A woman came out of the restroom and looked at the girl on the chair and then at her, standing by it with her arms crossed, then pulled the girl to her feet. "Moushiwake gozaimasen," the woman apologized several times, clutching the girl.

Now she and her chair were alone in front of the restroom. What if someone else came by to sit on the chair? She picked the chair up again. She was on the path leading to the Tokyo National Museum. Nearby was a guard post that was usually vacant, and to the right was a small but dense grove of trees.

There was one particular tall, large tree—a Kwanzan cherry tree. She'd chosen this tree after a long search through the park. A tree she'd selected as carefully as choosing good paper, studying it in the bright sun and in shifting light.

The death cleaner had been in his line of work for twenty years. He would know she wouldn't take her life in the apartment. She'd left a short note next to the envelope containing his fee. *Ueno Park, to the right of the fountain, beyond the zoo, at the cluster of cherry trees near the Tokyo National Museum.* She'd figured out that few people headed down this path in the evenings, that the Tokyo National Museum closed at five. The cherry trees looked strong and sturdy; a part of her wanted to try slamming her body into them. These trees in the interior of the park were especially pretty. Their trunks shone in a lustrous black, like healthy soil, as if they were yet undiscovered.

The cold air curled around her shoulders. *If you think of the chair as death*, she thought as she approached the tree, *the only thing left to do is to put the chair down.* She tightened the legs carefully to ensure the chair wouldn't tip. Everything else would be handled by professionals afterward. She took a deep breath. She felt a chill on the nape of her neck. She craved a hot cup of tea. She glanced at the sky, now a dark navy-purple. She climbed onto the chair and looked up at the dark tree she would be dangling from in a minute. She realized something. A person who was about to hang themselves from a tree did one last involuntary act, as natural as breathing—they lifted their chin. Because they had to find a place to secure the strap. With her head tilted back, her eyes scanned the branches, a tangle of thick and thin lines. At the very top, on the highest, thickest branch, sat a tiny person.

She rubbed her eyes. She wasn't dreaming.

It was quiet. An absolute quiet.

"Halmeoni?" she asked, shoving her hands into her pockets.

"How do you know who I am?" asked the tiny person atop the tree.

"Hello."

"You've never met me."

"I know you're Halmeoni."

"What are you doing here?"

"What you think I'm doing?"

"I can help you. If you want."

"If you're going to lecture me about hope or life, I can move this somewhere else."

"I don't know enough about things like that to tell you anything."

"You didn't even live that long."

"I didn't."

"I'm seven years older than you were when you died."

"When did I die? I forget."

"In 1951. In the winter. You were thirty."

"I'm sure you're right."

"You were wearing a long chestnut skirt printed with half-moons."

"Was I?"

"On that day, I mean. And your black hair was in a neat, ear-length bob."

"That was a long time ago."

"It was winter."

"February."

"Two days before the Lunar New Year."

"That's right."

"It was so cold that you thought your eyes and nose and lips would be raked off your face."

"You're talking about it as if you saw it with your own eyes."

"I lived with Abeoji for a long time."

"I see."

"What you did wasn't right."

"What wasn't?"

"You ruined his life."
"You shouldn't talk about your father that way."
"Just admit it. You were selfish."
"Aren't you also thinking only about yourself right now?"
"Yes."
"I was even younger than you. Don't you see?"
"But you had a family."
"It didn't matter."
"It did."
"So does that mean you wouldn't do this if you had a family?"
"I'm choosing this for me."
"I did, too."
"I chose how to live my life. And this right here is my choice, too."
"I know. I'm not going to try to stop you."
"Is it cold there?"
"It's the kind of place that makes you forget about being cold."
"What else?"
"It's the kind of place where you don't need things like conviction."
"But then, why are you here?"
"I wanted to see my son's daughter, just once. Before you die."
"You don't have the right to call him your son."
"I bore him."
"No. You abandoned him."
"You did, too."
"I didn't. I grew up and moved out."
"You shut your father out of your life."
"You're a strange person, Halmeoni."
"So are you."
"What do you mean?"

"You could have done this in Seoul, at home."

"It just happened this way."

"No. You came to meet me."

"You've been following me around all my life. Admit it."

"I don't live in your world anymore. There's no reason for me to follow you around."

"Aren't you the one trying to pull me into your world?"

"Depends how you look at it."

"You must have seen your children die. My aunts and uncles."

"I did."

"It's all your fault."

"That's what they chose. That's what you said."

"What?"

"That you chose this."

"Some things influence choices."

"Not me."

"You're a coward."

"How so?"

"..."

"Hurry. The guards will come by soon."

"I'm not scared."

"You're not? I envy you."

"Why?"

"You've conquered life's biggest fear. The fear of death."

"Yes. I have."

"That means, from now on, you're free to do anything you want."

16

Fifteen minutes by foot

He was standing at the entrance of Sensō-ji, which was mobbed. The oldest temple in Tokyo. People thronged before the huge lantern hanging from the Kaminarimon out front, taking pictures, forcing him to step aside each time. So many tourists—Chinese, German, Korean. The street leading to Nakamise Shopping Street and to Sensō-ji was about three hundred yards long. On either side of the long street were shops that had thrived for over a hundred years, generation after generation. Asakusa was a popular tourist destination in Tokyo, and the main attraction was this street, leading from the Kaminarimon through Nakamise. People were drawn to this area year-round. Soon pale pink cherry blossoms would bloom, arching over Nakamise Shopping Street, and flutter down. Construction was underway at the entrance to the main hall, the structure held up by horizontal and vertical supports. Pigeons flew between the supports, pulling the air up behind them. Or were they plastic bags? The sun was brilliant behind the people walking toward him, haloing them. All the faces looked the same, their shadows jumbled together on the ground. He was worried—not that she would blow him off but that he wouldn't recognize her. Shadows lengthened. Ignoring the tourists waiting for him to move out of the way, he stayed put in his spot right below the lantern. This was the most visible spot. She would walk up this path from the metro.

She hadn't recognized him at Tokyo Tower. He had chatted with her at the dinner but didn't even know her name. Maybe she had thought he was hitting on her. Thankfully she did remember meeting him last December. He mentioned the host's name, Park, the CEO. He referred to the candles on the table and the clay she had played with. If she hadn't recalled those details, he had planned to bring up the bald man who had sat next to her that evening. Lowering her guard, she'd pushed a section of her bob off her forehead. Her black nail polish was chipping and peeling. She seemed inattentive to everything. He had hoped he was drawn to her because she was unlike anyone else. Because she had nothing in common with any other human. Because she projected a lack of interest in nearly every kind of relationship, like the many skeptics in the world. But as she looked at him after pushing her hair off her face, he realized her gaze had changed. She appeared haughty, like most women who did their work with conviction. It was a brief moment, but he found himself disappointed that she might not be different from other women after all. Still, he was secure in his initial assumptions, in what he'd sensed before he had approached her. He had stared insistently into her dark eyes, gathering all his strength. She turned away first. That was when he knew for certain that he had been right: that she appeared haughty not to protect something within herself, but because she was fearlessly blank, having given up the most important thing in life. This subtle, resolute demeanor was why she stood out.

He had spotted Jun striding toward them, a hand raised high in the air. She had been about to turn away from him. Negishi, like Yanaka, was in Taitō-ku. Her place was fifteen minutes by foot from his. He had quickly thought of places that weren't far from where she was staying. Someplace easy to find and open daily. Only later did he regret suggesting a tourist attraction instead of Ueno Park. They hadn't had time to exchange numbers. She hadn't seemed to be paying much attention to what he was saying.

Now he would have no recourse if she didn't show up.

It was thirty minutes past the time he'd suggested. He didn't budge. He stood there, the anxiety that he might not recognize her in the crowd dissipating. Maybe she wasn't coming.

It wasn't for any particular reason that he wasn't dating. It was just that he had become accustomed to being with Sinae. Not much had been lacking from it, and he had no responsibilities in their relationship. At least until his brother died. Until then, none of his problems had required deep thought; he hadn't felt the need to reflect on his life. There was nothing more he could possibly want from Sinae. She was the kind of person who embraced all the positivity in the world. Her pleasant scent and laughter had pushed away the anxieties encroaching in on him. He hadn't seen any reason to be with anyone else.

But now he was waiting for another woman. Someone who wasn't Sinae.

His first impression of this woman had been that she seemed to be sinking into black water. Her hands were rough. He knew he should avoid her if he didn't want to get entangled in whatever she was going through. But he wanted to hear the stories that were submerged under that water. It was an unexpected desire. He didn't want to avoid her. It was hard for him to believe in love, but he believed in the power of attraction. He suspected he would be pulled along by these emotions. That was the other thing he knew for certain.

17

If I live

Her father loved Tolstoy. From what she could gather, Tolstoy's books questioned the meaning of life or, in other words, the reason for living. Books that questioned crimes and sought forgiveness. The moment the author felt he had achieved all that he had desired, he had wanted to die. Happiness and success had made him feel that what he had been depending on had shattered. Was that why Tolstoy began thinking of suicide? A too-ethical person wasn't able to choose death, because their principles would not allow it. It was not due to a lack of courage. Tolstoy hid any rope from his sight in order to avoid impulsively hanging himself, and he refrained from hunting to ward off the temptation for guns. Tolstoy thought of death differently from Dostoyevsky or Kafka—Tolstoy believed God would take him at the appropriate time. While fighting the urge to kill himself, Tolstoy began many of his journal entries this way: *If I live.* He lived as an ascetic, leaving everything behind and entering a monastery to spend his last years in peace and solitude. In the twilight of his life, Tolstoy caught pneumonia and died at the Astapovo station master's residence. He stayed true to his belief in God's will to the very end.

But maybe what he had been struggling against were less his own principles than the death drive. Maybe it was impossible to tease out a clear theory about those obsessed with self-destruction. Perhaps all artists worked in vain. Certain things could never be fully explained; you merely attempted to pull those unexplainable things, that urge to destroy, into your work. Her father's own urge for destruction must have been the source of his appreciation for Tolstoy's writings. Though it could be said that writers tended to write about their own experiences, and all experiences could be summarized into two things: life and death.

When she first attempted to incorporate silicone and air into her sculptural practice, critics described her work as embodying "deterioration and recovery." She had thought she was expressing life and death.

Her father's reading habits were anemic; he didn't read widely or creatively. His diary attested to his habits. When she happened to look through his diary, she discovered that each entry began with *If I live*. A mystic or a rationalist couldn't have written that. She had moved out, leaving her father behind.

Jumping once you climbed up a roof, looping a rope around your neck and falling once you scaled a tree—that was how you completed the act.

She silently traced her steps back to the apartment with the chair. She said to herself:

If I live.
There are things I want to confirm.
I might need someone else to help me.

Breathing in the curling smoke, she stood in the crowd by the incense burner at Sensō-ji. She was standing between the main hall and the entrance to the temple. He was below the red lantern hanging in the middle of the Kaminarimon. The huge lantern looked like it weighed more than two hundred pounds. He was looking down Nakamise Shopping Street, which led to the Ginza Line. As she'd walked up, she'd seen white cherry blossoms stretching overhead from either side of the street, creating a tunnel. But it was only January! She'd stopped and looked up. They'd turned out to be artificial flowers tied flag-like to rooftops. She'd ducked her head and walked on. The shadows of the tiny cherry blossoms looked just like the real thing. She had been here a few times on prior visits to Tokyo. It had been tranquil on weekday mornings. Today it was swarming with so many people that she'd wanted to turn around and leave. If he had been serious about meeting up, he wouldn't have chosen this tourist trap but an art gallery or a café.

He arrived twenty minutes before their agreed-upon time. She had already visited the Kannon figure in the main structure and the five-story pagoda on the temple grounds. She was placing incense in the incense burner when he stopped under the lantern. She stood among the people around the incense burner as they scooped the smoke toward themselves. It was supposed to chase away bad spirits. She stared at the bundle of incense burning down in the sand and then glanced back at him. They were so close; if he just turned to look toward the temple, he would spot her.

He was wearing a knee-length khaki trench coat, beige cotton pants, and yellowish sneakers. Though he had good taste, his choice of clothing and his facial expression revealed his desire to blend in; she had gotten this same impression when they had first met. At that party he had been seated diagonally from her, not too far, not too close. She could have struck up a conversation with him. That she hadn't was entirely because of his demeanor, she had thought when she met him again at Tokyo Tower. What she remembered about him from that evening was how he pulled his turtleneck sweater up over his chin and lips. He had looked timid and cowardly but also stubborn. She'd glanced at him as she molded a lamb out of clay. A docile, sensitive animal unable to take charge.

Even though it was now long past the time they were to meet, he didn't look around or glance behind him. He seemed certain she would walk up from the far end of the street. There was no point in disappointing him, nor was there a way for her to exit the temple without passing him by. As she walked toward him, she waved off the smoke that clung to her.

Part Two

18

THERE'S ONLY FISH THERE

She approached him on the platform in head-to-toe black, the same as always. He stood up from the bench. Four thirty in the morning. She was right on time. She must have taken a taxi from her apartment; it was too dark to walk. She had been the one to suggest taking the first train at four forty. Her gait was uneven, as though she were wearing ill-fitting shoes. As though she might totter right onto the tracks. Anyone would think that upon seeing her. And there were no railings or other safety features at Uguisudani Station.

She swung her arms irregularly as she walked toward him but then stopped short a yard. No, a yard and a half. This was the ideal distance between them. She nodded without saying anything. She looked like she hadn't slept at all. Five minutes until the train pulled in. He perched on the end of the bench so she could take a seat. She remained standing. He looked straight ahead but could see all of her. A wide wool scarf was coiled tightly around her shoulders and neck, making it impossible to worm a finger in. She had managed to get herself black plastic boots like he'd suggested. They would be sloshing around in the wet all morning. He wouldn't want to roam around in a place like that if not for her request. If it got colder, the constant drizzle would turn into sleet. She didn't seem to care about the weather. There was something striking about her—her black bob, her thick eyebrows, her dark eyes. But on the day they had met at Sensō-ji and walked toward Sumida River, he'd thought her face was hollowed out. She was neither beautiful nor alluring. She seemed melancholy and gloomy, much like his first impression of her. Maybe he had been staring too intently at her. Maybe he had been staring not at her but at another face, at someone barely clinging to life. As they'd passed the water bus stop, he'd wondered if he could come up with an excuse to see her again. That was when she asked if he could take her somewhere. Her offhanded tone suggested it didn't matter to her either way. That had bothered him.

The train pulled in. They would board the JR Yamanote Line and get off at Shimbashi Station, where they would take a taxi to Tsukiji Market. They weren't taking the Hibiya Line, which went directly from Minowa Station to Tsukiji Station, because the first train was at a later time. The market opened at six. There were quite a few passengers despite the hour, their expressions the same, stiff. She held the train strap, looking out the window. He glanced at the map and counted the number of stations. Their stop was the seventh.

"There's something I have to see there," she said to him.

He didn't think he had asked her anything. "There's only fish there."

"That's fine."

"I don't know if we'll be able to find our way around."

"You've been there before, you said?"

"A few times, when friends came to town."

"I'm sorry."

"For what?"
"It's so early in the morning."
"I guess so."
"It is."
"Then, this is what we'll do."
"What?"
"Next time can you come with me somewhere?"
"Sure."
"There are so many better places in Tokyo."
"All right, we'll do that."
"The weather's pretty bad today."
"It's still winter." She smiled.

He grabbed the strap so he wouldn't teeter. It seemed she would agree to anything he proposed. He felt oddly rejected. She looked as though she wouldn't resist, even if he grabbed her by her stick-like neck and shoved a hand down her top, her body swaying while he groped her as she blinked slowly, indifferently.

In the hazy, brightening sunlight, her face glowed with a sudden vitality. It was the first time he'd seen this expression on her, though of course he hadn't known her very long. Was he wrong about everything he thought he knew about her? Maybe she was more tenacious, more persistent, than he had realized. She wanted to visit the largest fish market in Tokyo. He wanted to know what she was seeking. She was concealing something; she could not see how tense she appeared. The train halted at Shimbashi Station. "We're here," he said brusquely.

19

What she saw at Tsukiji Market

Some things were difficult to classify. Like abstraction and materiality, regularity and irregularity. The gradually lightening early morning sky. Now a crimson glow ribboned up between buildings, as if pulled from deep underground. Dark pink and light blue bled over dawn, and above that, a blue tinged with yellow spread out like pigment in water. Standing at the entrance to the fish market, she watched and felt deeply the many layers of colors, colors stacked below a sky that was still mostly gray. It wouldn't be possible to depict what she was seeing. What the colors connected to might not even be part of this world. There was something else she couldn't easily classify. When he asked her why she wanted to visit Tsukiji Market, she wondered, *Am I drawn here because of Halmeoni or me? If neither, who? How many people drew me here?* But she could not ponder those questions here. She was shivering too much. The market floor was damp, and her feet were already frozen solid. The smell of the fish was precise and vivid. He was walking with her. She kept forgetting she was with someone else. She could not even remember this man's name. She followed him deeper into the market, to the auction.

Bells began ringing at six. Cold air swirled in the tuna auction area the size of a large gym. She felt she were standing in front of an open freezer. White light glared down from tubular fixtures on the ceiling. Tourists hustled from one end of the room to the other to nab good spots. If what he had told her was accurate, once an auction ended on one side, another would begin on the other. Massive quantities of huge frozen tuna were lined up on the ground, bellies gaping open. Their bodies were scribbled with red numbers: 十一, 三十一. Buyers beamed their flashlights on the cross sections near the tails and speared morsels out with hooks to feel the red flesh with the tips of their fingers, then popped it in their mouths and chewed. Their movements were efficient and constrained, not one part unnecessary, possible only for those who had long served in one line of work. She recalled how her father would plane wood. She studied the movements of the buyers handling the fish. Could they sort out the minute differences in taste and freshness? Handled by the buyers' expert hands, the fish were more like houses or valuable furniture waiting to be sold. Knee-high black boots, sharp hooks worn on the waist, white towels wrapped around foreheads, the sweat, the sharp tang. Only men, if you disregarded tourists. Only men worked in the auction area, like on fishing boats. The smell of fish, the smell of men. She felt ill. Sweat beaded on her forehead. She riffled through her pockets. She didn't have paper or a pencil. He asked if she needed something. She said no. Her hands moved swiftly inside her pockets, sketching.

The auction began. The most commanding man, who had been handling tuna and carefully writing in a record book, flipped a box over, got on top, and rang his bell. His speech sounded like a fast song or a language from the opposite end of Asia. People sold and bought tuna, hands snatching at the air. She suddenly felt hot. Tourists' cameras clicked, and the auctioneer raised his voice, and tuna were dragged out one by one, hooks through their open gills. The air buzzed with bells and voices.

Time was being violently sucked away. She picked up a foot and bent her knee, like a bird. *I'm not overheated, I'm not dizzy. I'm just freezing.* She switched feet. Her breath came out white.

They left before the auction drew to a close. The market was evidently several hundred square miles. She wouldn't see everything even if she poked around all day, even if she got lost and wandered. They followed a path to the inner market. The ground was slick and slimy with water and blood and discarded guts. The smell of fish crushed her temples. Tuna, yellowtail, snapper, mackerel, Japanese halfbeak, squid, octopus, stingray, shellfish, greenling, salmon roe, and herring roe, all displayed in wooden pallets and Styrofoam boxes. Narrow paths visible between the stacks of fish and merchants speeding through in electric carts. Merchants who had bought tuna at the auction were carving up the fish with short, sturdy knives. Red and vivid, the flesh gleamed.

They headed into a café she'd noticed from the taxi on their way to the market. She committed their path through the market to her memory so she could return alone later. She would no longer need his help. This café would be her signpost. He hastily slurped his coffee; he must have been freezing, too. A blue cast to his chin. The rain had stopped, and the sky had cleared up. She was in a strange place. Tokyo, the fish market, this cramped café where she had to sit shoulder to shoulder with strangers, her bag and coat stored in a plastic basket under the table, surrounded by Japanese people who seemed never to laugh or raise their voices above whispers. Her hair, even the hair in her nose, thoroughly marinated in the smell of fish. She thought about that man, the death cleaner, who had told her, "The smell of death is frightening because it never goes away, no matter how much you wash up. In the end, the only thing you can do is clip your nose hairs. Because the smell gets stuck there." That man had not seemed to be a good party guest. Her coffee was still hot. Was it good or bad that she had met that man?

He was gazing quietly out the window, his thoughts seemingly elsewhere. She looked out, too. "If we cross the street and walk down that way," he said, "we could take the Hibiya Line straight home." He suggested they head out. He told her about Hongan-ji, an ancient Indian-style building they would pass. He'd thought it was a temple and popped in. He seemed to be setting up a joke. Though she didn't really care, she asked him what it was if not a temple. "A funeral home," he said, "and a market sets up there some weekends." Her thoughts returned to the fish. In the future, if she were to recall the fish she'd seen today, she would picture an enormous, hard lump, frozen solid, the body white and frosted but the gills and cut-off tail a vivid red, powerful and stolid despite being dead.

"Were you able to see what you wanted to see?"

"No," she said, denying that last thought.

"What do you mean?"

"What I saw today."

"Tuna?"

"Yes."

"What do you mean, no?"
"I didn't see what I was looking for."
"And what's that?"
"Just . . . fish." She smiled.
He didn't smile back.
She said to herself, *I didn't see any blowfish today.*

20

Why only now

He buried his face in his cold sheets. The floorboards creaked as his mother walked around the house in slippered feet. Their house was old, wood-framed. They tiptoed up and down the stairs so his father wouldn't hear them. His mother double-checked the lock on the front door, turned off the downstairs lights, then stood by the calla lilies in the living room before going into the downstairs bedroom. An hour later she would get up, disheveled, and come into his room to close his window. He wanted to be asleep when she did. He tossed and turned. What was she waiting for? He wanted to ask her if she was satisfied with his father smiling at her only once a day. She had to know his father wasn't getting better. That there was nothing to do other than to keep a close eye on him.

His father had retired after his brother killed himself. Everyone had disagreed with that decision—his father's friend, the psychiatrist Dr. Suzuki; close colleagues; people who knew about his father's latent depression. Dr. Suzuki had insisted that maintaining one's daily schedule, not changing it up, was the best way to fight the shock. But his father would not be persuaded. Perhaps his father thought his eldest son's death was his fault. His father had gone into medicine because depression ran on the paternal side of his family. His father promised Dr. Suzuki that he would enter treatment again upon retirement. And that he would follow the regimen faithfully.

He never understood what undergoing faithful psychiatric treatment entailed. His father never left his room. Even when former colleagues came by, taking turns, at his mother's request, his father would bow silently and go back up the creaky stairs. The only promise his father kept was going to the clinic twice a week, taking medication prescribed to him. Otherwise, his father sat in his old rocking chair, staring out the window. Dr. Suzuki would stop by on his way home from work. But his father never cracked a smile, while his mother kept waiting for something to change.

He turned over, tucking his arm behind his head. He wanted to fall asleep. But he felt jittery, as if he might spring up and slap his mother across the face if she walked into his room. He wanted to see her with her eyes opened confidently, her eyes twinkling with rationality. It was past time to accept everything as it was. He rubbed his face with his hands. His mother might be able to suffer through another day as she watched his father, took a walk, locked his window. But how would she be able to live a year like that? Or three years? His curtains billowed in the breeze. He needed to find a way to fall asleep, his mind wiped clean. He didn't want to think about his brother, about Sinae, about his father dying. His mind wandered. Three-dimensionality—something that had length, width, and depth. Love was like that. Hadn't his parents taught him that long ago? An overwhelming sorrow shouldered past him.

He had to see Sinae again. Sinae, who believed he would return to her. He would tell her about his foolishness, about what he'd realized when his brother died. He was foolish to believe he could understand and accept and fulfill Sinae. He shook his head. He had been seeing her for ten years, from before she'd had her child. Still, he needed to say what he felt. He needed to tell her that love was three-dimensional, that the volume of this three-dimensional thing was difficult to figure out. He heard creaking at the bottom of the stairs. Why did he only now feel the need to tell Sinae these things? Quiet footsteps crossed the hallway. He remembered her silhouette, the woman who had seemed to limp with every step. He heard his door open. He squeezed his eyes shut. He began thinking about the eighteen ways of calculating the volume of a three-dimensional object.

21

HIS GAZE ANXIOUS

She dropped the knife. The phone was ringing.
    She lowered the flame and emerged from the kitchen to look around the apartment. The phone was on the side table by the sofa. Who would call this number? She had asked the staff at the Seoul Art Foundation and the Tokyo Art Center to reach out by email; she had told them she wouldn't be turning on international roaming. In fact, she'd disconnected her cellphone before leaving Seoul. The phone rang louder and louder. She sat on the sofa, her wet hands on her knees, palms up. It was evening. She had gone into the kitchen to make something to eat for the first time since she had moved in. This puzzling hunger was hard to sate. Food like convenience-store onigiri or beef hash over rice from a restaurant didn't do anything to chip away at it. Her hunger had suddenly resurfaced after a long hibernation. It demanded food that wasn't too sweet or salty or spicy. What kind of food could that be? When the phone rang, she'd been dicing carrots, onions, and shiitake mushrooms, boiling broth, and soaking rice to make mushroom juk. Thinking that this pang had to be something else if the juk didn't satisfy it. Water dripped from her hands. She could

feel the caller staring at her as she sat still next to the phone, which rang and rang with irritation. Was it Saim? But she was too far away to be of use even if Saim had collapsed. Maybe it was Baek. It wouldn't have been difficult for him to figure out how to reach her. She had only been away for about two weeks. But it wasn't like Baek to call. She waited for the phone to stop ringing. Emotions swirled inside her—she felt contrite, she wanted to argue, she felt longing, she wanted to avoid it all.

She watched the waterdrops land on the carpet. It wasn't like watching the vertical movement of a knife hurtling to the floor. She didn't have to worry that they would land on her foot, drawing blood. She felt she had moved into a different dimension, like she was hallucinating, like she was staring at a flame. The ash-colored carpet became wet, and these amorphous wet spots resembled small, faraway countries on the world map hanging in the bathroom. "I'm here," she murmured. "I'm still here, alive. Baek . . ." Her palms were now bone-dry. The spots on the carpet faded. The living room was devoid of humidity or the smell of food. She couldn't hear the phone ringing anymore, the phone she never used and never thought she'd use. No. That wasn't true. She remembered she'd called that man that day, the day she'd gone to Ueno Park with the chair.

She picked up the phone. She heard the dial tone. Her heart pounded. In her head she went over what she would say. She wanted to talk about dinner or the weather, just chitchat. She wanted to have a conversation that lasted less than two minutes, a conversation whose rhythm was off by half a beat. Her father didn't pick up. Six thirty. He would still be in the shop. Maybe he didn't hear the phone ringing over the machinery. She tried again. He didn't pick up. She could practically hear his rattling scooter. She pressed the phone to her ear. She had not been able to figure out her father when she had been beside him; even if she had lived with him forever, she would never have understood him. She moved out the year she turned thirty-one, not long after she found out about the existence of his birth mother. She had even worried over what to say if her father asked her why she was leaving. She needed an excuse. It wasn't enough that she was already thirty, because they'd lived together her whole life, just the two of them, peacefully, like flowing water, in sometimes intimate, powerful coexistence. Two stones becoming smooth.

This was what she wanted to say to him.

Abeoji. I couldn't stand listening to you talk in your sleep anymore. I was sick of everything: how you sob and flail in your sleep, how I had to shake you awake from your nightmares. You'd feel the same if you were me. You'd know how awful it is to hear someone over sixty shouting, "Eomma! Eomma!" Begging and sobbing. You have to understand. And it was like that every night. Every single night. We all get over disturbing incidents and painful experiences. But you never have. The way you talk in your sleep hasn't changed. Not in all the time we lived together. I didn't want to hear that anymore, to see you sweaty, your hands grasping at the air. I wanted to start over by myself in a new place. Somewhere brand-new, without you or Halmeoni or your siblings around.

One could say something like this only once. Carefully, never to be repeated. She put the phone down and buried her face in her hands.

Nine-year-old Abeoji. The boy who watched his young mother, his gaze anxious. The child who tugged on his mother's long, half-moon-patterned skirt when she lifted a bowl with two hands. His mother drank down the entire bowl in front of him and his father, then collapsed. Nine-year-old Abeoji saw everything. Every single moment. His mother drinking toxic blowfish soup and dying by her own hand. He would always remember that his mother had prepared the blowfish in the morning and simmered the soup for a long time, sitting in front of the kitchen fire. Nine-year-old Abeoji saw everything. His mother collapsing, his mother twitching, his mother stiffening, his mother vomiting blood, his mother's eyes bulging, and, finally, his mother's eyes closing halfway, his mother lying still. His mother, who had died.

Her father became nine years old again every night in his dreams. Not a single night was spared. Alcohol did not help. She could not stand her father anymore, this nine-year-old desperately calling for his mother. That was the only reason why she had left. She couldn't think of a more terrible reason than that.

22

This person, is she a woman?

The interiority encouraged by a space—he referred to that special quality as the thinking space. This feeling was elusive aboveground, most especially in a skyscraper. You had to be in a basement like this, in an appropriately dim space, populated with succulents, scented with cigarettes and alcohol. When he agreed to take on the renovation of Desert, Mun had asked him to turn the bar into a space one could think in. That was more complicated than being asked to squeeze in a set of stairs or a window in an impossible layout. He remembered studying the scruffy, rotund bar owner. Then or now he could not claim to understand Mun, but he could imagine the space Mun wanted. It was Mun's idea to hang black-and-white photographs on the brick walls, while his was to hang a heavy steel door at the entrance. A heavy, massive door that took effort to push open, giving you the sense that time had been reversed every time you walked in.

That door opened, and in walked Sinae, wearing a green skirt and a beige trench coat.

Which way will I end up going? he wondered as he wiped a finger across his sweating lowball glass. As Sinae sat down next to him, he detected a light scent—dried lavender, perhaps rubbed gently along the lining of her clothes. Sinae's scent, which he knew well. Lavender was what she smelled like, both on top and below. The air inside, which had been flowing in an orderly fashion, scattered, as if a breeze had barreled through. He was watching a glass bottle that had accidentally drifted over, bobbing and being pushed around before finally floating away. He sat up straight. He would try not to feel so uncomfortable. Because then he would get anxious, and that would open the floodgates for all the feelings that accompanied anxiety. He had buried his face in Sinae's chest whenever he'd felt that way. And somehow ten years had gone by. He pulled his stretched-out turtleneck over his chin.

Sinae sipped her mojito. Hemingway's presumed choice of cocktail, made with muddled mint. He glanced at the photo of Hemingway hanging to his left. The shirtless writer was wearing boxing gloves, looking into a mirror. Once Sinae had told him Hemingway had believed that a truly funny book could be written only by someone who had experienced countless ordeals. Overgrown beard and mischievous eyes. Something about the author reminded him of Mun. Next to Hemingway was a picture of John Steinbeck in his later years, sitting under a large tree with a woolly dog. He had noted that the two authors were an odd pairing, and Mun had responded apathetically, "There's no real reason behind it; it's just that they both liked dogs, and they both loved the desert." Mun had three dogs of different breeds. Rover, a mountain goat of a dog, lived in the bar. If Mun couldn't come to the bar for some reason, Rover would end up locked inside all day.

"What are you thinking about?" Sinae asked.

"Dogs."

"That's random."

"Is it?" He smiled.

"It's really strong today."

"Should we ask for more ice?"

"No." Sinae stared at him.

"It feels more humid this year," he mumbled.

Sinae finished her cocktail and ordered another.

"What do you think would be a hilarious book?" he asked.

"A book about eating and fighting and sleeping, and then repeating all of that the next day."

"That's a sad story."

"Same thing," Sinae said flatly.

He had never seen her like this. Had Sinae changed, too? She had been someone who considered eating and fighting and sleeping to be acts of beauty. The Sinae he knew would think that even death was something of value. If someone were to ask him why he'd been with Sinae all this time, he would have to say it was because she made a whole world of anxiety and suspicion vanish. When he was with her, he felt an intense, electric sense of relief, a momentary peace. Sinae knew how to make him feel that way. This quality of hers was why he had not been able to end things. He had not been sure what to make of the situation, even after she had married another man and had a baby. The one thing his brother's death had given him was the ability to reflect on himself. But that had unexpectedly dredged up big emotions. *What am I doing right now?* This question only brought up sorrow. What was there to do if what he believed was love was actually nothing of the sort? For two years after his brother died, he pondered this question as he continued to see Sinae. What he had ignited with her had turned out to be a small fire made of straw. The kind of fire that snuffed itself out if you didn't tend to it, feeding it with more straw. That couldn't possibly be love. He didn't yet know what to say to Sinae.

"I met someone like my brother," he said.
"Lots of people resemble other people."
"I'm telling you, I met someone just like my brother."
"Your brother's dead."
"I just don't want the same thing to happen to this person."
"What are you talking about?"
"I could have saved him."
"You're not the reason he died."
"I'm the last person he called."
"There was nothing you could have done."
"No, no. It wouldn't have happened if I'd been there."
"You're being too sensitive."
"I want to save . . ."
"Who?"
"This person I met."
"This person, is she a woman?"
"Or—I don't know. I just don't know."

23

Fabric Town

A bike rack for residents was installed next to the building entrance. It was a double-decker rack, perhaps to accommodate the many households with more than one bike. She had heard that the designated spots changed once a year by lottery. This year the spot assigned to her unit, number 605, was on the second level. Her shoulders cracked every time she raised her arms to pick up and pull down her bicycle. Her body had been gradually shrinking since she came here. Maybe it was her brain that was withering, not her body. Her brain, clean and soft when she was born, with hardly any wrinkles. But a yearning for death had taken root before blood began pumping through it. Now she observed herself skeptically as she struggled to take her bicycle down. Dozens of bicycles, lined up in a neat row, glinted under the morning sun. In certain moments she veered off track, forgetting about death. Like when she noticed something drawing light toward it. Maybe she'd first picked up a pencil when she'd realized that such a moment lasted a mere split second. She walked her bicycle around the right side of the building. Two trees wore signs that said ケヤキ, zelkova tree. The trees appeared ancient, and their branches had been trimmed short; perhaps they would be unable to grow leaves when spring came around. If she continued straight and took a right at the three-way intersection, she would end up at the south exit of Nippori Station. People referred to this street as Fabric Town. Twenty minutes round trip from her apartment.

In Seoul it was freezing. February in Tokyo, with its cool breeze, felt like late fall. It did make sense, since Tokyo had a more humid, subtropical climate. Seasons did not fit neatly in a box, as vague as the concepts of abstraction and materiality. Right now it was neither winter nor spring. It was part winter, part spring. A subdued olive light bathed the street, tinting everything around her. If a cool color exuded dissipation and a warm color suggested progression, a subdued olive might be perched right on that boundary. *Why did I choose form, not color?* She looked up at the sky and clattered her bicycle loudly on purpose. Colors and sounds entangled, and streets led to other streets. It was a straight shot to Nippori Station. This street was in a neighborhood, and this neighborhood was in a city. He had said he planned and designed such things for work. He got to know streets and built homes and decorated them with perfectly well-suited chairs. She had nodded, half listening. But she was troubled by the words he'd used—streets and homes and chairs. All the things she was planning to relinquish. Everything he had said might have landed differently if she hadn't already made her decision.

Sculpture was the transformation of materials. In this line of work, the artist constantly sought out mediums, mediums that were perfectly, specifically suited. It was an adaptive art practice. She found herself thinking about the scissors and the tape measure.

The box her aunt had given her contained scissors, a tape measure, and a handheld mirror.

Her grandmother's box.

Her aunt had kept it all that time. Both the scissors and the tape measure were worn as could be, liable to crumble into dust at the gentlest touch. But those simple objects transformed into living organisms the moment she opened the box. As though a blue pail drawn on a blank sheet suddenly burst off the page, water sloshing over the rim, soaking her feet. She couldn't bring herself to close the lid. She needed to think. About what the box was telling her. About the force that had made her bring it all the way here to Tokyo.

She was standing in Fabric Town.

She stood in the center of the district, in the flashiest, most bustling part. Of all the many neighborhoods of Tokyo, this area in particular got busy on early Saturday mornings. Stores flanked the road, selling leather, traditional fabrics, buttons, and specialized flame-retardant material. She would cross the street and head down an alley. The stores themselves were exotic and unusual, but so too were the shoppers: designers hailing from all over the world, folks in the fashion industry. It wasn't all that easy to cross the street; taxis and cars were jammed together. On a stand in front of a lace store, a wide length of white lace printed with red polka dots flapped like an awning; it reminded her of Yayoi Kusama. An hour later, when the sun would rise fifteen degrees higher in the sky, everything would glow brighter, in pure white. She looked down at her clothes. Baggy ash-colored pants and a thick travel coat made of shiny nylon twill. She was dressed in such a way that, if she covered her face, nobody would know whether she was a man or a woman. Ever since she'd begun to think earnestly about dying, she had felt she no longer had a gender. But as she stood there, she felt her dormant gender reawakening. This made her feel wretchedly embarrassed, a sharper mortification than what she felt when she was hungry. She stepped off the curb in front of a family restaurant called Jonathan's, ringing her bicycle bell as she hurried down the street.

24

A NEIGHBORHOOD WITH
SO MANY GRAVES

He looked back at her. She lagged a few paces behind. Maybe because of the cold, her face was bloodless, pale. The sun felt warm on his skin, but the wind was chilly; he wondered if they should forget about taking a walk. An anime character made of stone stood at the entrance to the temple, which ran a day care center in a separate one-story structure. She peeked in; he invited her to push the gate open and enter. The yard was empty except for a few colorful umbrellas on the far side. Perhaps the children had already gone home. He followed her lead and perched awkwardly on the edge of the day care's raised wooden floor. In the mornings he could see from his window a single line of kids in knee-high socks and yellow hats walking past, swinging their arms. Did they know this was a temple? Did they know it had been built over a hundred years ago?

He had not planned to sit with her in this remote temple. He had wanted to show her an empty lot called Kasu Harappa ONDI. The lot held a few egg-sized planters and a single sign indicating its availability for rent. Some people held a flea market or a bazaar, and others played music. Anyone could rent and use the space.

He'd thought she would be fascinated by that empty lot. Had it been an error to think that a sculptor would be drawn to spaces? She didn't show a flicker of interest in that empty lot or in SCAI The Bathhouse, an art gallery housed in a former bathhouse. She seemed interested in nothing.

They had met at Nippori Station. From her apartment, the station was less than ten minutes by bike. She had walked over. At least she seemed to enjoy walking. They walked past wood-frame residential buildings and small side streets, the public cemetery, a bagel shop. She had an even, unexpectedly long stride—twenty-four inches wide. She walked confidently, appearing to know exactly where to go.

A crow flew low across the sky into the silence of the Saturday afternoon. A minute passed so quietly that he thought he could hear moss growing in the shade. Anyone unfamiliar with the neighborhood would have a difficult time finding the temple and its day care center. He liked its simple, symmetrical design; it radiated permanence and conviction. Outside the temple gates was an open space as large as a playing field, dotted only with a few long benches—an earthquake evacuation spot. When he had first come here and sat on a bench, he'd felt relaxed as he watched people exercise or walk their dogs past the cones of light cast on the ground by streetlamps. But then, not even a week in, he had begun thinking that it had been a mistake to move here. In the afternoon, after the day care closed, all he saw were cemetery caretakers or elderly couples strolling slowly by, as though they had just relearned how to walk. Anyone would think his mother was one of them. They could have moved to a busier, livelier neighborhood, but he would have to wait until he could live on his own. It remained a question whether he would ever be able to.

He had wanted to show her this static design. Where stolid conviction hung in the air. He had thought about her even when he had been at Desert, sitting beside Sinae. Why did he want to tell her these things? Show her these things? He needed to interrogate himself. He didn't know when it had all started. When he thought about her, he was overwhelmed with the sensation that he was thinking about himself. He felt stymied, challenged. He drew a box in his mind. The way he did when he faced a complex, hard-to-solve problem. The basics of design resided in the idea that every object could be put into a box. Homes and cars and trees and furniture. He drew her inside a simple box. Whenever he drew a line, things that were fuzzy snapped into focus, almost as if he could reach out and grab them. Slowly a form took shape. If she were a house, her form would be incomplete. A house with broken windows.

"Have you been living around here a long time?" she asked.

"About two years."

"Where did you live before?"

"Somewhere a bit busier."

"Something about this neighborhood makes me feel like someone's following us."

"Maybe because there are so many graves?"

"It's quiet here."

"Tourists don't come to places like this."

"You forget you're in the city as soon as you turn down the alley."

"Yes, it's a nice place to think."

"And to walk."

"Have you been to Kyoto?" he asked.

"The Philosopher's Path, right?"

"Yes, it's really nice when it's cherry blossom season."

"I've walked it, all alone."

"Actually, you're right. It does often feel like someone's following me."

"Who could that be?"

"Someone dead, I'm sure."

"I get the feeling they're watching, too."

"Yes, always."

"Even now."

"Yes, even now."

In his mind, he erased her form. He wanted to draw her all over again. In the shade, her eyes were dark as night.

25

HER EYES LANDED ON THE BLOWFISH

Walking the entirety of Tsukiji Market would be an impossible feat. Not necessarily because of its size but because the wet, winding alleys resembled fish innards. She could go down an alley assuming it would lead to a dead end, but a new path would open up, dumping her out into yet another curved, hidden alley. She sketched a fish in her notebook, a few quick lines, glinting clear and blue. A single blue herring or a blowfish, though she couldn't fully grasp the shape of a blowfish yet. Her fish drawing wasn't bad. Her father's favorite writer once said something to the effect of: "Write what you know, but not too much." It was one thing to describe something you understood, another to overdo it. It was an old habit of hers to write and draw constantly, memorializing things as if taking a photograph. Some things vanished instantly, while others did so gradually. Making a record of that vanishing informed her next work. She could not begin to understand something she had never seen.

Only one shop in the fish market sold blowfish. This shop was nestled in a side street in the Tsukiji Outer Market, flanked by stands specializing in beans or dried seafood. She studied the shop from across the street; a plastic model of a round-bellied, fedora-wearing blowfish dangled at the end of the sign. It was only eleven thirty in the morning, but it already felt like the end of the day. She had been wandering the market since seven.

Early in the morning, she'd had a slice of toast and headed off to Ueno Park. She would sit in Pronto and watch people walk into the park if it turned out to be too cold. Suddenly she'd felt dizzy. She'd leaned against a tree. It felt like someone had blindfolded her and was now tugging her along by the hand. She surrendered herself to this force, headed to wherever it was taking her. It was something like the February wind, lights that randomly appeared, then disappeared, the dizziness she felt before starting a new piece or when she was focused on a single thing for too long. When she opened her eyes, she was standing in a wet alley in Tsukiji Market. She plowed out of the alley and uttered:

"Blowfish."

The name of a fish she had only heard about, the first articulation of what the blowfish was to her.

Now she went down the three low steps and crossed the street. Market workers in head-to-toe black protective gear sped by in electric carts. The blowfish shop was deserted. The proprietor was in the dark, dreary store, talking on the phone, his back to her. Something smelled fishy and bloody and cold; it hung in the air like old cigarette smoke.

She hovered outside, feeling sick to her stomach. Worried the proprietor would hear her gag and look behind him, she clapped a hand to her mouth and bent toward the display window. Her eyes landed on the blowfish.

A blowfish was laid out on a square stainless-steel dish lined with white muslin. Its body was patterned in black and white. Its tail and fins were spread open like small fans. She would have to venture inside to take a look at the gills and the eyes and the mouth. It was fat and stout, ridiculous-looking. She couldn't believe this one fish contained enough toxin to kill thirty-two people. The display window also included a bristly white bundle of blowfish skin and slimy yellowish blobs that appeared to be innards or roe, each on their own stainless-steel plates. That was all there was to it. Feeling less queasy, she straightened up.

The proprietor strode out, a cigarette in one hand and a knife aimed toward the ground in the other. The knife looked heavy. He had wild, tangled wavy hair and a bushy beard. He wore a plastic apron and knee-high boots, his eyes big and sharp and his physique beefy and imposing. He seemed to read her mind. Would he sell her anything? Still, she didn't avoid his gaze. She looked straight at him, as if she weren't there to buy blowfish. Standing a few steps above her, he tossed his cigarette butt over her shoulder and opened his mouth. "Irasshaimase!"

26

IF ONLY HE WASN'T AFRAID

Nanae would be transferring to KAC's Seoul office. In exchange, a KAC employee would move to their Tokyo office. Last fall the CEO of P&O, the multinational real estate company, had visited Tokyo to check out the Asian market. P&O had then entered into a seven-year cooperative partnership with P, a company betting on huge growth in the Asian real estate market. Seven years was a long stretch of time, during which they could build or buy or sell huge buildings in Tokyo or Seoul. The partnership was grounded in the expectation that the Asian real estate market, particularly in Seoul and Tokyo, would continue to boom. Even amid rumors of an economic downturn, Korea's vacancy rate was a mere 4 percent, and its market was acknowledged to be the most competitive in the world. Although it was unlikely that the Tokyo market would become more competitive overnight, P&O also pursued a partnership with Abe Kengo's firm, which of course had a branch within KAC. That a huge multinational like P was predicting Asian sales to increase to 40 to 50 percent of market share the following year was certainly a positive development. But many of his colleagues seemed skeptical about collaborating with a real estate company; there were no guarantees that the partnership would be profitable for either party.

His boss, Abe Kengo, had worked at P&O's Seoul office, consulting for and overseeing commercial real estate deals involving office buildings and warehouses. As everything in that company was linked to real estate interests, he wasn't sure how this development would affect him. He merely noted to himself that Nanae was going to KAC and that she would continue doing her work in Seoul. He didn't care about buying or selling buildings. But knocking something down was different; if you didn't control for speed and scale, it took only a split second for a city full of potential to decline. But he trusted Abe's business mindset. At Abe's firm they lacked as many things as they had perks. Like working late at night, busywork, layoffs. Abe was the type of businessman who believed that clients would be unhappy if the staff was unhappy. His staff could flex their time within their thirty-three-hour workweek. Personally that was his favorite benefit; he didn't need access to a cafeteria where you could dine while listening to classical music, or a massage room, or a gym. Most significantly Abe had given him the opportunity to work in architecture again. When he had to take his father to the doctor, he went to work around seven in the morning and left at two or three in the afternoon. He could probably have found a firm offering even better perks. But what he wanted was simple: to build something he'd drawn. A building that was a few stories tall or a residential home with trees and windows and chairs. He did not wish for anything more. He led a peaceful life. He wasn't living in disguise, but sometimes he would be overwhelmed by the feeling that he was crouching at the bottom of a glass bottle that didn't let in much light, his eyes covered.

Would I have continued working on the tower if that hadn't happened to Hyeong? he asked himself in the lively izakaya where they were throwing a goodbye party for Nanae. He took in all of Ginza below the floor-to-ceiling tenth-story windows. With glaring outdoor signs and neon lights that kept the night at bay, Ginza seemed to be constantly flashing and glowing, without a moment of respite. The streets were teeming with stores that each held at least a hundred years of history, no matter how tiny the establishment. In Ginza the streets were a grid, making it impossible to get lost, and there were as many traditional buildings as there were modern ones, which was why his mother liked this neighborhood. In the springs and summers, you could see women her age walking leisurely under flowery parasols. Her favorite shop in Ginza was an anpan bakery on 4-chome. The clock on the face of Ginza Wako indicated nine p.m. If he went to the karaoke after-party, he wouldn't have time to stop by the bakery before it closed.

The rush of pure delight you got when looking out at the night view from up high—he would be able to feel that if only he wasn't afraid. Something that wasn't grand could sometimes seem bitter and pitiful, whether it was a person or a work of architecture. For nearly a year after his brother died, he hadn't been able to go anywhere high up. Or, until recently, in elevators. Xanax and Prozac and Serentil didn't help. He wouldn't have been able to come out the other side without the compulsion to reject becoming his brother, without that powerful rage. For the first time since last winter, he was sitting way up above the ground, arms crossed, looking down at the world through a window. At one point he had thought he held that vista captive in his hand. Now he didn't think he would ever again be able to work on a tower.

Soyo, the construction manager, turned to him and topped off his not-yet-empty glass. There were more Korean staff than Japanese. Company dinners brought out a rowdiness in his coworkers. He loosened his tie and picked up a nicely browned shishamo. Nanae was sitting far away from him. Now whenever he went to Seoul for work, he could have lunch with Nanae. What would it feel like to work in Seoul? He reached out and grabbed a bottle of beer.

27

ONE WOMAN AND TOXIN

She was thinking about the proprietor of the blowfish shop. She would have to explain herself and confide in him. It would be difficult and awkward. She would have to make impersonal the problem she had been thinking about for a long time and take him through it step-by-step.

She planned to say: "The question of how to die is just as challenging as the question of how to live. Choosing death means entering another world, a different world from this one, a world without hope or despair or disgrace or rage or forgiveness or love. A world of darkness and loneliness that nobody else can understand. One needs to make this choice with as much passion as it takes to believe in love. None of this is easy to explain, especially a death chosen voluntarily. It's just that some people are fated to be sucked into death. I need to learn about blowfish to learn about my grandmother. I want to know where this fish will lead me."

No, maybe this would be better: "I want to learn about blowfish. Please help me."

In the end she did not say a thing.

The first day she bought blowfish skin displayed in the window. "A thousand yen," the proprietor said curtly, looking irritated. The second time she bought roe, packaged like white pollock roe. It was twice as expensive as the skin. The proprietor put it in a black plastic bag without a word and held it rudely out with one hand. She could feel his suspicious, mistrusting gaze on the nape of her neck until she exited the alley.

Back at the apartment, she placed the skin and roe—later she would learn it was actually shirako, blowfish sperm—on a tray on the table. None of it smelled like anything. The skin was so rough that it didn't seem like it could be part of a fish; it looked like leather from some exotic animal. The shirako looked like thick marble fingers. She could not believe these could be cooked and consumed. She'd never had blowfish before. Nobody in her family ate it, certainly not her father. She'd never even heard him utter the word *blowfish*. This taboo had weighed on the entire family.

She put the blowfish skin and shirako back in the black plastic bag and cinched it tight. She went down to the first floor and put it in the trash. Should she put it in the food waste bin? Which part of the blowfish held the toxin? Only after she got back in the elevator did it occur to her that the proprietor would have removed the toxic parts. She was ignorant about blowfish. This lack of knowledge felt different from not knowing anything about constellations or the history of rail.

On her third trip, she bought a plastic-wrapped tray holding paper-thin slices of blowfish. The proprietor grimaced. He didn't answer her when she asked how she should cook it. She didn't even realize that she'd purchased sashimi, which she could simply dab in soy sauce.

With her fingers, she picked up a slice of sashimi so thin that she could see, through the flesh, the flower pattern on the black container. It tangled like thin cloth. She couldn't tear it; it was tough, like mulberry paper. Despite the sashimi's chewy texture and thinness, she could tell it would taste sensual. Not a single part of the fish she'd bought contained the toxin. But she still felt as though she'd stepped just that much closer to the toxin. She slipped the sashimi, plain, into her mouth, without any soy sauce. It didn't taste all that unusual. A bland, leathery sensation remained in her mouth. It was close to having no smell or taste. She was deflated. She slid the whole thing into the plastic bag it came in and threw it out. Still, she felt light, unlike when she threw out the skin and the shirako, which had felt weighty in her palm. As though she'd completed a difficult task without realizing it.

On her fourth visit, she bought dried fins. The proprietor refused to even look at her. He took her money automatically and made change, gazing pointedly away. She bought a bottle of sake at the large supermarket near her apartment. She warmed the sake and dropped the dried fins, crispy like squid skin, into the sturdy kettle. She waited for the fins to steep, then took a sip of the lukewarm sake.

Ever since she had heard the story, she hadn't been able to wrap her mind around how her grandmother had killed herself. The moment someone decided to die, they began agonizing over the various ways they could take their life. The reason for all this fretting was because they wanted to leave in the cleanest manner possible. And because suicide could give rise to misunderstandings. They had to be thoughtful in choosing the death they wanted; a mistake could bring forth something unwanted. It had to be finished in one go. This last act required meticulous planning and attention to detail. Her grandmother could have used a knife or a rope, or she could have leaped into the well in the front yard or into the waters off the coast of Yeosu. She could have set herself on fire or swallowed pesticides or gulped down all manner of sharp objects. These possibilities had occurred to her when she'd opened her grandmother's box. Her grandmother could have used the scissors or the tape measure. She could have shattered the mirror and slashed her wrists. She hadn't needed to drink an entire bowl of blowfish soup she'd cooked herself in front of her nine-year-old son. Her grandmother's death was entirely too self-centered, she thought, a death that didn't deserve sympathy or compassion. One fact she didn't want to acknowledge was that her grandfather, a boat captain, had caught that very blowfish.

After she had overheard her aunts Jaehui and Sukhui talking one night, she began sensing that someone was tugging at her, following her. She had been preparing for her first solo show. Until then she had believed her grandmother had been an unlucky woman who married into a poor family and was swept away by waves at a young age. When her aunts first mentioned that story to her, they had said her grandmother had been swept away "like foam." That sounded so lonesome; she could see a young, urbane woman falling like a flower, then accidentally carried off by waves. She remembered how everyone had turned silent right at that moment. She realized then that silence could be synonymous with sorrow, even in response to a story that was untrue.

That night she had pretended to be deeply asleep in the corner of the room. Her aunts were talking about her grandmother, the one whose story they'd concealed from her. About her grandmother and blowfish. About one woman and toxin. Lying on her side, she feigned sleep, as though she would stay sleeping forever. Their voices carried, careless. She had understood her father in that instant. Finally she understood why he talked in his sleep, which she had to hear until she left home at age thirty.

One of her aunts said, "Keunoppa told me once that his own daughter looks and acts just like his mom."

She turned. Her father. *What had Abeoji seen in me?*

The hirezake was cold by now. It reeked of fish.

Then, on the third Saturday morning of February, she went to the shop for the fifth time. She didn't buy anything. There was nothing left to buy. The proprietor would never sell her blowfish guts or the toxin he removed from the innards. No matter how often she came by, he would never sell her a whole blowfish. She stood stubbornly in the entrance of the shop while the proprietor yelled, "You, what's your deal? Why do you keep poking around?" He sounded angry. He spat on the floor and threw his cigarette by her feet. She grew more composed, calmer. She didn't want to know what about her made him act this way. She hadn't done anything yet. Customers who came in looked at the two of them, then turned and left. They must not have realized that this was the only blowfish shop in the market. When another customer came by, she took a big step into the store to get out of the way.

While the proprietor helped the customer, she sat on a blue plastic chair facing a huge, blood-soaked wooden chopping block. The chopping block, scored by countless blades, was worn, the middle indented. A few blowfish squirmed in the fish tanks that spanned one wall. They didn't look all that lively or energetic. The customer left, and the proprietor strode toward her as if he were about to strike her across the face. She stood up and placed her bag down on the wet floor. He stood close to her. Blood vessels had burst in his bulging eyes, and his breath was awful. She bowed her head briefly, her hands clasped together. He paused. They didn't speak as they stared into each other's eyes. The truth, a metaphor, a lie. She could choose one of the three.

She felt she could say this now.

"Blowfish has become a new baseline for my senses."

It wasn't a metaphor or a lie. She wanted to speak the truth.

28

Who is beside a person

He was driving toward Wako University. He was careful to stay below forty miles per hour. His father was sensitive to speed. His father was in the back seat, looking out the window, having not uttered a word since they'd left home. The appointment with Dr. Suzuki was at three, and as always, his father wanted to arrive at the hospital half an hour early. While waiting for his appointment, his father would walk around the hospital grounds, lost in thought. This was the hospital his father checked into whenever he felt himself to be on the brink, before signing himself out again in a continuous, unending loop.

He glanced at his side-view mirrors and wondered if he should turn the radio on. His father was wearing a chestnut cashmere coat and a checkered scarf, along with a black fedora and thin tortoise-shell glasses. His brother had given their father those glasses for his birthday three years ago. Thanks to his mother, his father's silver hair was cut short, neat. His father looked like a university hospital doctor at the height of his career, or perhaps a dignified professor nearing retirement. But if you took a step closer, if, to borrow Mun's expression, you crossed the eighteen-inch line, you would notice the shadow of abject helplessness and resignation on his face.

His father tried his best to express how he felt. Dr. Suzuki explained that this tendency was why his father still remained himself despite his persistent illness. The courage to speak about what made him depressed, openly describing what made him sad, what weighed on him, what made him afraid. He didn't disagree. Dr. Suzuki was his father's friend and personal doctor, whom he had called Ojisan since childhood. But you weren't privy to certain things unless you were family, no matter how close you were to someone. Dr. Suzuki did not know how much his father's tendency for truth telling hurt the rest of the family. Especially his mother, who watched over every aspect of his father's life, day in and day out. Some things you knew in theory, others from experience. His mother was the receptacle for all of his father's feelings, isolated in a wordless house ringing with the midday cawing of crows. His mother, who had lived through his father being away by viewing possible future homes with good light, holding his little hand.

Once he'd asked his mother if they should just let his father be. His father would never be well. Like Dr. Suzuki had said, depression like his father's wasn't a minor cold; it was a chronic illness. Something without a miracle cure, something without the possibility of a full recovery. He would never forget how his mother had glared at him as she placed her teacup on the table.

Her cold, blazing eyes had pierced his bones like an arrow. It had taken him a minute to comprehend what her gaze was saying; nobody had ever looked at him like that. With eyes brimming with contempt and rage. At that moment she wasn't his mother. She was a woman who'd loved only one man. She was making her contempt known. A person who knew what love was, judging someone who did not. It lasted no longer than a split second. The brief moment it took for her to move her hand away from her teacup, then pick it up again. Just that sliver of time. His mother's closed lips had twitched as she'd collected herself, then she'd turned her head toward the living room windows. She'd said, "If I wanted to let him be and just have him be beside me, I could have had a dog." Her voice had been stern and cold. After that incident he had found himself wary whenever he spoke about his father. In their three-person household, his father was the only person who was honest about himself. His father's life without his wife—from a young age, he and his brother had understood it was best not to think about that scenario. But maybe his brother had shown other symptoms as a boy, and nobody had tried to understand them—it was a statistical fact that a parent with a heightened risk for suicide would have a child with a heightened risk for suicide. All his life, his father had been afraid of his own father's suicide, which had come at the end of a lifetime of significant depression. A never-ending illness whose most prominent characteristic was pulling the sufferer toward death.

His father was therefore that much more on edge and sensitive. He had glanced at his mother again. Maybe she was afraid his father would detect that her love was changing. He had studied her with suspicion, wondering if that was why she tried so hard to prove to herself that her feelings toward his father were steady. Thankfully she had avoided his gaze.

Now the tires spun over still-frozen patches on the road. His father didn't budge, his head turned to the side, as though he'd forgotten where he was. His father looked lymphatic, the severe angle of his once-strong square jaw having softened, and his half-open lips and puffy cheeks appeared tilted against his nose.

He parked in the hospital lot. It was best not to bother his father in that state, when he was staring silently in a fixed direction. His father wasn't staring at this world; he was weighing something outside of it. He turned the car off and sat still for a few minutes. He opened the back door and placed a hand lightly on his now-dozing father. Quietly he said, "Abeoji." His father ran a palm down his face and got out of the car with his assistance. That Saturday afternoon the hospital grounds were quiet. More people would be out taking walks in March and April, expressionless people floating slowly among blooming trees, looking surreal, absurd.

The temperature wasn't all that low, but it still felt chilly. In March his father would begin to take many—if short—walks. He climbed the stairs, a steady hand supporting his father's elbow. His father's arm, once taut and strong, was now gaunt, the bones nearly visible. Dr. Suzuki was in the hallway. He bowed to the doctor. He was planning to accompany his father all the way in today. He wanted to listen carefully to what Dr. Suzuki said to his father; he might need to tell her the same things at some point. He found himself relieved even as his father considered the world beyond this one. After all, his father had his wife and his old friend Dr. Suzuki in his corner. After his brother had died, Dr. Suzuki had said to him, "Wanting to die isn't the most critical thing. The better question is, who is beside a person thinking about taking their own life?" The doctor's comment had landed like a rebuke; his brother hadn't had anyone.

His father and Dr. Suzuki chatted about the weather as they walked into the exam room. He wanted to know: Did she have someone? He wanted to ask her. He stood in the corner of the room, his father's hat in his hands. When his mother had shut him up with that contemptuous look, he'd wanted to retort: *It's not that I don't know love. I've just never been able to ask for it, like I deserved it. Really, that's all there is to it.*

29

SHE MEETS THE DEATH CLEANER

They were to meet in an hour. Caricaturists sat by the entrance to Ueno Park, waiting for customers. One artist with long dreadlocks beckoned her over: "All you have to do is sit here." He grabbed a pencil before she could respond. *What would my face look like when someone else drew it? What would they notice first, what would they draw first?* She had the kind of face nobody would notice in a crowd. Bland, lacking remarkable beauty or any sort of characteristic. Other than her black bob and round forehead, she had the kind of face in which a caricaturist would struggle to find a notable feature. But maybe it was different now. Maybe her eyes were hollow, like two holes drilled into her face. She had made a self-portrait once—looking straight at herself in the mirror required more courage than she'd expected. For her, a self-portrait wasn't about confrontation with the self or an awareness of who she was; it was meaningless beyond the act of drawing. She had no idea why so many artists were absorbed by self-portraits, particularly at the ends of their lives. She found them uninteresting, even if they explained something about the artist's background or origins.

Dry twigs drifted gently to the ground from above her head. On the back of her bathroom door hung a calendar with all the days of the month printed on a single page, above the world map. She had to crane her neck while sitting on the toilet to see the tiny dates. Ipchun must have come and gone the first week of February. Usu was on the eighteenth, and after that would be Gyeongchip. Then it would be March, which brought the anticipation of spring. In March these wide walking paths would be mobbed by people coming out in droves to see the cherry blossoms. Not much time was left for her to stroll through the park in peace.

She was by the path that led to the fountain and the Tokyo National Museum. She stopped short. As the evening grew darker by the minute, nothing was visible: not the chilly breeze, nor the chair, nor the woman who had walked here, holding it. She looked up at a cherry tree, its trunk a glossy black. The tiny person on top of the tree wasn't visible, either. All of it felt real but as faint as a dream, as though she'd meandered down a hazy path in the pitch-black darkness before quickly returning to the beginning. She felt dizzy; she detected the slight metallic reek of raw egg. This would be the image of this day for her, at 3:00 a.m. on Friday, February thirteenth. She wanted to remember everything, record everything.

A crowd was gathered around the open space by the trees, exactly where she'd paced with the chair the other night. Her eyes were drawn to a man and a woman, dressed as a clown, standing on a white sheet, holding a huge yellow balloon. Throughout the park, people were playing ocarinas, and street performers were unpacking their saxophones. She stood at the very back, watching the balloon swell like an advertising balloon. The man inflated the balloon with all his might, urged on by applause from the clown. The man paused for a second and smiled mischievously at the audience. He shoved his head into the mouth of the balloon; now he had a balloon head, his arms and legs still human. The crowd grew loud. As the clown pretended to pinch and hit the man's limbs, his body went deeper into the balloon—arms, torso, then legs. The balloon had fully sucked him in. He was now a balloon.

She could not breathe, as if a plastic bag were over her head. She took a step back. The man sat down, as quiet as could be.

Silence.

The audience and the crows and the wind hushed. She reached out and grabbed at the air. Maybe that ridiculous round yellow balloon felt to him like an unbreachable wall. The man seemed to be shrinking. Air was slowly leaking from the balloon. "Daijoubu?" people murmured. The balloon man began bouncing around like a ball. Everyone clapped. The clown yelled, "Hup!" at the balloon. The balloon man stood up, at attention. The air had all leaked out, and the yellow balloon was now plastered against his body. He looked like a giant penis in a yellow condom. The man pulled the balloon off, sweat drenching his hair and face. He looked spent. The applause grew and the clown began to work the audience, holding out an empty hat.

As the crowd disbanded, she saw a man walking up the straight path. Two crows and half a dozen pigeons sat pecking, in his way. The crows seemed to be eyeing the pigeons. The pale, light gray ground was wet. Three months had passed since she'd met him, but she instantly recognized him. He looked like an office worker, a flat file folder tucked under his arm. She could have brushed past him without a word. If she had not wanted to be noticed, she should have worn something other than black; black overpowered and absorbed all other colors. The death cleaner recognized her, she thought. He was walking toward her, his gait sure. She glanced at her watch. It was thirty minutes before their meeting time.

30

Accommodation and reinforcement

She was glowing gold-orange, like the setting sun. He almost tripped, walking as he was with his head turned toward her. The glow wasn't overpowering. It gently lit her and a wide area around her. If light had a demeanor, this would hesitate, waver. She was looking straight ahead as they walked into the airy second-floor café of the National Art Center. At first she'd seemed unapproachable, like a dark, ominous shadow. Which was precisely why she'd stayed rooted in his mind. He never imagined he would see her glow. His heart was pounding. *Does she listen carefully to what I say? Does she look closely at what I'm wearing? Does she study my expressions? The way I'm attuned to her?* She turned her gaze toward him.

Every time he came to this Kurokawa Kisho–designed National Art Center, he was reminded of the Guggenheim in New York. Frank Lloyd Wright had puzzled over creating a space that could accommodate specific intentions and experiences in a form that was not an ordinary cube. In Wright's design, each space was separate but still contributed to an overall open concept. There was no clear beginning or end, and you could see both the lobby and the ceiling from anywhere in the building. The National Art Center was quite a different design from the Guggenheim, but because of the tempered-glass-clad exterior and steel support structure, it felt open to the outdoors. In both buildings, he found himself contemplating accommodation as a concept. The power inherent in a curved line. Accommodation and reinforcement—characteristics that needed to be carefully considered when designing a new space, especially one that transcended preexisting forms. He watched her. He thought about her. All along, ever since that evening at Tokyo Tower when he had seen her again.

He was glad this was only their third encounter. They could share more, confide more deeply in each other. But she was a mystery. She rarely talked about herself. He realized this only after they went their separate ways; he didn't notice it when they were together. She didn't seem to be a woman; she didn't even seem alive. She seemed uninterested in everything. He wanted to delve a little deeper into her history.

"Have you had a chance to see Park again in Seoul?" he asked as he dropped a sugar cube into his coffee.

"Who?"

"The CEO of KAC."

"Yes, I saw him at an auction. And I've been to his Nonhyeon-dong place for a dinner celebrating an artist opening."

He wanted to ask if she'd seen the picture hanging on the fourth floor of that office. He'd brought Park up because he was the only person they both knew. At that point he didn't know he would be meeting up with the death cleaner who'd sat next to her at the Shibuya party.

"How long will you be here in Tokyo?"

She didn't answer. She merely looked down at the museum lobby, her head tilted, gazing at the round tables dotting the ground floor. The light changed and moved as time passed. The orange glow bathing her had retreated to her left, now tinged a light gray. At this time of day, shadow overtook light. February afternoons were short. It suddenly felt easy, like they were sitting in a garden, not in a sealed space filled with strangers and unfamiliar objects. Things felt just right—not too tight, not too loose. Maybe the discombobulation her glow had caused was the reason why he felt so relaxed.

Out of the blue, he blurted that the anniversary of his brother's death was approaching.

She asked him how his brother had died.

"It wasn't long after I got to work when he called me," he said.

"He called you?"

"Yes."

"He was sending you a sign."

"And that was the end."

"He must have depended on you."

"I thought we were close."

"What did he say on the phone?"

"He just laughed. So I thought he was joking."

"Anyone would think so during a call like that."

"But I felt a chill down the back of my neck."

"Why?"

"He'd never called me at work before."

"This was in the morning?"

"Later, when I thought about it, I realized it wasn't the best way."

"What wasn't?"

"The call."

"What did he say?"

"'Hurry up.'"

"'Hurry up'?"

"Yes. Then he laughed. He wanted me to hurry home."

". . ."

"And weirdly I got it."

"I think I understand."

"I knew it would be too late even if I immediately ran out. I knew it was the last time I was hearing his voice."

"You must have known that instinctively."

"Or maybe I expected that things would end like that."

"Maybe you were afraid?"

"I might have wanted to ignore that possibility."

"What was your brother like?"

"He tended to believe that he didn't really need to live."

"Someone from the Epicurus school of thought, I see," she said, flashing a lonely, crooked smile.

"You know how some people don't think it's joyful to be alive?"

"People always thinking about ways to escape the pain they're feeling, yes."

"It sounds like you understand my brother."

"There's a sculptor I love."

"A sculptor?"

"Yes. She once confessed that she'd wanted to die all her life. You can't put yearning like that into words. It's—it's a shocking, unusual energy that could conversely feel invigorating. Once she turned seventy, she said she couldn't remember how she was able to escape that urge. Each time she felt like that, she made art, and then she found herself to be seventy. It's a little sad, isn't it?"

"What is?"

"That she couldn't remember."

"So what happened to that sculptor?"

"Well, not killing yourself doesn't make you famous, right? As she got older, her work became larger in scope but simpler in concept. I have to wonder if her art practice was what prevented her from acting on her urges. She made very original work. In the end she wanted to live in a more beautiful, peaceful world."

"So she was a mystic."

"Or maybe paranoid."

"What do you mean?"

"To endure that kind of urge, you have to hold on to something, whatever it may be."

"Maybe my brother didn't have anything like that to hold on to."

"Even if he did, he might have let go, just for a moment. Or maybe it crashed over him suddenly, like a wave."

"By the time I grabbed a taxi and got home, it was too late. Even though it took me only fifteen minutes. He jumped from the window."

". . ."

"Our parents had gone to the doctor. So his call had been more serious than ever. He was telling me to hurry home and take care of the aftermath before our parents came home."

"Was your brother a good person?"

"In the usual sense, yes."

"What about in the unusual sense?"

"There was something about him that was hard to understand."

"Everyone has a side like that."

"Not everyone."

"You can't expect people to be something they're not."

"Is that sculptor still alive?"

"No, she's dead."

31

Underdrawing

On her seventh visit to the blowfish shop, the proprietor beckoned her over. She was across the street, standing on the stairs. The temperature had dropped suddenly over the past several days. Icy wind razored in from all directions. She was frozen solid. But her every sense was alert and open to the world. If she were a fish, tens of thousands of her minute scales would have been bristling like feelers, reacting a split second before encountering cold air, warm wind, and water. It seemed her entire body had transformed into an enormous sucker. She couldn't tell where this sensation had come from; it was unexpected and vivid and persistent, unpleasant and hot and sudden. She burst into abrupt tears while eating soup and rice. Her body itched, and she couldn't shake off the feeling that some kind of root was slowly, but with furtive strength, crawling up from the soles of her feet, along her spine. As soon as she had woken up in the morning, she had run over to the fish market and prowled near the blowfish shop. She watched the proprietor and the proprietor watched her, this narrow street separating them. There was nothing else to do. Except for one thing. But before that, she wanted to know. She wanted to understand deeply. She could not remember the last time she had felt such intense emotions. She had turned into someone unrecognizable. She mocked herself for how much she had changed, as she might have said to someone who had suddenly given up their blind faith in something. None of it was of any use. She came to Tsukiji Market, her face swollen. Her soles felt as though they were cracking wide open. White frost bloomed like salt flowers on every window in sight. She bit her lip, wanting to quiet the thing writhing inside her, and wished she could freeze, stuck flat on glass. That was when she saw the proprietor, who had been smoking in front of his shop, beckon, his face a grimace.

Twelve steps between them. She wiped off the surprise that might have remained on her face and headed toward the shop, yanking her frozen feet off the ground, one step at a time.

She spoke.
    He ignored her.
    She spoke again.
    He seemed to listen, a little bit.

He was silent. Not for long. She stood there, rooted in place.

His name was Abe. He pointed at the fish tanks. Two light purple blowfish with fat bellies and one agile blowfish with a dark blue stripy back waved their fins lazily. Two long, roomy fish tanks were stacked one on top of the other, taking up an entire wall inside the small shop. She knew blowfish got stressed and perished if the tanks were too small. *Look at this*, Abe-san said without speaking. From that very first day, he conveyed everything he wanted to despite speaking only rarely. Abe-san pressed a finger into her shoulder. It was so painful that she nearly screamed. That jab was telling her, *You can't understand something you haven't observed for years.* She nodded. You understood some words only after hearing it many times. You saw some things only after looking at it many times. Most things were like that. Especially things that remained for a long time in her heart. It was the same when she was looking for materials. Blowfish were alien to her, something she'd never handled. Observing something for a long time was the first step toward comprehension. She'd learned that at the beginning of her art career.

The twenty-watt fluorescent light gave the blowfish a gloomy, rusty green tinge. "That's karasu, that's shimafugu." She committed those names to memory.

Was it when they had been walking along Sumida River? She remembered what he'd said. He had talked about the fear that overcame him when he drew the first line on a fresh sheet of paper. She knew this feeling intimately. She felt it before mapping out a work, before sketching an idea for the first time. He'd told her he didn't erase the underdrawing even after completing the shape he was going for. He believed those preparatory lines had a vital, inherent force. She stared stubbornly into the fish tanks, trying to remember the first line she ever drew.

The next day Abe-san dragged over a plastic folding chair. She sat. Abe-san opened a notebook. On an empty page, he drew a straight line and connected the ends with a curve below. On one end he drew a small rectangle. A knife. In his staccato way, he stabbed each part of the drawing with his pencil. The spine, the flat, the cutting edge, the heel, and the tip. "Okay," she said. He must have believed she could not handle blowfish without understanding how to use a knife. She knew a little about blades. But fish knives looked entirely different from sculpting tools. They looked more real and more specific and crueler. She looked not at the notebook but at the knife placed on the thick wooden chopping block behind Abe-san. A middle-aged man peeked in from the entrance, then left. "I can tell from a single whiff," Abe-san mumbled without turning to look at the customer, "whether someone's going to buy blowfish or not." *And me?* She didn't ask. She wanted to plug her nostrils against the reek of fish. Abe-san blasted out a fishy stench just by sitting diagonally from her. The stench was pervasive, sticky; it melted out of his pores. She didn't turn away. The smell of unvarnished rawness softened his strident demeanor. Abe-san said, "When the knife leaves the chopping block, the tip must always point down." It sounded to her like the law of the knife. He closed the notebook, as if to dismiss her for the day.

32

WHEN ALL BEAUTY VANISHED

His ribs cracked open in half, launching thousands of beelike things into the air. Tiny white butterflies as small as fingernails. They fluttered an arm's length away, unable to fly far, having lost their sense of direction, as though they had sprung out after being sealed in a box for far too long. How could butterflies be so tiny? He lay back down. He wasn't feeling any pain. Even for a dream it was a weird one. His eyes were open, but the dream continued. He stared at the flying creatures. Even though they weren't bees or some other kind of insect, there was something unnerving about white butterflies. His mother would turn away, looking sad, if she spotted a white butterfly. And there were so many of them. They were infinitesimal; they were like foam, like someone's tears. When he squinted at them, they looked like the words you saw when you flipped through a book, not yet linked together to form decipherable sentences. When would this dream end? He laced his fingers behind his head. Maybe they weren't butterflies. He tensed at that thought. He couldn't fall back asleep. The room turned foggy and bright. He felt like he had been living, fossilized, in this state.

The maybe-butterflies sparkled like fish scales. Something chilly fell onto his forehead. He picked it up. It was damp and twinkled like a shard of glass.

He opened his window. Icy air rushed in. He thought about what he'd just seen, what he'd felt. Maybe they had been nothing more than specks of dust. He glared out at the night streets. Somehow he'd become a different person, more sensitive, more cowardly, since his brother had died. His hypersensitivity made him unable to sleep through the night. After a consultation, Dr. Suzuki diagnosed him with stress. He was on alert, even at the smallest noise or the faintest smell or the most modest of heights. It had gotten better for a spell, but then he had turned even more sensitive, his nerves honed to the point of a needle. What was this dream telling him? What he'd just hallucinated weren't butterflies about to fly far away or peaceful foam or dust falling in futility. They were unstable crystals gathering to build a house in the air.

On the day he met her at the National Art Center, he'd spotted in her bag a book in Japanese: *Understanding Blowfish*. Her Japanese wasn't perfect, but it was good enough that she didn't seem to have issues navigating daily life. Was reading a book about a fish a good way to improve your Japanese? He couldn't tell. Maybe she had esoteric interests. There was no better city than Tokyo if you wanted to find books about your unusual interests. After all, Japan was the country where you could find a book explaining the various ways you could kill yourself. He had noticed her bag on her camel-colored chair when she had gotten up from her seat. Her scarf fell off her bag and onto the floor, and the book revealed itself. *Understanding Blowfish.* He couldn't tear his eyes away from the title. It felt different from a book about the ocean or animals or gardening. He had been telling himself that he hadn't been drawn to her from the moment he'd seen her, but when he saw the book, he realized he had been fooling himself. His meeting her had pushed him into a confounding space filled with unanswerable questions. Like now. The latest clue he had about her was that she was reading a book about blowfish. He picked her scarf up from under the table and placed it back on top of her bag.

Someone had once said that nighttime was when all beauty vanished. For him, nights were when he could sense the changes in light, when he was in a state of utmost sensitivity and purity. It required deep wells of patience, like keeping your eyes trained on a bird flying by. He didn't know much about sculpture. But he did know that understanding and interpreting light was critical to both architecture and sculpture. The two disciplines were related, the way music and language were related. Making architecture or sculptures without an understanding of light was as foolhardy as designing a seventy-story building without planning for an elevator. At this very moment, he was standing in the night, taking in the cold, dark air.

He could not put out of his mind the way she'd appeared in profile at Tokyo Tower, her face steeped in death. *Blowfish?* He gripped the windowsill. This fish contained toxin so fatal that it was dangerous to ingest a mere two grams of it; it was ten times more lethal than cyanide. Was that why she had wanted him to show her around Tsukiji Market? He felt himself being snatched up, yanked aloft. *Hyeong, what is about to happen to her?* His brother had been the one who'd said that nighttime was when all beauty vanished. That nighttime was when you couldn't truly be happy. He shook these thoughts away. It was late. Nighttime was merely when the rhythms of daily life shifted.

33

THE POWER OF AN OBJET D'ART

He seemed different that day. He didn't ask for her thoughts or pull the neck of his sweater over his chin. He wasn't hesitant or timid. He seemed to have planned the entire day from beginning to end. As if he'd sensed she no longer needed him. She followed him into the bar. He was like a boy wearing too-large clothes, playacting at being a grown-up with an older girl. The kind of kid who was always hiding in a hard-to-find spot in the house. She hadn't given him much thought. Still, when she was with him, images popped freely into her mind. She could have refused when he'd suggested going on a walk, invited her to dinner, and asked for her contact info. She now knew how to get to Tsukiji Market, and she had found the blowfish shop on her own. She didn't need his help with anything.

Just as they were about to go their separate ways outside Desert, she realized why she kept meeting up with him.

She had immediately understood that this bar was a meaningful place for him. She noted how awkward he was when they said hello to the owner of the bar. She sensed the owner studying her. As they waited for their drinks, she found herself thinking about the woman, the woman who existed in the glances exchanged by these two men. Maybe she was the one who grew calla lilies. He'd mentioned her once. A calla lily was a beautifully tall perennial, an elegant, virginal flower. He'd said that water dropped from the tips of the flower petals all day long. That they sometimes looked like tears. The woman crouched to tend to those flowers every day. He'd turned noticeably gloomy when he spoke about her. She couldn't bring herself to tell him that the bulb of the calla lily was toxic.

Perhaps his careful movements made the big, tall owner of the bar seem discreet and reserved. She figured that was why he came here often. She took a sip of her gin and tonic. He was being circumspect, looking nervous. His nose, which appeared bent to the left, depending on the angle you looked at it, was sharp and sensitive. He had worn this same expression when he'd told her about his brother.

Was it the night she'd heard about his brother? She'd pictured his dead brother, a man who would have looked like his twin. It would take quite some time for him to emerge from the shock of his brother's death. She'd slept fitfully that night. Though she'd never met his brother, he seemed familiar to her. His brother might have made the right choice, assuming he wanted to live in a more beautiful world. But when he'd said, "My brother should have been in this world longer," his voice tamping down his rage and sorrow, she'd found herself nodding. Why had he told her about his brother, about someone who'd killed himself? She'd felt uncomfortable, as if someone she didn't know had shown her a great kindness. Like she'd picked up a test filled out with all the wrong answers. The way someone approached you said a lot about that person, though you wouldn't realize this until after you got to know them. If he were a composer, he would have written a contemplative song, not a romantic one, a song containing the poignancy of a tragedy. One that concealed sadness and kept turning away from those emotions, hitting all the elements of a song. There was something systematic about him. When she mentioned that, he let out a weak laugh.

"I haven't heard that before. I think of myself as offbeat and disorganized."

"It seems like you have your own framework. Your own structure."

"Is that a compliment?"

"Yes and no."

"And what's that structure made of?"

"Wood, maybe?"

He laughed. "I think it would be something more artificial than wood."

"Maybe glass?"

"Yes and no."

"So I was partly right."

He turned earnest. "You can't build something with just glass."

She turned her attention to the music. She watched as the bar owner carefully selected an album after handing them their drinks. Thomas Quasthoff began to sing Franz Schubert's *Winterreise*. It started with "Gute Nacht." *What an overplayed song.* She was disappointed. He was staring at the bottom of his cocktail glass. She could not believe this bar had been in the very same spot for twenty years with so few customers. The music spread deep and wide. It walked boldly inside her. Emotion welled from within, the way it did when she listened to Jan Dismas Zelenka's *The Lamentations of Jeremiah* or *A German Requiem*. It pierced her heart like a burning arrow. She wanted to ask the owner to change the album. She gripped her hands together so she wouldn't be moved. *Wer sagt mir dann von ihr?* Quasthoff sounded listless. Then came a resonant melody, meandering slowly, like a river. She looked around, bewildered, as if awoken from a deep reverie. The owner was standing in the corner of the bar with a beer bottle before him, reading the paper. Next to her, he was tapping on his sweating glass, and on the wall were black-and-white photographs.

"He might have been a great artist, but he had very bad luck," she blurted out.

"Who do you mean?"

She pointed at the picture of Hemingway.

"Because of how he died?"

"For Christmas his mother sent him the gun his father shot himself with."

"That can't be."

"It's true. He didn't have an easy relationship with his mother."

"So was that the same gun he killed himself with?"

"No, he used a rifle."

"You sure know a lot about Hemingway." He looked at her. Sinae would talk about the author's favorite drink, how the mojito was refreshing and sweet and how the crunchy ice clinked lightly in the tall glass. This woman knew all about the depression and defeat and fear of failure that had dogged Hemingway, as well as how he had killed himself and what weapon he'd used.

She looked at him quizzically, as if to ask, *What?*

He erased Sinae from her face.

Her face remained its own, independent of anything else. Pale, boldly peaked lips. Those lips parted and said, "I'm learning about blowfish."

"Blowfish."

"Yes, the fish." She laughed, but it sounded like leaking air.

"Why blowfish?"

"I want to know more about them."

"About blowfish?"

"Why, is that weird?"

"No." He shook his head. "What made you interested in blowfish?"

"I was just drawn to them."

"Just naturally drawn to them?"

"Something like that."

"Without any end goal?"

"Like . . . the way my right hand leads my left."

"So the blowfish is an objet d'art for you."

". . . 'An objet d'art.'"

"Right. Something that draws you in and moves you. Isn't that how artists choose what to make?"

"You mean in their art?"

"Right. It's how you choose something with artistic value, isn't it?"

"'Something with artistic value.'"

"Right."

"Do you have this concept in architecture, too?"

"Yes, in architectural design. What you draw is the architectural form. In other words, the objet d'art."

"Then, the remaining area must be white space."

"That's right."

"That's the same in art, too."

"And that's the basis of architectural design."

"What interests me about an objet d'art is how it always makes me do something."

"In what way?"

"I make it or reconstruct it."

"Sometimes I just look at it."

"That's still doing something."

"Right. It's exactly that force that catches your attention and makes you want to understand it and pushes you to discover it again, like it's fate."

"Like fate."

"Yes. That's the power of an objet d'art."

"That power . . ."

"That's what the blowfish must be."

"What do you mean?"

"It must be an objet d'art for you."

34

ARTISTS DON'T MAKE ART TO MAKE PEOPLE HAPPY

He was scheduled to give a special lecture, "What Is an Architect?," to architecture students graduating from Musashino Art University. *An architect is like a carpenter in that utility is the goal*, he would say. *An architect is like a conductor in that both create things of value, and an architect is like a politician in that they hope their work is well received. An architect is like a philosopher in their pursuit of interactivity and in the way they value process over result. An architect and an artist both seek beauty. The fundamental purpose of architecture is to make people happy, but that quality is what sets architects and artists apart. Artists don't make art to make people happy. Artists consider themselves more important than anyone else. You need both intention and desire—passion—in architecture and in art.* Would these proclamations be helpful to graduates? Japan's unemployment rate, which had plummeted to an all-time low, was still hovering around 4 percent. What he'd sensed at the lectures he'd done so far was that students were interested in gleaning tips that might help them land jobs. Each time he saw his reflection in the metro window, he asked himself, *What is an architect? Am I a carpenter or a conductor or a philosopher or an artist?* He didn't know.

He'd lost certain things. Intention and desire, now too faint to see. That passion. It was hard to admit he no longer had any of them.

Pain and sadness and despair and happiness were everywhere. But passion was the kind of thing that darted away if you weren't paying close attention.

What if I had a cherrywood cane of my own?

She had told him about her great-grandmother—her grandmother's mother. Whenever something valuable went missing or when her great-grandfather was late coming home, her great-grandmother would stand in the yard, holding her cherrywood cane, and pray. Perhaps because she had been a little tipsy when she told him this, she had stood up and acted it out, as if she'd watched her great-grandmother herself. She'd closed her eyes, grasped an invisible cane with both hands, and prayed, miming the tapping of the cane. He'd looked up at her silently. Mun, drinking beer in the corner, had glanced at her, too. It had been late at night, the bar empty. Her forehead had grown damp. She had been sweating, even though she had just been acting it out.

"And then," she'd explained, "the cherrywood cane would move in a certain direction. My great-grandmother would let the cane lead the way. That's how she found a clock a peddler had hidden in a pile of straw to later steal, and how she found my great-grandfather at another house or a bar in the neighborhood. As a young girl, my grandmother stayed hidden in the closet, terrified, when her mother brought out her cherrywood cane. My great-grandmother always wore white, and her cherrywood cane looked just like a burning tree."

He'd asked if her grandmother also had something like the cherrywood cane. He was more curious about her grandmother peeking out at her earnestly praying mother.

She'd stayed silent. Maybe she was thinking about her great-grandmother's cherrywood cane. She'd stayed mum even as they parted ways outside Nippori Station after having managed to catch the last train.

He was afraid that the things he had just recalled, those passions, would fall to the ground, hot like candle wax, and solidify in an instant. He wanted to bang on the ground and speak. He wanted to pray. He wanted to be led by the cherrywood cane. Toward the things he'd lost, the things he wanted to recover. Sometimes you had to suffer through certain events without complaint. And sometimes you had to hide certain things but find other things. He did know one truth: that a new interlude in his life had begun. He sweated as he walked along the long, dim corridors of Musashino Art University.

Part Three

35

The Mori Art Museum

From the fifty-second floor she took the elevator up a flight. Perhaps because of its location, the Mori Art Museum was sometimes referred to as the art museum closest to the sky. The ceilings were more than twenty feet tall. The exhibition space was around four thousand square feet. The biggest contemporary art museum in Asia. The exhibition *Medicine and Art: Imagining a Future for Life and Love* was on view. The show explored the interplay of art and science in six thematic sections, featuring works that examined the human body. *Childhood* (fourteen by twelve by nineteen inches, 2002) was displayed near the end of the second gallery. Next to it was Gilles Barbier's *Nursing Home*, an installation that included a man with one freakishly elongated arm and leg, sitting at a small white desk with an open paperback on it; behind him was a nurse in a Wonder Woman costume, standing beside a patient on a stretcher.

Childhood depicted a boy's head. At first she had put it in a glass box; visitors would touch and soil the white silicone sculpture as the air slowly leaked out of the boy's face, turning it into the gaunt face of an old man. But when she sent it here for this show, she'd removed the glass box and asked them to raise the platform about twenty inches. Sealing the head inside a box had always made her uneasy. She actually did want visitors to get the urge to come close and touch it. That needed to be part of the work.

Not too many visitors were in the gallery. She watched an elderly Japanese couple and a white woman with a huge backpack pause in front of her work before moving on. Once no one was in front of *Childhood*, she went up to the platform. The boy glowed cool and blue under the lights, his pupilless eyes open listlessly.

She had made this sculpture for her master's thesis exhibition. Her advisor and fellow students had wondered why she had made a boy, not a girl. For her the question of gender seemed an unnecessary boundary between man and woman, self and other. At the time she hadn't thought deeply about deterioration or transformation. She had wanted to try using inflation in her work. At that time it had felt like a huge spinning ball hurtling toward her had been momentarily suspended in the air. She'd felt at peace, as though the ball's trajectory had been deleted. She'd worked on this sculpture night and day, taking full advantage of this unfamiliar sense of peace. And she'd completed it; in those years she had struggled to find something that clicked. She could have decided to mold the face of an adult, but she'd found it difficult to represent the expectations and advantages of an era, of a society, on a grown-up face. A boy retained things that were mostly lost by adulthood. Boyhood was a moment in time before peril hung over one's life. When she'd first started sketching, she'd figured he would be around eleven, the age at which one was statistically least likely to die. By the time she'd made a plaster mold of the face, he looked older but still at an age that hadn't yet faced much danger. With silicone she'd made the old man's face, which would go inside the boy's. She'd connected the air hose. It took three minutes for the boy to turn into an old man. She'd stroked the boy's head as he slowly turned into an old man, whispering, "Everyone dies, kid." The dormant adult, the boy who hadn't yet hit puberty, had stayed silent.

The boy looked the same even though quite some time had passed. She had worked on this piece in a tiny, barely eleven-pyeong basement studio in Sangsu-dong. When Baek had first visited that place, he hadn't even taken his shoes off as he towered in the entrance. Late at night, after their second date. His expression had contorted, betraying a rebuke: *How can you possibly work in a place like this?* She didn't think she was deserving of such disdain. Calmly she'd taken off her coat and turned on the oilstove. Under her blithe refusal to acknowledge Baek's distaste had been a mixture of self-confidence (most poor young artists' studios weren't as nice as this) and pride (she knew she was making her best work). Those years would have been difficult to survive if she hadn't felt that way. A few months later, Baek showed her the Naesu-dong house.

Why she was thinking about Baek right now?

She remembered what Baek had said one day. She still remembered that day clearly. Like always, Baek had shown up out of the blue as she kneaded clay in the studio. He'd caught her at a bad time. She hadn't wanted to stop working and have sex with him. Baek had leaned against her worktable: "Why don't you take a break?" She'd asked him to give her thirty minutes, something she'd never requested before. Baek had muttered something, his tone curt.

"What did you say?" she'd asked.

"I said, do you have to keep doing that?"

"What do you mean, *that*?" She'd straightened up and looked back at him.

"What, you think you'll finish a masterpiece in thirty minutes?"

She had seen the shadows in Baek's eyes. She had seen his derision. His simmering derision, bottled up for a long time without a chance of release. "What do you mean, *that*?" she couldn't help but ask again.

"Isn't sculpture just making dust?" Baek had said. The way he said it had been clear. It had been neither criticism nor an attempt to get under her skin. "Can't you do it any old time?"

She had not taken her eyes off Baek. Her face had felt raked by a blistering wind. She'd gritted her teeth to stop herself from blinking or curling her lip. Tasting salt in her mouth. In that brief moment, she'd made the decision she had been struggling with. Baek had been probably in the dark, even to this day, that this was why she'd broken up with him.

She'd felt insulted.

That was the one emotion that would linger for an artist, even if all others disappeared. She had been deeply relieved that the feeling hadn't been love.

The museum was quiet; it was a Tuesday morning. A vast silence flowed, as if she were in a dense forest from which you couldn't see even a sliver of the sky, let alone a skyscraper. In a three-minute loop untethered to anything else in the world, *Childhood* deflated, turning a boy into an old man, then inflated, changing an old man into a boy. That consistency almost made her embrace the boy. She was now so removed from when her sole wish had been to become an artist, one who believed in herself and in what she made. She wanted to cover her eyes. Then she heard a voice from behind.

"It's a breathing sculpture."

A woman was standing behind her, speaking to her in Korean, her voice ringing out clearly. "Isn't it?" asked the woman.

She was at a loss for words. It had taken her some time to move on from Baek. She could have disagreed vehemently when he'd said those things to her. But she knew exactly why she hadn't. He had highlighted her anxiety that she might end up only making dust. Baek would never know how painful it had been to hear those words. She took a cautious step back. *Childhood* was breathing. It was moving. Proof that she had lived through that time in her life. It stood witness to that time in her life.

"Yes, that's right," she said to the visitor. She wasn't sure what she was answering. The woman held up the thick exhibition catalogue and pamphlet and said, "I know you're the artist who made the sculpture." The woman invited her for a cup of tea. She finally took a closer look at the woman. The woman had long dark hair pulled up in a ponytail and was wearing red lipstick and a classic white tweed Chanel suit, holding a hard clutch. If she measured this woman's face with calipers, it would be in perfect symmetry. Her ears also seemed to be evenly placed. It wasn't all that common to encounter such a symmetrical face. The woman smelled like lavender. "All right," she said, taking a step back, away from the scent.

"There's a café downstairs," the woman said, her eyes sparkling.

36

Two kinds of lives

He had just returned to his desk after a meeting with the general managers and the interiors team. The fax machine spat out several pages with a groan. He knew without turning around that they were from his friend Jun Lee. It was early morning in New York. On the last page would be silly sketches that Jun always included. When Jun had a girlfriend, he would send a doodle of her, and when he bought a manual typewriter at a flea market, he would draw a typewriter. Jun was the only person he thought of as the perfect friend. The years during which they'd vowed, full of ambition, to design a tower together in a global city somewhere had scattered into air. The fax machine cranked out the message. Five pages. He took all the pages and stapled them together. He looked down at Jun's large, lively scrawl in black marker.

The message was simple, despite the many pages. It was about Jun's uncle, who headed an architecture firm in New York. The three of them had enjoyed a few meals together in Tokyo and Chicago. The redevelopment of New York City's Meatpacking District was underway, and Jun's uncle's firm had won a major bid. Jun had recommended him, his old friend, for a spot on the planning team. Interest in the revitalization of cities was growing all over the world. The goal was to balance the built environment within the space of an entire area, keeping in mind functional and design needs, with being environmentally conscious. That was the kind of project he wanted to challenge himself with. And New York was far away from home. It would give him a good reason to leave Tokyo and his parents. There had been many opportunities, but he hadn't jumped at any of them. He hadn't wanted to flee this city. He'd needed a real reason. Was now his time?

He hunched over his desk and imagined moving to New York and taking on a new project. Redesigning a part of a city, a specific space, would be like transforming an ordinary rectangular eraser with twelve edges into the plastic Kadokeshi eraser on his desk. After a few uses, the twelve edges of an eraser became rounded; it was hard to use it for intricate work. But a Kadokeshi eraser, made of ten cubes, had twenty-eight tiny edges. In addition to its superior design, it was firmer than a regular eraser and easier to use. Which boosted your productivity. Jun would tell him that redesigning a city wasn't like creating a new eraser but was work that was inspirational, closer to achieving their youthful dreams of building a significant architectural marvel. Jun would tell him it would be the manly thing to do. Maybe Jun was right. He couldn't keep sitting at a desk, playing with an eraser, thinking about erasers. How long could he live like this? He pictured the possibility of leaving and the possibility of not leaving. If he left for New York, he'd think about why he'd left, what he was doing there. He imagined the other possibility. If he didn't leave, he would keep asking himself why he'd stayed. The former was intuitive and the latter was inductive, and neither was the best way to figure things out. All he could do was make an educated guess, but he knew he didn't have the heart to leave. In fact, more than ever, he thought he should stay. But it would be hard for him to turn Jun down. Would he regret his decision?

There were two kinds of lives. A life you were born into and a life you built. It was all a question of choice. He turned to the last page of the fax. Jun had drawn a beer mug and a slice of pizza, along with the twenty-two-story Flatiron Building on Fifth Avenue. As large-scale city planning projects boomed in the early twentieth century, the pointy building had been built on a triangular plot just off a street that had remained from its Native American days. Jun loved that building. Jun was telling him to hurry over to New York so they could have a drink there. He folded the pages neatly. The question of whether to leave or stay was entirely different from, say, searching for a lost bag. He stood up. The sky was starting to clear. He needed light, and for that he had to swivel the blinds. The right answer wouldn't require deduction or an intentional choice. He decided to trust that the correct decision would walk out on its own, from his subconscious.

37

NAMES

Abe-san slammed the side of his knife against the head of the blowfish. The creature leaped into the air and landed on the chopping block before ricocheting back up. Water sprayed everywhere. She recoiled and took a step back. Moments earlier Abe-san had scooped a three-pound blowfish out of the tank, placed it onto the chopping block, and wiped it dry with a rag. The movement of his knife had been swift and sudden. She wasn't sure she'd even noticed Abe-san holding the knife. The dark purple blowfish writhed, its tail and body flailing. Veins popped in Abe-san's left arm as he held the fish down. He was knocking it unconscious, not killing it. This fish didn't die easily. In her book the blowfish was described as having a strong instinct for life. Abe-san slid the fishhook out of the gills and tapped the resisting blowfish's head with his knife. Time to cut out the tongue. He slammed his knife down. With the tip he removed the bean-sized brain. He sliced the fins off either side of the body and the belly and shoved the blade deep into the head. He yanked the knife toward the tail and began to peel off the skin, as if dissecting it. The blowfish stopped moving. Abe-san used two knives, one after the other. A thick, heavy knife around the bones, a long, sharp knife to remove the skin. Abe-san had a special philosophy about knives, though not necessarily about blowfish. Of the three ways of using a knife—gripping it, pressing it, using it like a finger—he was handling the knife as though it were an extension of himself, allowing for the greatest flexibility. But even for him it didn't look easy to skin a blowfish. He gripped the thick skin with one hand, and with the other he scored the flesh to remove it. He didn't discard the skin; he scraped it clean and pushed the bones against the grain to detach them. The skin looked rough, even when wet. She wanted to touch it, to feel that sensation with her fingers. But she'd promised Abe-san that she would only observe. Instead, she felt through her eyes what her hands would have sensed. She sketched Abe-san's motions in her head: Slide the knife between the fresh red gills and cut off the flesh, do the same on the opposite side, press the head to remove the innards, detach the flesh from the bones. All this was performed mechanically, without a single mistake. Perhaps still wanting to scare her, Abe-san held up the trailing innards he'd pulled out of the fish and shook them in front of her face. They were large and voluptuous, as if the fish were composed entirely of organs. The dark green gallbladder and the fingernail-sized heart, the spleen and the bladder. The gallbladder was the largest among them. It looked like a slippery pebble plucked from the water. Plump, too, as if it would pop pleasingly in your hand if you squeezed it, like a Chinese lantern flower. Abe-san shoved his knife into the cartilage of the spine and cut the fish into thirds. He wiped the blood away with a dry rag and trimmed off the bits of skin and fat remaining on the flesh. Only the organs and skin stayed on the chopping block, while the flesh was placed on a clean, dry rag, ready for sashimi. Seven minutes. That was how long it had taken him to prepare the blowfish he'd lifted out of the water tank. Two knives, one wet chopping block, water, blood. Abe-san went outside for a smoke while she was thinking these thoughts. When he returned, he washed his hands, placed the sashimi on a disposable tray, and put it to the side. He wiped the chopping block with a rag and laid out the innards and the bone and the skin. Their lesson resumed. Abe-san pointed at each part with his knife and identified it. What she'd thought was the gallbladder was in fact the spleen, and what she'd guessed was the kidney was the heart. Abe-san pointed at something that looked like a couple of thumbs. Shirako. Blowfish sperm.

"Is it poisonous?" She finally asked her first question.

Abe-san snapped his head around. "Not shirako. But the roe is."

"Is that the only poisonous part?"

He looked flabbergasted. "Did you think the toxin was all in one place?"

She stayed quiet.

"A blowfish is more structurally complicated than you think. Here and here." Abe-san pressed the tip of his knife into the spine and the gills. He poked an eye with the knife. "And here."

The eyes. She gazed down at the blowfish's eyes.

"The most toxic part is the ovaries. This one's a male, so I can't show you the ovaries, sadly." Abe-san laughed. He seemed to be laughing at her. He listed the names of the blowfish that one could not eat. Oharafugu, moyofugu, shippofugu, hotsufugu, mushifugu, futashiboshifugu, komon-damashi, senninfugu, takifugu, shimikumafugu, kumasakafugu, fukitsufugu. She asked Abe-san to tell her which types of blowfish were edible. He laughed. He stopped, then started to laugh again. *Bastard.* She suddenly felt unwell. The shop pulsed with the smells of wet metal and fish. They hadn't bothered her before, but now she was suddenly repulsed.

"What you have to remember is this," Abe-san said, and paused. He seemed to be pausing to ensure that she would understand him.

She looked at him.

"It takes about a decade to figure out which blowfish are edible and which aren't."

She smiled. She was certain he would take it to be a smirk. She looked at him coolly and laughed.

Was it because of that?

Abe-san opened his cashbox and took out a bundle of keys. She didn't want to look, but she couldn't tear her eyes off him. He seemed fully aware of that. Abe-san stalked over to the entrance and pulled down the plastic blowfish hanging above. He opened the hat like a lid and tossed a key inside. When he let go, the blowfish sprang up. Nobody was walking by the store. All this happened in a matter of seconds.

"You lied to me," Abe-san said, crossing his arms.

She stopped smiling.

"Do I really look like I'd help you?"

". . ."

"As I promised, I'll show you how to prepare blowfish. It's up to you what you do with that, whether it's to understand the fish like you told me or whatever."

"I'm very grateful." She wanted to say that correctly.

"I don't care if you make a mockery of your own life or of me. But remember this. You can't handle or eat this fish without trust. I decided to trust you. Right now." He started to laugh again, so hard that his shoulders shook.

She bit her lip. She felt she was being sucked into a weird game. It didn't feel good. She wanted to leave. But she was already in too deep.

"Important things are always kept close," Abe-san said. "But that's the case for dangerous things, too, right?" He untied his apron and threw it onto the chair before turning around. Water roared into the sink as he washed his hands. It was time to close up. The innards and bones and skin were drying out, strewn across the immaculate chopping block. The thin sheath of skin already looked desiccated. From her bag she took out an envelope containing enough money for one blowfish and placed it on top of Abe-san's blood-speckled apron.

38

THE SHADOWS FACING EACH OTHER

It wasn't easy to avoid the gazes of cats in this neighborhood. Black eyes that glared intently, cruel eyes that seemed to pierce through every concealment. When he encountered a cat in a narrow alley, it would refuse to move and would stare at him. Maybe because he'd never had one, something felt different about a cat than a dog or a duck or even a goat. A cat made a chill go down his spine; he found himself whirling around to look back. Graves, though, didn't bother him. They were round or flat and didn't move or make noise or give off any smell. Cats were different. They appeared and disappeared at will and went around on their own and smelled rancid when it was humid. At night they emitted their own sharp white light, as if wearing a cape of special glow-in-the-dark fabric. He turned the corner, burrowing into the lapels of his coat in an attempt to avoid that glow. A cat slunk along the top of a wall, watching. It was an old cat with a missing leg that acted like it owned the place; everyone in this neighborhood knew this cat. It was close to midnight. He rummaged through his bag and found his key. *Meooow.* The cat wailed long and low, like it was trying to tell him something.

He stepped inside the house. Mottled silhouettes were reflected on the sliding doors. He heard faint murmurs. He realized the shadows facing each other were those of his parents. The shadows of his old, dying parents. It wasn't sad or depressing or tragic; this was something spluttering to an end. They must not have heard the front door open. They drew close enough for their foreheads to touch, then backed away. He stood there in the entry, unable to take his shoes off. He couldn't decide if it was better to go in and disrupt whatever was going on, or stand there until the conversation was over, pretending he hadn't noticed anything.

He had seen so much in his life. Sad, happy, tragic, depressing things, things that couldn't be turned back. He rubbed his eyes. He had never looked closely at them like this, a big shadow facing a smaller one. He crept outside.

He didn't want to hear any of what his father was saying, what his father wanted to say, to his mother. It was probably about a decision his father had made in an effort to convince her of something, and his mother would be doing everything she could to stop him. He could tell from their shadows. Maybe they had started talking in the early evening, maybe in the afternoon, and continued all this time. Maybe they would continue into the morning. The bamboo planted beside the front door rustled and swayed. He lowered himself awkwardly onto the steps. The cat meowed from its spot. *See, I told you not to go inside.* It looked down at him, dignified. *Certain things shouldn't be interrupted.* The old cat yawned. Strangely he didn't feel spooked, even though the cat was close by. Sometimes he felt glad to have a home. Like tonight, when he saw the shadows facing each other, when he realized that home wasn't somewhere you lived but a place with someone who understood you, who listened to you. As it was for his father. But he'd learned that home wasn't always like that. Pale air surrounded him. Across the way, an empty plastic clothes hanger dangled on the veranda. Next to the near-full moon, a first-magnitude star shined brightly. He wanted to hang all his father's words in the air, all the words his father was using to persuade his mother. That way they would all disappear in the morning, blasted by the sun. His father was the kind of person who would tell his wife that he'd decided to kill himself. His mother had once said to him, "We have to remind your father that he can be happy." But as she had said that, she had looked like she'd regretted verbalizing that. She knew better than anyone that his father's ability to be happy was dependent solely on himself.

It was the beginning of a long night. Nights were always long. Nights were cat-black and briny and damp. *No*, the glowing yellow moon seemed to say, floating above him. He felt better whenever he gazed at something round for a while. As he did when he looked at a grave. Was it his neck or his heart that was hurting? He imagined a long line coming down from the moon. Now it was a big round yellow balloon. He imagined another moon next to it. The world's huge eyes. He imagined drawing a pointy triangle inside the moon and a few lines radiating outward like a fish tail on the opposite side. Now the moon was a blowfish, puffed up in response to danger.

39

Someone who was neither stranger nor friend

She glanced at her reflection in the glass door of the convenience store. She looked angry. Sometimes she was disappointed in herself or felt sad or wallowed in self-pity. When that happened she slept or roamed the streets to feel better. She tried her best not to cry. When she cried alone in the dark, she had a strong feeling that someone was watching her. Sometimes she was embarrassed to stand before her grandmother.

It was snowing over Fabric Town. She'd heard the snowstorm would continue into tomorrow. It wasn't too cold. Crows flew calmly by, holding the gray horizon between their beaks. From far away she saw a familiar shape, coming quickly toward her. The light at the crosswalk turned green. If she crossed the street and went around the recycled paper plant, she would be at her apartment. But she didn't move. He was biking over from Nippori Station. They'd made a vague plan to have a drink together if it snowed that night. Even without those plans, she would have come to the convenience store to buy onigiri and oolong for dinner. She tightened her grip on the plastic bag in her hand. He got off his bicycle and came up to her. His hair was tousled, and he smelled like cologne.

She followed him and his bicycle down the street. As they walked he told her about the neighborhood shops, saying, "This oden place is a hundred years old" or "It's not an exaggeration to say the tonkatsu here is the best in Tokyo." He sounded goofy and excited. People were going in and out of houses and stores and izakaya beginning to hang noren in their entrances. She felt like she was in a small town, not a city. A familiar small town that might remain as a faint memory. She looked up at him as he searched for a good spot. He was the kind of person who would walk past the right street. The kind of person who would read a book and forget everything about it. She felt her anger subsiding. Maybe she was wrong; maybe what she was feeling was different from what he was feeling. She followed him confidently into an izakaya.

He asked her how her study of blowfish was going. She stopped shelling the edamame they'd ordered. Time seemed to whip around and head down a different direction.

They were in the neighborhood's oldest, smallest bar. Partitions barely separated the half dozen tables, and solo diners were seated at the bar, watching the owner as he cooked. The air smelled sweet, of katsuobushi being cooked and freshly steamed rice, scented with a woodsy aroma. It was snowing harder by the time they finished a small bottle of sake. People entered, brushed snow off their coats at the entrance, and found seats. She wasn't getting drunk. He didn't seem to be drinking to get drunk, either. His eyes looked clear, as if he felt more alert the more he drank. But she could still detect the intense exhaustion that always clung to him. Her hands had frozen in place when he'd said blowfish, but she now picked up another edamame pod and put pale green beans in her mouth. Had it been a mistake to tell him about blowfish? She wanted to study him from a distance, the way she had when she'd first met him. There wasn't enough room here for that. He was using his chopsticks to slice neatly through tamagoyaki.

"What is it?" He put his chopsticks down.

"It looks like it'll snow all night."

"And it doesn't usually snow this much here."

"Maybe it's telling us spring is coming."

"You said you're going to Seoul in the spring, right?"

"Yes, in March."

"In March."

"Yes."

"When will you be back in Tokyo?"

"I'm not sure."

"Let me know when your next show—"

"I'm not sure about that, either."

"What do you mean?"

"Whether I'll be making more work."

He didn't speak. He looked disappointed, like he had been expecting something else from her.

Through the lattice in the door, she saw snow blowing around outside. She felt impatient. As if it would be March as soon as the snow stopped. In March blowfish tasted different. "It's hard," she said.

"What is?"

"Blowfish."

"Oh, I see."

"You asked about blowfish."

"I did." He sat up straight, looking serious.

"When my grandmother was young, she lived along this street for a short time."

"Which grandmother? Your great-grandmother with the cherrywood cane?"

"No, her daughter. My grandmother."

"So around the 1920s or the thirties?"

"Yes, as a young girl she lived in Shimonoseki. She would come all the way to Tokyo, transferring trains, with a tire on her back. Evidently she would make a decent amount of money if she sold a tire. And then she would wander through this area until it was time to catch her train home. She'd get distracted by the colorful fabrics and miss her train. She wanted to be a seamstress. She got into Ochanomizu University to make Western clothing, but she couldn't afford to finish. Then she had to go back to Korea."

"You said your grandfather was a sailor."

"At nineteen my grandmother married someone she'd never even met."

"You must have been close to your grandmother."

"No, I never even met her."

"No?"

"I heard about her from my aunts and uncles."

"Did she have something like a cherrywood cane, too?"

"She would have been too young, I think."

"I see."

"I wonder what she would have prayed for if she'd had one."

". . . Is it because of your grandmother?"

"What?"

"Why you're here?"

"No. Not at all."

"She must have passed away at a young age."

"What makes you think that?"

"If not—"

"Otherwise I would have met her, you mean?"

"No?"

"Apparently she was the best seamstress around."

"You're saying her talents were wasted."

"She wasn't afraid of anything as long as she had a needle and a pair of scissors."

"I see."

"Sometimes I wonder where I came from."

"From your grandmother?"

"Maybe my grandmother made me this way. Before my father even existed."

"Do you mean your temperament?"

"That, too."

"Or artistry?"

"I'm sure that, too. Like, what makes me who I am?"

"If you're talking about influence, I'm sure it's not just from one person."

She wanted to laugh. It sounded like he was insisting that she'd chosen to pursue art not because of her grandmother's influence but because of all the people she had known, the people she'd seen and heard and imagined. But he didn't sound firm or decisive. His voice was faint, as if it would flicker off at any second. March. His voice had changed ever since they'd started talking about March. His head was turned slightly away. She almost reached out to put a hand on his. She wasn't sure how to talk to someone who was neither stranger nor friend. All she knew was that she didn't want to make any assumptions. Because then his heart would slam shut.

He offered to walk her home. She declined. He brushed snow off his bicycle seat. The light changed, and she stepped into the crosswalk. He grabbed her by the elbow. His grip was urgent and tight. She turned toward him. His lips were moving, but she couldn't hear him. She rushed across the crosswalk. Maybe she was still angry at herself. Maybe what she thought they shared wasn't only connection forged from pain. Her anxiety grew. Anxiety was no longer anxiety, and anger was no longer anger. Snow melted and trickled down her face as compounded sorrow enveloped her. She needed to say it. To him. Like this. *I'm not in competition with a blowfish's toxins.*

She looked back. As though someone would be standing there.

40

IN THE DESERT WITH ONLY A DOG

It was past midnight when Mun called him. He was flustered not by how late it was but by the fact that Mun was calling. He tried to remember if Mun had ever called him. Mun called it a favor, but it sounded like a regular request to him. Mun asked if he could go to Desert and check in on Rover. Mun explained that he'd popped out to buy cigarettes and bumped into an acquaintance. But someone needed to be with Rover, who was several days into a bout with enteritis. He hesitated. Something about Mun's story just didn't make sense. Mun stayed quiet, as if acknowledging that fact. Who had Mun run into, and if he was nearby, why couldn't he go check on the dog himself? He wasn't sure if he should ask these questions right now, over the phone. Eventually he agreed. Still, there was one thing he wanted to confirm. Had Sinae asked Mun to orchestrate a meeting at Desert? The other man said no. In fact, Mun retorted, even though he and Sinae were the regulars Rover knew the best, he couldn't call Sinae up at this hour, could he? "I guess that's true," he said, nodding despite himself. He'd already missed the last train to Omotesando. He would have to hail a taxi in the middle of the night to go look after a dog. Someone else's dog. He shook his head in disbelief.

Just as Mun had explained, the spare key was nestled under the stainless-steel fire extinguisher. He pushed the heavy doors open and heard a faint moaning. The lights were still on. An empty glass was still at Mun's favorite seat; he must have gone out mid-drink. "Rover!" he called. Rover stumbled over from the direction of the kitchen. He sniffed the air twice. Recognizing his scent, Rover relaxed and slobbered all over his legs. Following Mun's instructions, he found Rover's medicine in the kitchen and put it into his bowl. If Mun wasn't able to come right now even though he was close by, maybe he wouldn't be able to come tomorrow, either. After all, some people promised to be back soon and never returned. He filled the food and water bowls generously. He'd been coming to Desert for years, but this was the first time he'd stepped foot in the kitchen. Everything was immaculate: the huge fridge and freezer, the liquor bottles on display, the sink, the blue tiled floor, the kitchen cloths, and the cutting board. He looked around, expecting to see fruit peels or peanuts left on the floor, but there was nothing. It was as if he'd opened a dresser organized by a neat freak.

Near the kitchen entrance was a burlap sack that must have once held coffee beans. It was big enough for a child to fit inside. He stopped and untied the cord at the mouth of the sack. Rover approached, sniffing. Inside were three 1.5-liter bottles of water and packaged nurungji, tuna cans, biscuits, and chocolate, all stacked neatly. A stash of earthquake provisions. It was enough for one person to survive a week. Embarrassed, he told Rover, "Your food's in here, too," and retied the sack. He couldn't tell if the sack helped him understand Mun better or not. Once Mun had told him that thinking about commonalities, not differences, was better for a relationship. If he lived his own life following this principle, Mun should have had at least three or four people to call in the middle of the night to help with Rover. It was confounding to him that he was the one Mun had called. He had never thought about the commonalities he shared with Mun.

He selected a dark beer and perched on a barstool. Rover came over and flopped down, laying his face against his shoes. The dog seemed okay, despite Mun's concerns. Other than being tired, he seemed symptom-free. It did occur to him that he knew next to nothing about dogs. From time to time, he called out, "Rover!" and each time Rover looked up before settling back down. A sick dog would have only instincts left. By his third beer, he realized Mun would not be coming back tonight. He didn't think he could go home and leave Rover alone. Who had Mun bumped into tonight? How would the unexpected encounter affect Mun?

He turned off all the lights other than those above the bar. It was almost three in the morning. "Now I'm left in the desert with only a dog," he mumbled. His careening emotions settled, locked inside him. Nothing would shock him tonight. Even if Sinae came by. Even if his brother walked in and sat beside him. It was a weird night. It was quiet, and the dog below his feet was asleep, and he was drinking beer after beer, not getting tipsy in the least, alone in the empty bar. He cracked his knuckles. This solitude seemed to be trying to teach him something. He kept startling and looking behind him like someone was there, nervous about what might happen if he were left forever in the dark like this. Nobody was there. The world wasn't there. She wasn't there.

41

Where was Abeoji?

She had one thought and one thought only in the shuttle bus from Incheon Airport to Hongeun-dong.

It was the evening of the third Wednesday in February. She leaned against the window, her handbag on the seat next to hers. That was all she had for luggage. Inside she had a toothbrush and underwear; a small, thin notebook and a pen; her wallet. She didn't know what else she had. She thought about the things she'd left behind in the Negishi apartment. Packing had been easy, but she'd had to take care of a number of things before locking the front door behind her. She had thrown out the trash and locked the veranda doors and emptied the fridge of perishables. A home sometimes felt like a living organism, especially when it was time to leave. Some manner of organization and tidying was needed. As she stared out the window, she realized she had let out a smile, if faintly. If he were beside her, his expression would become concerned as he told her, "You can't think of a home like that." He was the kind of person who would talk about stairs in a home before talking about the home itself.

Once he'd explained to her why there was always an odd number of stairs. He had said that the foot stepping onto the first stair had to also be the one stepping onto the last stair, so that the foot you favored started and finished climbing the stairs. Apparently this was guidance from *de Architectura*, written by the Roman architect Vitruvius. He'd insisted that a home was a space created by stairs. With her finger she traced stairs on the window. A single step wasn't enough to divide a space. You would just trip and fall. Three steps—that was the bare minimum that would create difference between levels. He had said he wanted to build a house one day that could withstand earthquakes. She didn't know much about the architectural meaning of a house, but she had wanted to say, *Wouldn't you need to design a house with more detail, with more consideration?* She hoped she wouldn't have the opportunity to say that to him. She rubbed away the stairs. Every time it occurred to her that she wanted him to tell her a lot of things, that *she* wanted to tell *him* a lot of things, she felt her face shriveling, as though the air around her was constricting. Her face, which she couldn't bear to look at in the mirror.

She had to think about so many things in order not to think about her father. When she spotted the Hongeun-dong overpass, she realized that she hadn't been obsessing over the concept of home or her father or him. A single thought remained rooted in her mind, unmoving.

It was two days before the Lunar New Year. The anniversary of her grandmother's death.

The woodworking shop was empty. The door was unlocked, and the light was on. The shutters were lowered on her aunt's restaurant next door. Her aunt closed shop every year on this date. But her father never took a day off. She stood forlornly on the sidewalk before heading back into the woodworking shop. She placed a hand on the stove. It was warm. The old-fashioned cast-iron stove. She picked up a piece of wood from the floor and put it in the stove, making the embers crackle and bloom into fire. She didn't see Mr. Song, the apprentice who had been learning how to make lattice doors for the past ten years. Maybe they had stepped out for a moment. She pulled a wooden chair over to the stove and sat down. She hadn't been to the shop in a long time. When she had been working, she'd come by often to grab pieces of wood for supports. The smell of burning sawdust infused her body. The smell of larch trees. The smell of her father. Maybe it wasn't that hard to disappear, unnoticed by anyone. Maybe what was hard was breaking away from yourself. Breaking away from your own gaze. She who left the Naesu-dong studio, she who no longer worked, she who only thought about dying—that was who she was right now. She felt her heart splintering. Maybe she shouldn't have come to see her father. It was evident that someone continued to work here. The heap of sawdust used for kindling and the incomplete doors leaning against the wall, the orders and to-do lists written on the whiteboard, the two ventilation fans on the ceiling, the chain saw, the circular saw, the grooving drill, the sharp grinder—they all smelled and creaked and moved, unaware of her presence. She rubbed her hands together. Hands that had held a knife just yesterday. Hands that did not know what to do right now.

Where was Abeoji?

She scooped sawdust with her hands and poured it into the stove. Smoke leaked faintly out of the stovepipe. There must be a gap somewhere. Winter wasn't over yet. She would have to tell her father to get it fixed. Maybe he wouldn't come back tonight. Maybe her aunt and her father hadn't gone to shop for the jesa table.

Scenes from past jesa felt distant. Usually her father, her aunt, and she, just the three of them, indifferently performed the jesa. The food on the table always looked sad, like they were plastic models, even though her aunt fried jeon and dried fish and parboiled namul and bought fruit in the days leading up to the rites. Sometimes her younger uncle or her eldest aunt came up to the city by train, arriving in Hongeun-dong with Styrofoam boxes full of fish. Everyone looked a little broken on the day of her grandmother's jesa.

The shed. The shed next to the woodworking shop, where red pine, oak, and alder stood, leaning against one another. That secretive, special place, forest-dark with high ceilings, redolent of wood, where nobody could enter without her father's permission. She'd loved the shed since she was young. It was the perfect place to hide. Whenever he managed to source special wood, like aged pine or fir, her father would take her to the shed to show her, boasting in a low-key way. He was the kind of person who took a long time to select a single piece of wood. Maybe he was in the shed now, looking for the best wood for something he was about to make. She glanced at the drawers hanging on the wall. As a young man, her father had made the wall hanging with fifteen small drawers. It was just to the right when you walked into the shop. He'd said even large sums of money never disappeared from it. The key to the shed was in one of those drawers. If her father was selecting wood in the shed, there was nothing she could do but wait. Or maybe they were somewhere else. They might still be at the traditional market down the hill. They could be buying young zucchini for jeon, fresh tteok, warm tofu, bracken, mung bean sprouts, spinach. Since the Lunar New Year was always two days after the jesa, they shopped for New Year's at the same time. The chore often took a long time. Her aunt would lead the way with her bags, and her father would follow, walking his scooter. Right about now they might have finished shopping. They might be enjoying a simple meal of makgeolli and pajeon in the market. They might just be taking a little longer than expected.

The embers crackled. The flames were bluish, the tips yellow. The fire was hot and ferocious. The air warmed. She began to feel calmer. She'd be starving by the time they returned. After the jesa, they would mix rice and various namul in a huge brass bowl to share. Her father and her aunt would drink jeongjong together late into the night. Darkness settled over the sidewalk. Cars sped by on the overpass. White cars looked black, and black cars looked even blacker. Everything had turned into anthracite. Her eyelids began drooping. Ever since she had been jarred awake in the middle of the night, she'd only been thinking of her grandmother. Could she lean her head on something for a second? She shouldn't fall asleep. She looked around the shop and sleepily murmured something she'd never been able to say out loud. "Abeoji, why are you looking at me like that?"

42

THAT NIGHT HAD FELT AS LONG AS A WHOLE MONTH

Yesterday she had not shown up. He had waited on a bench in front of Mori Tower, which had been mobbed. A huge spider sculpture had arched before him, one leg reaching behind the bench he had been sitting on. An hour past their meeting time, he'd wondered if the plan to meet there had been his alone. But she'd suggested the place. She'd said there was something she wanted to show him. Something that had to do with her. He'd looked up at the bronze spider, its eight long, sturdy legs spread wide. A black net was wrapped around large rocks forming the spider's body. This sculpture was by Louise Bourgeois, who said that the purpose of art was to overcome fear. Just looking at the spider had made him so terrified that he'd felt unable to breathe. As if something vague but certain was approaching. She was two hours late. Waiting had grown into doubt and doubt into fear.

He had left then, taking the Hibiya Line and getting off at Minowa Station. He had exited the turnstiles to the south. Maybe she was unwell. Maybe not showing up was her way of saying goodbye. He would actually be relieved if that were the case. He had picked up the pace, covered in a cold sweat, like when he'd rushed home after answering his brother's call. He would accept anything as long as he could keep at bay the feeling he'd gotten when he saw her at Tokyo Tower. Her apartment building was known for its two old zelkova trees. Twenty years ago, when the building was being built, the landowner had allowed construction only after extracting a promise from the builder that the trees wouldn't be damaged. Her building was five minutes from the station. He'd decided not to think about anything. That hadn't helped at all. He'd imagined the worst possible situation that could be unfolding that night. Countless things could happen in life, and the worst possible options were always among them. He'd wanted to remain skeptical.

The glass doors to the building were closed, and the intercom was on the other side. He'd spotted her bicycle on the racks. It had a green seat, one side peeling. Around the corner was the street that led directly to Fabric Town. At the end of that street was Nippori Station. He couldn't remember when he had trailed her after they'd parted ways. He'd gone toward the side street he'd assumed her unit faced. Where the tire recycling plant was, the one she'd mentioned in passing. He'd looked up at the apartment building. She was on the sixth floor. That was the extent of his knowledge. Some verandas had laundry and blankets hanging from drying racks, or were cluttered with plastic toddler tricycles or huge stacks of cardboard boxes. In the dusk he had seen shadows moving inside the units. Scenes of homes that weren't hers.

He didn't know much about her. All he knew was the following: She was living a life dogged by a continuous urge to die. That was her true existence.

He'd turned around and looked into the distance. Toward the place where next year she would be able to see from her living room a part of the new tower, which would be about ten stories by then. Right in front of her, even though you couldn't see a thing now. He'd begun walking away. If he hadn't quit that project, he could have shown her that very special tower. He'd sped up so his regret wouldn't feel like an ominous sign of his attachment to her. Not even noticing that, usually, very few things made him rush home.

That night had felt as long as a whole month. In his dreams, she'd stood on cold, hard ice, looking as though she didn't care that she was about to fall through. She gazed at him silently like that before he woke up.

It was early in the morning, but the streets were as deserted as they were at the end of the day. He sat in the rest area of the Tsukiji Outer Market, watching the shop across the way. Watching the man who came out through the noren with blowfish drawn on them, smoked a cigarette, then went back in. She had mentioned the proprietor, Abe; that must be him. The man was disheveled, unlikely to make anyone want to buy fish he handled, and looked mean to boot. The shop was also far from inviting. He stood, his body tense, and went outside. He avoided a puddle as he crossed the street. The proprietor, sitting with his arms crossed, didn't bother getting up when he walked in. He hesitated. It occurred to him that he might not seem interested in buying blowfish. He quickly turned his gaze to the two large tanks behind the owner. Three spotted blowfish were huddled at the bottom. They looked like heavy, immovable rocks. They didn't betray any animalistic vitality. Disappointment flooded him. He wanted to announce that blowfish no longer interested him. He managed to tear his gaze away from the tanks. The owner got up. It was a tiny shop. There was a chopping block with a noticeable dent in the middle and a few knives. The smell of fish assaulted his nose. The man's gaze was sharp. This was the man she spent her mornings with.

This hadn't been his plan. He had no idea that he'd be asking this man for a favor or asking about her. From the other man's perspective, his questions would be no different from threats. Maybe there was no difference between a question and a threat. He had to emphasize that she should never be given a whole, unprepared blowfish, no matter what. It was clearly illegal in Tokyo. It would be more effective to threaten the man. But he anticipated that what he wanted to say would sound like a plea. He was meeting this man much sooner than he'd imagined. Things didn't always unfold in a predictable way. But you had to be mindful of all the possibilities, even if unlikely. After all, it was about her.

The proprietor said she hadn't been by.

He searched for something to say in response.

The proprietor said they'd agreed to meet the first week of March. He was going to Fukuoka tomorrow for a blowfish festival, he explained. Though he'd invited her along, she had refused, saying she had to attend to something in Seoul.

He shoved his hands into his pockets. He felt like he was hearing about a family member from a stranger.

"Then is she in Seoul right now?"

The proprietor took out a cigarette and lit it. "How would I possibly know that?"

He asked the man to tell him what he did know. He was fully aware that his tone wasn't polite or subtle.

The proprietor seemed to be grinning at him.

43

TWO MIRRORS

The city at night was like a larch tree, thorns concealed in its bark. She wanted to lean on it but was afraid of getting hurt. She was at the Gwanghwamun intersection. Her bag was starting to dig into her shoulder. She kept stumbling, left foot tripping over the right. There was only one place to go. She was trying with everything she had to avoid going there. She walked the same streets over and over again. She didn't see the birds flying or the stars floating askew in the sky. As she walked across the street, she felt a woman glance at her. She looked familiar. But she couldn't remember who she was. The honking horns and the crowds and the lights glowing from the outdoor billboards made it hard to tell if it was the middle of the day or night. She knew these streets very well, even the back alleys. But she was bewildered. Too many lights shined in her face all at once. She had descended into an indecipherable hierarchy of the city, into a trap. Her feet went down the stairs to the underground passageway. Something light and metallic fell by her shoes. Someone tapped her on the back and held out a button. It had fallen off her coat. She was about to say thank you, but then she clapped a hand over her mouth—the person who'd picked up the button looked just like her. She had to hide somewhere, somewhere safe. She wanted an overwhelmingly bitter cup of coffee.

She told herself to calm down.

When she'd opened her grandmother's box, the first things she'd seen had been a pair of scissors, a tape measure, and a tarnished silver hand mirror. Her grandmother had had this mirror for a long time. In front of her bathroom mirror, she'd held the hand mirror up, her image reflected in the larger mirror. The bathroom mirror had reflected the hand mirror and her face in it. The two mirrors had sucked her in, a black hole. A tornado from which light could not escape. In the two mirrors she had seen dozens of her own face, replicated in smaller sizes. The last face had been so far away that she hadn't seen it properly, but she'd known it was hers. She'd seen dozens of her own face through her grandmother's mirror, and her face had been the second thing she'd seen when she'd opened the box. The women in the mirror had spoken, their lips closed firmly. Uttering a very short sentence. She'd put the mirror down and crouched on the floor to avoid the bathroom mirror. Seeing so many of her own face at the same time had made her feel a surprising pang of sadness. She hoped to never experience that again.

The restaurant was nearly empty. She sensed people sitting, and getting up from empty tables like smoke, and walking boldly among the tables. Some had her face. She quickly downed her espresso. She wanted to wake up from this dizzy state. But she felt she was still standing before the bathroom mirror, holding her grandmother's hand mirror. It felt different from facing death in the dark. She sat, her head hanging, avoiding everything, afraid. The food was ice-cold, and the tablecloth was so white, it glowed blue.

She passed Gyeongbokgung Station and went down a side street. A dark, narrow street. The streetlight was broken, and stray cats meowed listlessly. Snow was piled on either side of the street. A woman was coming down from the school for the blind, sweeping her cane. It clacked as it made contact with the ground. She turned her back until the woman passed so she wouldn't have to see the woman's face. She shook from fear, drenched in cold sweat, as she stood by the street leading up to the Naesu-dong studio.

This truth was what had been reflected in the two mirrors. That the parts were the same as the whole.

44

BEING ANXIOUS DOESN'T PROTECT ANYONE

Dr. Suzuki brought out two cups of mint tea. He took a sip. "Ojisan," he said, trying it out. It was the first time he'd called the doctor that since his brother had died. Dr. Suzuki nodded in encouragement. He began telling the doctor about her. It felt like he was opening a box he'd long kept secret in an inner pocket for the first time in someone else's company. He hadn't told anyone about her. Then again he didn't have anyone in his life he could tell. Maybe things would have been different if his brother had still been alive. His brother had left too many things behind for him. That was the main reason why he'd felt so enraged after his brother died. Before his brother died, he'd never known loneliness, though he'd known fear. He told Dr. Suzuki all about her, getting everything off his chest.

"What's the main feeling you get from that person?" asked Dr. Suzuki. *That person.* When Dr. Suzuki referred to her as *that person*, he could finally, clearly see the fragmentary thoughts he had about her.

"Fear."

"Is she a tower or an elevator or something?" Dr. Suzuki laughed heartily. Then he stopped and asked, "Fear of what?"

"Fear that she might vanish."

"Well."

"What is it, Ojisan?"

"It occurs to me that I'm extremely incompetent."

"It's my fault."

"The consultations we had haven't helped you at all, it seems."

"This is completely unrelated to that, Ojisan."

"How so?"

"This, well, is about a girl."

"A girl."

"Yes."

"When did you say you started seeing her?"

"The first week of January."

"So about two months now."

"Yes."

"And you said you thought of Yunjae the first time you saw her."

Yunjae. His brother's name. The name he hadn't been able to utter in a long time.

"Has it ever occurred to you that you're seeing everything through her eyes?"

". . . !"

"You're worrying your father might do something terrible, worrying she might do something like that as well."

"I didn't think we were close enough for her to have that kind of effect on me."

Dr. Suzuki smiled. "Do you happen to have a talisman?"

"I'm sure it's pasted somewhere in my room."

"I imagine your mother would have put it there."

"Yes."

"Have you ever wondered why your mother would do that?"

"She probably finds it comforting."

"Right. Everyone thinks it's superstitious to have talismans, but nobody can fully dismiss them. And you know how much we Japanese believe in talismans. I have one right here, myself." Smiling, Dr. Suzuki tapped his right back pocket, where his wallet was. "Superstitions are a manifestation of fear."

"Which is why they aren't rational or logical."

"Are you able to explain your fears rationally?"

". . ."

"It would be great if everything could be explained by logical reasoning, but there you have it."

"But you can't possibly encourage someone to use talismans."

"Then, how else would doctors like me survive?"

"Please don't make jokes, Ojisan."

"Do you think there's a way to rationally explain why someone is afraid of a broken mirror?"

"But that can't be explained rationally to begin with."

"You mean like the feeling you got when you first met her."

He stayed silent.

"Everyone feels nervous the moment they break a mirror, even if it's by accident," Dr. Suzuki continued.

"Then, I have to find something that will help me get rid of that anxiety."

"It won't work if you don't believe in it."

"Ojisan, isn't it a problem for a talisman to take on that role?"

"Why?" Dr. Suzuki leaned forward.

His throat prickled. Dr. Suzuki had told him all manners of stories. Ridiculous and dispiriting and sad and terrifying stories. Stories he'd remembered and stories he'd forgotten the moment he'd left Dr. Suzuki's office. He still remembered the one about someone who'd slashed his own Achilles tendon with a razor blade, a man who hadn't wanted to go anywhere.

Dr. Suzuki continued, "The fact that you're feeling anxious, the fact that you want to rely on something to make you feel better—none of that is possible without passion. Being comforted by something like a talisman is an act of hope. You want to believe in something. What's wrong with talismans if they can give you that kind of hope?"

"I'm not sure I understand."

"Don't you think there are appropriate and inappropriate passions?"

"You're saying I have more of the latter."

"Right. Fear isn't passive. It's active."

"Ojisan."

"Go on."

"I don't want to lose her."

"Then hold on to her."

"I don't know how."

"Do you know what you need to get used to when you love someone?"

". . ."

"You have to learn not to want everything all at once. It's the same with the truth."

He nodded, still confused.

"You don't have to worry too much about your parents. They're fully aware of all that."

"I guess they're wise, even though they're not happy."

"They know what happiness is."

He didn't answer.

Dr. Suzuki continued, "And show her."

"Show her what?"

"That you believe in her."

He could see the sun setting behind Dr. Suzuki. The sky was framed by the window like a painting in violet and navy; a bird flew across it. The sun could be setting or rising. It felt as though all he could see was what was encased in the window frame. He didn't think he could show her anything. He thought, *This is just who I am.* "Ojisan," he said, his eyes still glued to the window. He wanted to ask, *What kind of person am I?*

I have never desperately prayed for anything.

I don't know anything about things like constellations.

I only wanted advice I could act on.

I—I have never loved anyone.

He opened his eyes. Why did sadness accompany realizations? The sun was definitively setting. The sky grew darker. Silence settled, thick and dense. He got up from his seat slowly, as if checking to see if his body could move. He felt air being pushed back about four inches. He left, taking his coat from the entryway. In the hallway Dr. Suzuki thumped him on the shoulder. The doctor seemed to want to say the following: *Keep in mind that being anxious doesn't protect anyone.*

45

WHEN YOU EAT IT, IT TASTES LIKE DEATH

Confusion bubbled up from an unexpected source. She had thought she could discern what she believed in from what she didn't. If she handled something and it gave her a certain feeling or sensation, that was something she could believe in. Like when she handled clay, when she touched flower petals, when she laid a hand on another person's body, when she wiped away tears. Even when they were mere inanimate objects, they left behind a particular sensation and impression. And of course there were things she didn't believe in, even when she touched them. Shadows, forms reflected in the mirror. Sentences like *I love you* and *That hurts* didn't trigger any sort of feeling. But her confusion had begun with the vertigo she'd felt when she first saw blowfish writhing in Abe-san's shop. Blowfish. Fish she hadn't handled yet. Without convincing Abe-san, she would never be able to handle them; it was something completely out of the realm of possibility for now. Whenever Abe-san cleaned and gutted and fileted blowfish, she migrated all her senses to his fingertips. Furtively, as if slipping into his body for a brief moment. Even though she'd never handled a still-living, still-breathing blowfish, she realized that now, when she thought about blowfish, when she watched one being butchered into edible and inedible parts, toxic and nontoxic parts, the blowfish became a real, vivid being for her, like it was her own physical body, one she believed in implicitly. Did touching and feeling Baek's body mean she could trust it? Did looking at her reflection in the mirror mean she couldn't? She wasn't sure if it was her or the blowfish asking these questions. Just as every movement started with the movement of light, everything right now seemed to arise from being one with the blowfish. She remembered how he'd suggested blowfish would become a special objet d'art for her. An energy as strong as a tidal wave overpowered her as the blowfish lay on the wet chopping block in the process of being deboned and gutted, sucking in her gaze, sucking in all her senses.

Today's selection was a four-and-a-half-pound karasu with a glossy black body.

Abe-san's movements were efficient as he wielded the knife lightly like a pencil, made precise cuts, and placed the knife neatly down. He had turned out to be completely different from her first impression of him. She'd never seen anyone use a knife so masterfully. Though she wasn't schooled in the taste of fish, as she watched Abe-san using the knife like it was an extension of his hand, she realized the common saying had to be true: The taste of fish depended on the skill of the person handling the knife. As he struck the big, strong blowfish, chopping and skinning and pushing and slicing, Abe-san occasionally barked out a tidbit about blowfish: That blowfish were the most difficult fish, the tastiest fish, the fish that kept you on your toes every time you handled it, the fish with toxic ovaries. This karasu was persistently alive, even under Abe-san's knife. His forehead glistened. She wanted it to fight on for longer. She knew Abe-san would stop talking once the karasu was cleaned and fileted. She looked up at Abe-san's profile. Regardless of the kind of person he was, he would remain forever etched in her memory as the first person who told her all about blowfish.

Abe-san unfolded a dry cloth on his clean chopping block. He placed the cleaned blowfish parts on top like specimens. To her they looked like two heaps. On the left were the inedible innards. On the right were the edible flesh and skin and bones and fins. She looked at the pile on the left, the kidney and heart and bladder and eyes and brain and ovaries and spleen. Light green and yellowish white and cloudy red and murky orange-yellow. She counted the items on the right. The backbone, dorsal fin, pelvic fin, tail, skin, pectoral fins, belly, inner skin, cartilage, skull, ribs. Eleven parts. The parts that wouldn't kill you. Abe-san pointed his knife at the innards on the left. He sank his knife into the reddish heart and said, "If you want to die, there's no point in learning how to handle the toxin. Right?"

She nodded.

"You need to know how to handle the toxin so you don't die. Right?"

She nodded again.

Abe-san asked if she knew what blowfish tasted like.

"No."

"It's a grotesque taste," Abe-san said. "When you eat it, it tastes like death. That's what it tastes like."

She reminded Abe-san that they had one more lesson left.

Abe-san nodded indifferently. He looked out at the rainy street. "It's March now," he said. "March is the end of blowfish season."

She left the outer market holding a black plastic bag of blowfish fins, flesh, skin, and skull. She didn't go straight out toward the main road; instead, she turned and went down an alley, taking a shortcut to the metro. She would find herself at the café on the other end, where they'd fled the cold when he'd brought her to Tsukiji Market the first time. An enormous fish head hung like a billboard on the roof of a three-story building by the main road. The head sparkled like marble under the sun and got drenched on rainy days like today, grinning through it all. Every time she entered and exited the outer market, she shot a glance at the fish head in the air. Today, as she looked up at the fish head, she felt the world spin. She took two steps forward. In that brief moment, she wondered if she should buy an umbrella or just get wet, if she should leave the plastic bag on the train or throw it out back at the apartment. What did Abe-san do from the end of blowfish season in March through the fall? Something heaved her up. She stumbled and fell. Workers who had been shoveling ice into wooden crates, shop owners, and tourists scattered and ran. Her pants had gotten wet. She shook her head to clear her vertigo. People rushed away in the same direction. "Ah!" she cried out; the ground was shaking. It was a vertical motion, that of an organism deep underground picking her up and dropping her. Someone rushed past, shouting at her, "Nigete! Nigete!"

She couldn't move. She sat there, hands braced against the ground. She looked far ahead, as if she would run forward. A bell rang faintly out there somewhere. The world was layers of gray. The river flowed, and a flock of long-necked white birds were aloft above the wetlands. As if a crack had formed in her consciousness, she could see even farther away. She felt she was farther away. A deep silence settled over the alley. She dropped her head and wept, as though blazing eyes were glaring at her. She couldn't overcome or rid herself of her sadness. Her father was dying. Sadness that couldn't be overcome or eradicated was the same as death. It was always right there, in the same place.

46

Body

The long, wide sofa was more like a twin bed. It was one of the pieces of furniture he and Sinae had chosen when her husband had bought this house to celebrate their fifth wedding anniversary. Sinae had wanted a sofa big enough to lie on, even with a few decorative pillows on it. The Dacron-and-polyurethane seat cushions were springy but cozy. Sinae had decided on this sofa the moment she sat on it. He'd wanted this sofa for himself but hadn't been able to buy it just yet. Many such things populated this house, most selected by him. Like the Philippe Starck crystal candlestick lamp in the library, the fifty-five-inch Bang & Olufsen TV, the green lamp with free-flowing curves hanging from the kitchen ceiling. The only thing different from most other times was that he was naked right now. Butt naked.

Was he embarrassed right now because he was surrounded by the things he'd selected? Or was it because it had only now fully occurred to him that Sinae lived here with another man? How much longer would he have to be here? That was the real question. No matter what happened, he would leave at some point. He was certain that, as soon as the door closed behind him, both he and

Sinae would accept that this was the last time. He'd had no idea what Sinae had wanted when she'd told him to take off his clothes, when he'd met Sinae's eyes squinting with hurt. All he'd known was that doing as she said was the right way to end their affair. Love that trampled you. A farewell ceremony for that must exist somewhere in this world.

Slowly he had taken his clothes off, as if giving Sinae permission to trample over his body. The light slanted in through the large window. He'd never imagined doing something like this. Standing before a suit-clad Sinae, he silently took off his jacket and then his shirt, his pants, his socks, and his undershirt. Even as he took his clothes off, it felt like he was fastening buttons one by one. He must have hesitated for a second when he was down to his underwear, because Sinae quietly ordered, "Take it off." He took it all off. His clothes were in a pile by his feet. He realized for the first time that none of it was erotic when one person was naked and the other was fully clothed. It didn't make him embarrassed or angry. Maybe eroticism existed only in between parted lips, parted fingers, parted clothes. The attraction that had pulsed between them for ten years evaporated as he alone took off his clothes. Sinae didn't look in his eyes, at his face, or at his asymmetrical scrotum, which she'd loved. She didn't look at his penis, drooping and heavy. Empty and numb, her gaze raked over his face and body. They stood there, facing each other. Two bodies that remembered everything, peach fuzz to peach fuzz, bone to bone, blood to blood. Two bodies walled off from each other right now. Nobody would be home for the next two hours, this home he couldn't leave, and so he stood in a space taken over in its entirety by Sinae and her timeline. He didn't budge. If this was how they could go their separate ways, he would do it. He erased shame and guilt from his mind. This was the decisive moment.

He couldn't put it off any longer. If he didn't make the choice himself, the world might force on him a choice he didn't want.

Sinae stood there, frozen in place. It wasn't Sinae's reddened eyes but her dark hair brushed neatly into an updo, without a single loose strand, that announced her sadness, her even bigger sense of loss, and her decision to be done with him. He wanted to smile at her. Something fizzled in his throat like water being sprayed on a fire.

It felt like a long time had passed. But he wanted to stand there across from Sinae for as long as he could, until his body could be perceived as one of many nameless bodies.

Sinae went into the kitchen, saying she would make some tea. He slumped heavily onto the sofa. Only the bouncy, cool sensation on his ass reminded him that he was naked. Sinae didn't return. He didn't hear water boiling or teacups clinking. He picked up the English-language book on the table. *The House Gun*. A novel by Nadine Gordimer. Sinae had told him she was reading it. That it was about a gun that happened to be in a house, causing one person to drive another to death. A book that questioned the issues of individual and societal responsibility. Sinae had told him it was hard to accept a situation in which a gun just happened to be there. That it was just a contrived novelistic setup. He couldn't remember what he had said in response. He must have thought the same thing then as he did now: *Dangers like guns are everywhere.*

He went to the window. He could see the yard from his vantage point on the second floor. It contained well-maintained trees and rocks, a child's swing. He leaned against the glass. He didn't want to know how he must look. His body had changed. It could no longer conceal his feelings. He wanted Sinae to come back and look at his body that could no longer hide. He wanted to look at Sinae's body, which his body had needed like he needed water, at his own body that now wanted to say that everything had been a response to Sinae's desires, not his. He wanted to stare into his mutant body, as though looking into deep waters. The floor swayed. He felt vibration. Air scattered. A glass cup fell onto the tiled kitchen floor. One second. No, two seconds, three. He waited for the time to pass, for the small earthquake to end.

Nobody came into the living room. It was as if he were in an empty home. As if he had always been alone.

47

ANY LIGHT OR SOUND

For two years Saim had focused on incorporating geometry into her art. This had been after she'd established herself in the Asian art market with her paintings—in other words, two-dimensional works. Collectors had lined up to buy Saim's pictures despite the waiting list; her work had been exquisite in the way miniatures could be, and her work had taken a long time to complete. Then Saim had suddenly stopped painting and ejected herself from that world. Some people considered this period of inactivity to be a positive development. Unlike most young artists in slumps or grappling with the trajectories of their careers, Saim hadn't gone on a trip or attempted to force herself to have experiences for the sake of her art practice. People who knew her well had whispered that it would be hard for Saim to have new experiences because of her illness. She had visited Saim's studio often around that time. Saim had seemed the same. The only difference had been that she'd draped white cloth over her worktable and chairs. Like someone who was about to leave for a faraway destination. She and Saim had chatted, sitting on wooden chairs covered in white cloth. You couldn't tell with the cloth over them, but her father had made two of the chairs from high-quality red pine for Saim. When they had been in college, Saim had liked accompanying her to her father's woodworking shop, and when Saim had gotten her first studio, he had gifted her two chairs of a simple design.

It was true that her father felt a special kinship with Saim. He knew she didn't have close friends or colleagues other than Saim. One day her father had said something interesting to her. Saim had just gone home after killing time in the woodworking shop, as she had on many days, drinking a cup of coffee her father had had delivered. Her father had asked her what she thought friendship was. She remembered looking at him, puzzled. It was such a strange question, and she'd never imagined having a conversation like this with her father. Was he joking? Should she laugh? She'd hesitated while collecting her bag to leave. Her father's voice had been colored with a vague and unspecified but deeply rooted concern. "A friend is someone who tells you who you are," her father had said, and then—perhaps feeling awkward—he had gone to the shed. His words had made sense. But it had been strange for her father, who didn't have a single close friend, to tell her something like that, and she'd felt miffed, like he had pointed out a flaw she was well aware of. *Someone who tells me who I am? That would be you and Halmeoni and her mother, wouldn't it?* she would have retorted, but she hadn't had the chance.

Saim talked and she listened. On days she talked, Saim listened. They never talked about art. They ignored the fact that everything they talked about was related to art. Saim talked about reputation and pride. About understanding and sacrifice. About compassion and fear. About love.

One day she'd said to Saim, "Everything you talk about can be boiled down to one thing."

She still didn't know if Saim had understood what she'd meant. She hadn't said the word *death*. Because it was a word that could gain greater meaning by not uttering it out loud. She waited for Saim. Saim watched her as she made art. Saim, who was thoughtful; Saim, who suffered. That was how she defined Saim. That was also the best way she could express her belief in and friendship with Saim. Everyone went through gradual, irrevocable changes. As an artist, you couldn't avoid that.

Saim's new exhibition exploring geometry was highly acclaimed. Saim had wanted to push the universe of mathematical order, systematic and pure, to new frontiers. In her pursuit of order, her practice had been closely aligned with minimalist art. The difference was that she had pulled in noise, considered an impurity in minimalist art, and woven it together with light. It was the kind of art that was impossible to make without challenging her own worldview and infusing discovery with hope. Saim had used engineering calculations to make a realistic spherical image of a bird. She'd created it with a mathematical formula derived from a world without room for even the most minute of errors. Saim had focused on the unfamiliar order that arose from repeatedly creating darkness out of noise. A never-ending, intricate, systematic world, like the universe at night.

When she received her aunt's call that her father had passed away, she thought of Saim's picture. Whether it was a bird or a sphere, she wasn't entirely sure. She felt she had seen a small object within an endless universe, within an order of enormous magnitude. An object whose movements weren't predictable. She gripped the phone. "I'm sorry," her aunt kept saying. She tried to keep her focus on the object that had escaped order. "Gomo, Gomo. Sukhui Gomo," she said, calling her crying aunt's name as she shook her head.

Her father wasn't the right fit with that kind of object, with Saim's picture.

He had kept his head bowed, fists covering his eyes. He hadn't always been in that position, but it sure felt like he had. Like Van Gogh's *Sorrowing Old Man (At Eternity's Gate)*. Like that shabby, poor old man in that painting. He had always looked like that. Her aunt told her he had hanged himself. Her aunt apologized to her for failing to keep him safe.

She had expected something like this, something she'd believed inevitable. Her aunt's quiet weeping pierced her eardrums; it felt heavier than her father's death. *Don't cry, Gomo*, she wanted to say. She wanted to tell her aunt that everyone died from their own mistakes. She stared into the darkness. *Did the thing that sidestepped me pull Abeoji under?* She was standing all alone in the middle of an inescapable forest. She couldn't detect any light or warmth or sound. Like the home she'd grown up in, the place that had felt like a comfortable ruin.

She raised her hand and covered her eyes.

48

IN THAT FEAR

A small calendar marked with lunar dates hung behind the bar. It included pictures of Seoraksan in each of the four seasons. Today was Thursday, March fifth: Gyeongchip. He checked his watch. Eight thirty in the evening. The numbers were clear and trustworthy. But he still felt trapped in an uncertain time and space. He'd been feeling this way for an hour, since seven thirty.

The seat beside him was empty. By now everything was gone—the traces of someone having sat there, the conversation they'd had. Nothing remained that could prove it had happened. He hadn't been nervous or displeased when he'd met up with the death cleaner. He'd merely understood more clearly that he had started down a path that would be hard to reverse out of. He stared at the seat next to him as if the man were still sitting there. The death cleaner had left ten minutes ago. He could hear conversations at other tables and smell peanuts and fruits others were snacking on. He poured himself a drink. He hadn't even brought his glass to his lips when the death cleaner had been there. He could have easily decided not to meet up with the man.

But an hour ago, he had met the death cleaner at Desert.

He'd been eating a late lunch alone at a bakery near his office after having spent the morning at a client's house. He couldn't stop thinking about her. He'd finally seen her the day before, and she'd told him she'd gone to Seoul for a few days. She had said Seoul was colder than here and so windy that she'd managed to lose a scarf tied around the handle of her bag. He'd asked himself, *Was it really a scarf she'd lost?* He thought it was preferable when she didn't talk at all. She didn't speak to reveal or express something but to conceal and evade. Even worse was how she never disagreed with any suggestion he made, her gaze lacking any emotion or curiosity. In his imagination he did all kinds of terrible things a man could do to a woman as she stared intently at something other than him. He ripped off her clothes and beat her and spat vile words and cursed and begged for her love. As they went their separate ways in front of Nippori Station, she had suddenly looked at him and smiled. A bright, open smile. It hadn't been the first time he'd seen her cracking a smile. But he couldn't bring himself to smile back. He hadn't wanted to smile in a way that could make her feel nervous, the way her smile was making him feel. "Bye," she had said, still smiling. He'd knitted his brows. He had felt like he was overpowering her to look down her dark throat, like in most dreams he had about her; *defeat* was the only way to describe it. Though she had been smiling, she hadn't looked beautiful or happy or animated.

He'd left his cooled soup and sandwich uneaten and trudged back to the office. He'd unfurled the blueprint the client had asked him to revise. He would have to start from scratch, this project that had been progressing for several months. The design featured base isolation technology, where a rubber mat or hard bearing was installed between the ground and the building to dampen the movement of the earth. Buildings with base isolation didn't collapse, even after a strong earthquake; they were left with their steel frames standing, resulting in less damage. But it wasn't yet widely used because of the enormous cost and time required to install. Abe Kengo, who'd experienced a magnitude 8.0 earthquake when he had studied in California, was enthusiastic about this technology. But he was still skeptical that a building could refrain from shaking when the earth moved. He was more interested in designs that included vibration control, which didn't avoid movement but took it full force and absorbed the shock. This technology had been implemented in just a few places, as a pilot. There was something ironic about the fact that architecture was being advanced by earthquakes, of all things. Before his next meeting, he had to review what could be carried over from the existing plan. But he couldn't focus. Maybe what she'd said as she'd left wasn't *Bye* but *Thank you for everything.* Maybe she hadn't been smiling but trying not to cry. He'd kept tugging his shirt over his chin.

And that was when the death cleaner had called. He might have ignored the call if he hadn't been thinking about the way she had smiled. He hadn't been too keen on that man's line of work to begin with.

The death cleaner had arrived at Desert ten minutes early. He hadn't seen this man since the party at Park's Shibuya apartment. The man's hair looked thinner, and he was in a neat gray suit. The death cleaner had ordered sparkling water with ice. Mun, who had furtively stolen a glance at him and the man, had nodded.

He had looked down at the business card the death cleaner had handed him. The first question the death cleaner had asked was when he'd seen her last.

He'd wanted to scoff at the man and criticize his line of work. Yesterday he'd answered truthfully. They didn't know each other, but he couldn't bring himself to tell the man anything but the truth.

"She's at risk," the death cleaner had said, his tone businesslike.

He hadn't responded. He had felt his face splintering. He'd wanted to rage at the circumspect death cleaner. He had been angry, remembering his brother's voice saying, "Hurry up." He sat through a huge wave of rage. He considered that rage, that rage that always took and took and never gave anything back.

The death cleaner had told him that once she'd arrived in Tokyo, they'd met in Ueno Park several times, drinking tea or taking a stroll. And about what she had been thinking about for a long time. How last January she had called the death cleaner to ask him to pack up number 605 and how she had called again this morning, asking him to do the same thing. Apparently he was the only person she was friendly with in Tokyo, which was why the death cleaner had reached out to him.

Before the death cleaner had left, he'd told the man there was something he wanted to ask. The death cleaner, already halfway up, had awkwardly sat back down.

"Why do you do this work?" He had still been angry. He hadn't expected an answer.

"Because it feels like I'm helping."

"Helping who?"

"The deceased, of course. They're usually all alone."

"I'm sure they are."

He had watched as the death cleaner had opened the heavy door and left. The death cleaner must have told him the truth. He'd turned away, feeling like he was emerging from a state of suspension. Maybe he had been sitting here all alone all evening, alternating between malt whiskey and water. He was afraid he'd imagined everything he'd seen and felt since yesterday and found himself hoping that was the case. He could hide himself in that fear. He called out to Mun, "Was I sitting here with someone?"

"How would I know?"

"I don't know."

"You don't know what?"

"What I should do."

Mun's face was blank.

He wanted to ask if a person who thought long and hard about one thing and one thing only could love another.

49

THE EYES AND THE BONES

The taxi pulled up in front of the building at precisely 11:00 p.m. She exited her apartment quietly, closing the front door behind her. Umbrellas hung from each unit's windowsill along the hallway. The floor was puddled with rainwater. It had rained in the afternoon, and more was in the forecast for tomorrow. The forecast was more often accurate than not. She went down the emergency stairwell to the ground floor. The stairs were steep and dark. It smelled like the tire recycling plant. A black Nara City taxi idled before the entrance, hazards blinking. She settled into the back and felt the driver looking at her through the rearview mirror. She named her destination.

The driver repeated it. He seemed to be wondering, *Why is she going there at this hour?*

She looked out the window to indicate that he should start driving. The taxi began moving smoothly. They turned the corner and went straight toward Showa-dori Avenue. Away from Nippori Station. Red taillights and the yellow glow of streetlamps dappled the wet road. Not a soul was out, no elderly pedestrians nor bare-legged children in thin school uniforms. Not even anyone drunk. The wide avenue was deserted, perhaps because they were due for a few days of unseasonably cold, below-freezing weather after the rain. Although her desire was to drive through busy streets, everything looked closed, austere. The driver didn't turn on any music or try to speak to her. Thick frost shellacked the windows. Once in a while she opened her window for a brief moment, in a futile effort to get some fresh air. She sat ramrod straight in her seat. She felt matter-of-fact, and when they arrived at the market, she realized she'd become surprisingly calm. The driver told her he could wait for her if she paid a little extra. She declined and got out. The taxi idled for about a minute, as if expecting to witness something important. She stood on the sidewalk, waiting for the taxi to leave. The car gave up and drove slowly away.

A cat stared at her, its eyes deep-set, from the stairs of the rest area. "Go away," she murmured in a thin voice. Her vocal cords weren't working. The cat didn't budge. The street was desolate; nobody would even know if something unfortunate or tragic happened overnight. On this street stands began to shutter in the afternoon. A seventy-yard-long street that looked like a dark shadow, as though the night had managed to drag it along. Only the cat's eyes shined in the street. The eyes of a cat weren't what she wanted. She rummaged through her pockets. Her notebook. She tore a few pages and crumpled them. She threw them at the animal. The cat, which hadn't been tense or prepared for attack, swiftly leapt onto the divider between the sidewalk and the road. She looked around. Nobody was there. Right now the street resembled a ruin, but at two in the morning, noren would be hung over the stands and the lights would turn on one by one. The cat returned to the sidewalk and meowed, then slowly followed the white lines painted on the road.

She was under a streetlamp. She was standing all by herself. There was nobody else around. Her shadow, cast long on the ground, could have been that of a young woman or an old woman or even an old man. It was as if she were standing with two others, not by herself. All dead but not yet fallen over.

She reached up and pulled down the plastic blowfish hanging from the S hook above the shop. She stuck her hand into the blowfish's hat. She remembered the drawers hanging in her father's woodworking shop. Like Abe-san had said, maybe the important things were kept close. If the key to the shop was a test, she was failing. If this was a game, she was losing. Or maybe nothing was clear-cut. Did Abe-san trust her or not? Who started this strange game, Abe-san or her? She found the keys.

She opened the outer door and the inner one, then raised the shutters about three feet. Once inside she turned on the lights and pulled the shutters down. The two water tanks each contained three blowfish, their stomachs grazing the bottoms. Two shimafugu and one nameradamashi. She pulled a plastic chair up to the tanks and grabbed a big scooper that was face down by the chopping block. She climbed onto the chair and scooped some water. She put it on the ground and went back onto the chair, a net in hand. She lifted a shimafugu from the topmost tank: three pounds. Not too big, not too small. This wild blowfish had come in from Shimonoseki three days earlier. Abe-san didn't work with farmed blowfish. He said farmed fish didn't taste like nature; they didn't have the taste of the ocean in Shimonoseki, his hometown. Farmed blowfish didn't have something else—toxin. Only wild blowfish were poisonous. The fish thrashed in the drooping net. But the more it did, the more it got tangled in the top part of the net. She took a black garbage bag from her pocket. She carefully slid the net into the bag and shook it. What if she couldn't handle the force of the blowfish? She twisted the bag closed and held it tight. The fish fell to the bottom of the bag. She took the net out and poured in the water from the scooper. As if sensing impending death, the blowfish flopped around ferociously, angry. Blowfish were sensitive to small spaces and changes in water. It might end up dying from stress before she got home.

She held the black trash bag with the blowfish in one hand and walked along the streets, using her other hand to shield her face from the neon signs and car lights. She thought someone would grab her by the nape of her neck. Water dripped to the ground as she walked. The waterdrops would be nearly invisible, but some might consider them irrevocable evidence. Sweat trickled down her spine.

An hour later she was standing on the footbridge by Minowa Station. A corner of the sky to the east was being dyed a saturated topaz. The rain forecast must be wrong. Was the blowfish doing okay in the trash bag? She shook the bag, its opening still tied up, and placed it down. The black trash bag slumped to one side, and she felt a flapping from within. Ten more minutes—ten more minutes and she would be at the apartment. In her mind she was already in number 605, standing before the table, a clean, dry chopping board and knife in front of her.

And now she would be handling the blowfish, which she still hadn't ever touched whole. She'd learned a lot from Abe-san, with her eyes and senses and mind. First she would slide the fishhook out of the body, then swiftly hit it twice in the head with the side of her knife to knock it unconscious, slice off its mouth, split the head in two, and remove its brain and eyes and spine. That was when she would stop. She didn't need to filet the rest of the fish. This was what she wanted. The parts that contained the toxin.

The eyes and the bones.

In her apartment she looked at the far side of the dark living room, as if expecting someone. She was standing in the living room, stinking with the smell of fish and water. She waited for a sign, something subtle, something that was clamoring to be noticed. Something that had followed her deliberately for a long time, making fun of her. Something she thought she would never be able to avoid, something that made her feel trapped. Abeoji. She thought about her father. About her father's dead body stiffening. About his face, expressionless, as if he were already dead, even when he had been alive. About the lives of his family, oppressed by the complex rule of death. She felt a cold draft. She opened the living room window a crack so her soul could escape. She wanted to smile with dignity. "Let's start," she whispered.

She was looking at the blowfish's bones. At the blowfish's eyes.

LISTEN TO ME, PLEASE

Everything the death cleaner had told him was correct—the code to enter the apartment building, the location of the key to number 605. It wasn't that he hadn't believed the death cleaner. He hadn't wanted to believe him. He went to the apartment six hours earlier than the time the death cleaner had told him. He couldn't just wait for 1:00 p.m. He kept hearing laughter. He remembered how she had smiled so brightly, as if that were her best defense. He rang the doorbell repeatedly before letting himself in and walking through the front door. A fishy smell clobbered him in an instant. She was collapsed on the living room floor. Only later did he realize that he'd gone through two doors and maneuvered past the dining table and a side table, like they were an obstacle course, before reaching her. But all he saw when he entered number 605 was her, prone on the floor. His eyes were drawn to her, as if she were a long, dark figure lying in a completely white room, the darkness absorbing all other light. It was a dull, unremarkable darkness, but he realized that it was pulling him in, this darkness that was like savage noise.

He went to her.

He picked her up and laid her on the sofa, peered into her eyes, then called 119.

She was having a minor seizure.

When the paramedics left, he called Dr. Suzuki, who told him he would send a doctor as soon as he could. He was to make sure she didn't drift back to sleep once she woke up. Her tongue would be stiff for some time, making it hard for her to speak. It didn't even occur to him to shake or bite her awake. Heat crawled up his legs to his torso, to his neck. It wasn't sorrow or rage or pain. He put his hands on the tea table, leaning against it, waiting for the emotions coursing through him to leave. She was breathing evenly, her face reflecting her habitual gloom. He didn't know when she would open her eyes, or whether it was night or day. All he knew was that right now the two of them, she and he, were together, in this space. He'd managed to pry open a door that wouldn't open or close easily. A door he'd been watching for a long time. He felt time pass him by. Like an omen of pain, time penetrated him as he stood there at 7:47 on Sunday morning. He hugged himself, protecting himself. He felt he was finally living his life. He let out a long breath. A sigh of relief that this had actually happened, this looming event from which he'd fled. A sigh of relief that she was alive. A sigh of relief as he realized that he was a man, not a beast who could never shed tears.

She woke up two hours later.

Her eyes searched the air. She blinked. He was sitting in an armchair perpendicular to her head. His hands were knotted together, trying to control himself.

"Has—has it been a long time?" She sat up. She didn't touch her hair or look at him. She just looked straight ahead.

"I came here around seven." He stood.

"What are you doing?"

"Getting you some water."

"I'm okay. Just stay there."
"Okay."
"I didn't want you to see this."
"It's okay."
". . ."
". . ."
"My lips feel stiff."
"You'll start feeling better soon."
"It hurts, but I'm not sure where it hurts."
"That means everything hurts."
"Were you sitting there all along?"
"I was standing, too."
"Why?"
"I wasn't sure when I should go."
"You couldn't go before I woke up."
"It's good to see you smile."
"I'm sorry."
"About what?"
"Everything. From the beginning."
"You don't have to talk. It must hurt."
"I'm okay."
"I'm glad."
"I was scared."
"I bet."
"I didn't think I would be."
"Here, a tissue. Your nose is running."
"We met when it was really cold."
"We did."
"It's going to be spring soon."
"The cherry blossoms will be out soon."
"I bet they're beautiful."

"They are."
"Really?"
"Really."
"Okay."
"We'll go to the park together."
"All right. I'm going to lie down for a bit."
"I'll bring you some water."
"I'm okay. Just stay there."
"Thank you."
"For what?"
"For everything."
"I should go, even though it's too late."
"Where?"
"To my father."
"Where is he?"
"At home."
"In Seoul?"
"I want to talk, but I'm getting sleepy."
"How's your stomach?"
"I don't know."
"Talk to me. You can't sleep right now."
"I'm tired."
"Talk to me."
"Later."
"No, you have to talk."
"What should I . . . ?"
"Open your eyes."
". . ."
"You can't sleep. You can't."
". . ."
"Listen to me, please."

51

She wasn't sad or scared

Layers of white and light pink cherry blossoms weighed down the tree branches. They would soon be in full bloom. People were walking along the paths, excited. They were elderly, their gait looking less like they were walking than stepping purposefully on the earth, praying for a large harvest. In the afternoons it was hard to feel vitality in the park. But today the entire park felt different, maybe because of the cherry blossoms. It was as if the usual pale cotton cloth had been lifted and replaced by fabric as colorful as tropical fruit. The only constants were the strutting crows, showing off their sheer size and boldness, and the placid pigeons scattering, rashly pecking at the ground without realizing the dangers the bigger birds posed. Most of the pigeons had a missing foot or a torn wing. In the brief moment when she sat on the curb by the flower beds, she watched an eagle snatch a pigeon by the wing. The pigeon had been sitting on the walking path, not even a yard away. She turned away from the flailing feathers. She had learned while walking through Ueno Park that eagles always tore at the wings when going after pigeons. The pigeons were always taken helplessly. Gray feathers scattered across the sidewalk, dripping blood. She was no longer shocked by it. These were the lives of eagles and pigeons. Life was quick in that moment. The wind blew, bringing along a musty whiff from the zoo. The eagle, gripping the pigeon's neck, flew leisurely west, toward the grove of trees. Cherry petals fell one by one around the ruby blood drops. The petals looked even more startlingly glamorous there than when they were adorning the sky. An image of white cherry blossom petals falling like a snowstorm on a red river bobbed up, then vanished. It was still cold in the shade. She had never seen cherry blossoms in full bloom. She didn't know the splendor of such a sight. He had told her that in a week it would be peak cherry blossom season. He had told her about the plaintive beauty of the flowers. *Beauty*. Somehow that word felt like it was imposing sorrow on her. There were too many things to think about and too many things she didn't know about, as though the only thing she'd done since the moment she'd dropped into this world was count the days until she could exit this life. Clouds and birds and flowers and trees and people. The park was the same park she had seen all along; it didn't look different now that flowers were blooming. Maybe she wouldn't be able to learn something new about beauty or about anything else. She did know that one thing had disappeared from the park. Her standing under the cherry tree back in January, looking up at the sky, the wooden chair in hand. But the cherry blossoms were making it impossible for her to even recall that memory. She heard a loud sob. A sudden burst of tears. She looked toward the zoo, and the people around her looked back at her placidly, as if crying under a shade of flowers were entirely normal. Her shoulders shook as she wept loudly. She wasn't sad or scared, but she couldn't stop crying.

She got up once the sun disappeared beyond the horizon.

The afternoons were long, but the nights were short. She packed her suitcase, then called the airline to confirm her ticket. She turned off all the lights and pulled the blankets up to her neck. She tucked her hands under her head, wrist on top of wrist, and closed her eyes. She fell into a deep slumber. The darkness seemed to be telling her that it looked like she was protecting her head, her face.

Part Four

52

Seoul, December

It snowed hard twice during the first week of December, just three days apart. He tried not to look out the window. The snowdrifts and the hazy clouds and the dark green pine trees next door growing tall above the wall around the KAC building—they all seemed to be conspiring to draw him outside. Every morning he crossed the river to get to KAC before anyone else, and after work he picked up a meal in the department store food halls by the office and went straight home to Hyehwa-dong. He no longer dwelled on the cold, having bought himself a few heavy coats. He'd even discovered a walking path only he seemed to know about. It required some practice to convert his days to be simple and unexciting, but it hadn't been as hard as he'd expected. But late at night was when he had to be on guard; it was when he tended to get lost in his thoughts. These thoughts and questions weren't rational; they were more often vague. It was always at night when he felt he was constantly going around and around the same wrong path. So he struck his heels purposefully against the ground when walking.

When it snowed he went outside and cleared the paths, wearing the thick gloves kept by the front door. Diligently, as though the snow could pull him into a deep, inescapable reverie. The snowfall three days ago had broken records. His labor didn't make any difference, no matter how much he swept. The KAC building was well-known for its design, as well as for its mature pine trees and large yard, increasingly rare in the middle of the city. After a few minutes, he would look behind him and discover that newly fallen snow had already undone his work. Panting, he cleared and cleared the snow. He felt he was getting rid of old, useless things, and this unexpectedly hard work made it impossible for him to think about anything. He could do this forever.

Earlier Nanae, who sat at the end of the table diagonally across from him, had messaged him. *Dinner tonight? To celebrate your 6 mo anniversary.* He'd glanced at Nanae instead of responding. She'd raised her hand briefly. He'd nodded, and Nanae had sent him details about when and where to meet. He'd looked up again to send her the okay sign, touching his forefinger to his thumb. Everyone worked at the same long table. There weren't partitions or anything that could stand in as partitions, other than books and files. Park loved to talk about open space in architecture, about how open spaces made open societies and open people. When he had first realized there were no private offices or partitions in the space in which he would be spending most of his day, he was so dismayed that he'd wanted to whirl around and leave. For him this space was much too open. Rather than allowing freedom, it seemed designed to control emotions. Maybe what he needed right now was a utilitarian space like this. And yet he still felt awkward in this space, as if he were sitting in the middle of a plaza, feeling tentative, even when he didn't need to.

The taxi he was in came to a halt in traffic. Gray high-rises and trees with lopped-off branches and signs had been rushing by. Empty sites looked like spooky pits. Some things had disappeared, and he was seeing other things for the first time. Seoul always seemed to yearn for something new. Perhaps all cities shared that quality. Strangely he had this thought only when he was in Seoul, not when he was in other cities. He wasn't sure if six months was a brief or long period of time. If Nanae hadn't mentioned it, he would have forgotten that it had already been six months. Summer and fall had come and gone, and he'd traveled to Shanghai for work, and he'd had the flu and a stomach bug. None of the days had felt long. There had only been a never-ending moment during which he'd waited for the night to pass.

He got out at Fradia near Banpo Bridge, by the Han River. Soft orange lights illuminated the exterior of the restaurant. He sat by the second-floor window and looked at the river rolling outside. The river was a huge, gleaming mirror lit by colorful reflections of lights on the bridge and the restaurant. Long, swift-looking boats docked outside swayed lightly, as if to suggest that they had once shot across the water. Nanae would be here in thirty minutes, after her meeting wrapped up. He ordered a beer and some snacks, keeping his eyes on the river of unfathomable depth. No words were necessary—that seemed to be the meaning conveyed by the deep. He shook off that thought and looked to the south, where the brightly lit Banpo Bridge was reflected in the water. He took a sip of his beer. Then another sip. He felt he could speak. He felt he could answer the question he had asked himself when he'd suddenly decided to come to Seoul, as abruptly as using his paddle to stop a boat short. He could now answer that once she had disappeared from his life, he'd realized that he'd been with her his whole life. Now he would be able to say that to anyone. He finished his beer and ordered another. Nanae walked in, wearing pink headphones resembling huge earmuffs.

53

No matter where

After they toured her studio, she led the curator to the veranda by the front door. The curator was smart and young, with a keen eye valued by the gallery director. In awe the curator looked out the floor-to-ceiling windows at Naesu-dong and N Seoul Tower, standing tall like a steeple. From up high every part of the city looked glittery and special. Especially at dusk, when the cityscape turned a vibrant red, making you long desperately for the deep silence and peace of night.

Flipping through the file the curator had brought, she paused at the work of Jaume Plensa. His work was to open in two days at Art Basel Miami. K Gallery director Hyeon had left yesterday. Dealers and collectors from all over the world would gather at the largest art fair in North America. She had been set to participate in a conversation with up-and-coming artists. She had agreed to it after last year's show. But three days ago she had called Hyeon to cancel. She had told Hyeon that her work wasn't finished, that she was afraid it might take longer than anticipated. She had a slate of shows coming up at the end of the year and couldn't push them back. "But it would be such a good opportunity," Hyeon had said, disappointed. Major galleries like Gagosian and White Cube would be there; with so many collectors going, the fair had become the talk of the art world. Her *Vacuum Packed Boy* would be on view. Displaying it required a large space with high ceilings. A few Korean galleries had pulled out, concerned about last year's stagnating market, so K Gallery and other booths had enlarged their footprints. Hyeon had said they were planning to hang *Vacuum Packed Boy* in the most prominent place. She imagined it hanging like a bat, like a mummy, from the ceiling. Although it was an exclusive fair that was hard to get into, she'd decided against going.

All she'd done since returning from Tokyo was cancel or delay her plans. The only things she opted to do as scheduled were a charity event to help children in developing countries and her new show opening at the end of the year. She had been so beset by anxiety last night in her studio that she'd thought for a moment that she should cancel even those. She wrapped up her appointment with the curator by choosing which work should be featured on the cover of a monthly literary magazine and deciding when to photograph works for the publication accompanying her new show. She asked the curator to get her a picture or a postcard depicting Jaume Plensa's *Anna's White Head*, an enormous human bust created by linked letters of the alphabet. You could see straight through the closely entwined letters that formed the head. It was the kind of work that made you think. It seemed appropriate that this year's fair was being dubbed "the return of times past." What artists battled against wasn't merely fear or pain or desire or guilt; they also struggled against time that couldn't be rewound and their younger selves who had lived through those times. Only when she was engrossed in her work did she realize that her life brimmed with fear and pain and desire and guilt. And that these feelings formed the basis of her life. These were things you realized after repeated, brutal practice. Not wanting to go anywhere was a decision made out of fear. She had lived through so much time and so many events only to return to her studio. Only to return to where she had started. The anxiety that she would never return if she left, no matter where, woke her up in the middle of the night and made her work with focus every day. At night she went up to the frozen roof and sat on the squeaky swing. Maybe she wasn't wasting time if she learned the difference between what was important and what was dangerous.

At the beginning of winter, she had realized she was waiting for something. She felt herself splicing into many versions of herself. They weren't the ones who had been dogged by death or interrogating one another. Instead, there was one wandering through deserted alleys, one cooking, one observing her past, one who just waited. As though hinting at a schism, countless copies of her followed her around, splitting into even more versions. She stayed glued to her worktable, trying to express her emotions through art. Sometimes sorrow rushed in. What came at the end was a deep, familiar exhaustion. Strangely she did not necessarily want to avoid it. She frequently fell asleep in the studio, curled in a wooden chair. She who worked would speak to the one drowning in sorrow. She who cooked would bring home the one wandering through the alleys. She observed time flowing by. At summer disappearing, at winter progressing. One of her remained in Fabric Town, pacing.

After she saw the curator off, she headed to the parking lot just up the hill. The white church building was hunched against the cold. She couldn't hear the singing or praying that was usually audible even through closed doors. Down the gentle slope, lights gathered like shivering people; winding roads linked together in the darkness like veins. She turned her gaze eastward. She looked to the west and then to the south. She would never be able to forget herself entirely, no matter how far she looked, no matter for how brief a moment. Perhaps that would be impossible until she finished her sculpture. She went home and closed the gate behind herself. She opened the front door. Before she went down to her basement studio, she stopped and looked back.

54

Why don't you go to her?

The only drastically different thing about being in Seoul than in Tokyo was that he was alone for long stretches of time. Especially on weekends. At first he would find himself standing lost in the streets, not knowing what to do with himself. He didn't need to go to the doctor with his father or trail his mother when she went for a walk. The workload wasn't as heavy as it had been at Abe Kengo's firm, and there were fewer client drinks and work dinners to attend. He wasn't sure if it was good or bad that he was alone for long periods, but he would have to consider himself content, since he didn't feel sad or lonely. He felt a touch melancholy, though, which was different. He didn't feel that way because Seoul and Tokyo were so different or because of the change in environment. He felt melancholy when he watched himself walking around, tense and stressed, preoccupied by the fact that he wasn't doing what he had to. Even when he wore soft-soled sneakers, he thought his feet clacked on the pavement as if he were wearing soccer cleats. There were other strange things that happened, but he didn't have anyone to tell. Or anyone he wanted to tell. But he did feel calm when he wandered around Hyehwa-dong, where he was staying. Maybe because this neighborhood had a concentration of redbrick buildings—the ARKO Art Center and the Korea Arts & Culture Education Service theater and the Samtoh building.

He looked back at the house he'd just locked behind him. It was also made of red brick. Park had shown him the basement guest quarters when he had been looking for a place to stay in Seoul. It was noisy from the street and the parking lot right in front, but the studio space was perfect for one person. On one wall was a fifty-two-inch LCD TV and an L-shaped bookcase filled with books on architecture and art. There was no kitchen, but in a corner there was a coffee machine and a minifridge and an electric teakettle, along with a black leather sofa that could stand in for a bed. For one person there was nothing more you would need or want. At night chilly air blew down the old-fashioned spiral staircase that went up to the first floor. Park lived on the first floor, and Park's eightysomething mother lived on the second. Some weekend mornings he would go upstairs and join mother and son for a late breakfast. Eating jeon made of mashed lotus, he would be reminded of his own mother's cooking; not many people knew how to make that. Once he hit a year in Seoul, he would need to either move to another place in town or return to Tokyo. Everything felt uncertain, suspended in air. But he felt safe when he was sitting inside the redbrick house.

It was Sunday morning. Wind blew from the southwest through the streets of the still-slumbering city. Black plastic bags, newspapers, flyers, and playbills fluttered at knee height before settling back onto the ground. He couldn't spot the pigeons he always had to take care not to step on or the chickadees that would flit away in a panic. He passed by Hyehwa Station and headed toward Hansung University Station. From exit number six, he walked about a hundred yards to the three-way intersection. He turned right and began climbing the hill. It was about a mile to the Bugak Skyway trailhead. About a forty-minute walk. He walked briskly. He knew it was good to work up a sweat when he felt like this. He tensed his calves and swung his arms. When he stood at the observatory across from the Seongbuk-gu Community Center, he could see all of Dobongsan. This was where the trail began.

He had walked constantly over the summer and fall. He hadn't walked for fun but to overextend his body so he wouldn't be able to think. Sweat trickled down his spine. Parts of his body he had never used and had never thought he would ever use—the muscles leading to his calves and hip joints and femoral region—had awakened slowly and strengthened. There was something spontaneous and vigorous about the sensation of his body coming to life. He had felt his body was under duress, with some parts damaged and other parts trapped. He had felt that way for a long time, and he had worried it would be like that forever. He had been thinking about the heat he'd felt the last time he saw her, when he had spent hours wide-awake beside her as she had slept. He had moved her sweaty hair to the side, then held her fingers, which were curled around a piece of paper. He'd opened her stiff fingers one by one. He'd unfolded the paper, which hadn't had anything written on it yet. He'd placed her hand on her chest. Then he'd rested his palm lightly on the back of her hand, gently pressing down. But then he'd yanked his hand away; something hot and stinky was gushing up from her chest like blood. He had dropped his hand, shaking, scared he would feel death emanating from her.

But death hadn't been what he had felt from her body, her body that had nearly gone over the edge. He hadn't seen her since, but here on this trail, he was just now realizing that it had been the sensation of a terrified body fluttering awake. She had once said to him, "Isn't half of life embarrassment? And the rest of it fear and greed?" She hadn't explained herself, but he'd understood that *the rest* meant *death*. He had to tell her that the truly embarrassing thing wasn't always thinking about death and being pulled toward it, but having never loved anyone.

He passed the trailhead. It was near his brother's apartment. He walked by the restaurant he and his brother had gone to often for breakfast. Nobody knew why his brother had died. Why he had decided to die. His brother had been unable to disappear in the memories of those he had left behind. If his brother had wanted to physically disappear, he'd achieved that perfectly; anyone could do that. He let out a breath as he looked out at Namsan and the tower through the sparse, light brown branches. His thoughts always galloped ahead of his stride. Even when he walked briskly, it was impossible to push away his thoughts, to empty his mind. Cool air brushed against his face. The air changed subtly. His brother was standing beside him. Placing a hand on his shoulder, his brother pointed at N Seoul Tower beside the peak and said, "That's N Seoul Tower." His brother explained that if he went straight at the fork, he would reach a road, which would end at the barbed-wire fence after the three-way intersection, and told him how he should get back down.

He nodded without turning his head. Sullenly, he retorted, "I know my way around. Did you forget we walked here all the time?"

Looking straight ahead, his brother said, "What do you think? Doesn't that look like a beautiful pattern or something?"

He looked down at the early morning cityscape. Morning sun was dyeing the space between the buildings red, and a cumulonimbus resembling a humped camel hung low and faint on the horizon. It might rain in the afternoon. Everything was quiet. A chilly wind shook him awake. Nothing all that loud or showy; it was too early for that. Maybe this view really could be seen as beautiful. Everything his brother was saying was correct, because he was dead. Was his brother calling his name?

"What?" he responded tersely.

"Why don't you go to her?"

"I'm just not sure."

"About what?"

"I'm worried I might take her down a path that's too narrow for us both."

"Go tell her."

"Tell her what?"

"You need to tell her."

"Tell her what?"

"That the future is always closed off—"

"Hyeong, that's a terrible thing to say."

"—when you're dead."

"Yeah."

"When you're dead. You hear me?"

"Okay, all right."

"You'll go?"

"Yeah."

55

Saim began speaking

She avoided meeting up with Saim in the depths of winter. Especially out in the city. It was better to be in one of their studios. They were always worried that Saim might collapse at any moment. That worry grew as the years passed; it was part of the formula of her friendship with Saim. As always Saim walked into the Seoul Museum of Art looking like a huge bundle of fabric, wearing a thick double-breasted coat and a wide orange cashmere scarf. Her warm, practical coat could be folded up and stored in a bag. Saim selected clothes with padding so she would be protected when she fell, and she wore layers upon layers of these garments. *It's so hard and cold*, Saim would say, grinning, her expression suggesting good-humored resignation. Her expression was the kind only Saim could make, one that gently pushed away any sympathy and compassion coming her way.

She began strolling around the first floor of the museum with Saim, who walked quickly through the galleries. It was a Wednesday afternoon. Something smelled ferrous, like a wet pipe. The exhibition, which was divided into three sections and titled *Resistance Against the Sculptural*, questioned the fundamental concepts of sculpture. She walked by cubes made of A4 sheets of paper piled on the floor like bricks, floating up thanks to the breeze from a fan; soap that had been carved into a thornlike point; and a huge inflated transparent plastic envelope. Most of the works explored daily life and personal emotions, avoiding the questions of *What is sculpture?* and *What roles do objets d'art have?* Some works were dramatic; others were lighthearted. At this moment in time, an artist's inspiration and philosophy seemed more relevant than grappling with the essence of sculpture. These works interrogated the boundary between what was sculpture and what was not. Saim had long been interested in the boundary between painting and sculpture, in how the divide between three-dimensionality and two-dimensionality was becoming fuzzier, and how that gave rise to experimentation and exploration. That was also where Saim's practice diverged from her own.

She felt disoriented as she looked around the galleries and saw another artist's work. Everything was so current, so brilliant; some were creepy, and some ignited feelings of terror or anxiety. Some artists and critics would say that this was the role of twenty-first-century art. She had once said that she didn't strive to master new techniques or to transform her work. She might have been reacting to her own lack of understanding of such things, her unconscious fear of them. But when she'd begun working with air, she had felt that terror diminish. Everything was destined to return to the very beginning, and that, she understood, was the essence of art. She had focused on her own interests. The emptiness of the in-between times, representing deep liminality. Absorbed in that, she had despaired that she couldn't go deeper, to where she wanted to be. Now she realized she had been using the past tense when referring to herself. It had been a long time since she'd come to see art. Though it would be more accurate to say that Saim had dragged her here.

"What do you think art tries to evoke?" Saim asked in front of an installation piece of copper pipes and refrigeration equipment.

"Reason?" she suggested.

"Desire?" Saim countered.

"Understanding," she and Saim said at the same time.

"Life," Saim said.

"Death," she said.

Saim turned to her. Her expression was serious, without a hint of a smile or good humor. Saim looked straight at her, then absently touched the pendant around her neck. Saim's voice was almost guttural when she began speaking again. "I'm about to tell you something. I've thought about saying this for a long time, but I didn't want to bring it up. I've always liked you. I still do. But I don't know if I can keep liking you. I don't think you have the right to talk about death. I mean, I don't either. That's basically what I want to say to you. The other day I had a seizure while frying fish. I fell on my kitchen floor. When I came to, I was lying on the tile floor, all alone. I wanted to live. I actually bit down during the episode. So dangerous. I cracked a molar and cut my chin. I was lucky I hadn't spilled oil all over myself. It was fine. I didn't bite down on my tongue or anything. I went right back to the studio. Because I feel like I haven't done enough yet. I haven't met my potential as an artist. Death isn't chasing me down. Instead, I have this huge desire to create. I could die from eating something bad, or I could collapse in the street. I could walk down the street and get hit by falling glass or a drunk driver. None of that's happened yet. It could happen tomorrow or maybe never. But I'm not weighed down by that stuff. I know you think you've experienced too much death. But really think about what you've actually experienced. It's just your father's death. And his death and your grandmother's death aren't related to yours. Of course a family member's suicide affects the people left behind. But people who are still living make this mistake. They scapegoat the dead person and consider that person to be the source of all their problems. Why do you think about death all the time? It's not because of your family history or genetics. All that is an illusion. You're hanging on to the specter of death and you're resigned in everything you do, because you're secretly worried that you might not be a great artist, that you might be nobody special. You've probably never given a thought to what your legs are doing under a table when you're with a group of people. Right? But I have. Once I went to pick my napkin off the floor, and I noticed how your legs were positioned. After that I made sure to take a look whenever possible. Your legs are always turned toward people. You just don't want anyone to know that about you. Think about your life. You know you don't have love; you don't have responsibilities. Have you thought about your father after he passed away? As seriously as you think about yourself? You only think about yourself. You can't claim to be always thinking about death when you're like this. Death should be something that comes to you once in a while, not something you drag around with you all day long. Your father actually called me a few days before he passed away. He asked me to take care of you. That you don't have anyone. I understood what he was telling me, but I wasn't about to change his mind. Because that was his decision, his life. You need to be generous about what you want and really think hard about it. I hope you'll respect your own passions. What was sculpture to you, in the very beginning? What made you want to make art? You have to get a grip on yourself. Properly. You can't come back to life once you're dead. Nobody else can keep you safe."

56

WHETHER HE WAS GLAD SHE WAS ALIVE

When he arrived at the hotel, he got a call from Park saying he would be about thirty minutes late because of traffic on Teheran-ro. He had the invitation. In his coat pocket, actually, folded in half. The corners were already worn. When he walked through the revolving doors, he got a whiff of an air freshener commonly used in hotels. He went to the lounge and ordered coffee. The lounge chairs were made of simple curved lines, without any adornments. They looked sensuous but weren't comfortable to sit in. He felt as though he were sitting in an unpolished concrete chair, though he knew it wasn't the chair's fault. He picked up his coffee cup. People in suits came and went through the sliding wooden doors across from the lounge. That was where today's charity event was to be held, an auction organized by a pharmaceutical company famous for its philosophy of giving back to society in partnership with art directors at major agencies. He'd heard that all proceeds from this event, which drew well-known art collectors and celebrities, would fund childhood vaccines in developing countries.

He'd seen a half dozen copies of the invitation on Park's low table covered with magazines and documents. Huge green ribbons adorned the invitations, and he'd absently untied one as he listened to Park talking about university libraries that could be considered comps. Printed on one side of the invitation were the names of donors to the auction and of the galleries and agencies organizing the event. He hadn't known any of the names. Except for one. He had stared at the name. At her name, which he'd been afraid would remain only in his memories of last winter.

"Oh, are you interested in going?" Park had asked.

"What's the date today?" he had asked. It was still November, a Sunday morning, one in a series of dry days, without a drop of rain or snow.

"Why don't you come along?" Park had suggested, grunting and scratching his exposed ankle.

Paintings and not-too-large sculptures were displayed in the room, which had three large pillars. Round tables with place cards dotted the space, and a large, gleaming ceramic jar held a bouquet of lilies. People with champagne flutes were chatting in small groups. Hardly anyone was seated. They were greeting one another and talking about the art while a man and a woman with boutonnieres looked down at a sheet of paper together; perhaps they were the MCs. The event would begin in ten minutes. He asked for water from the catering staff just inside the entrance and waited, rubbing his chin.

She hadn't been the kind of person who had stood out. She had often worn black, as if not wanting to drawing attention to herself, and she had never worn anything eye-catching, not jewelry nor peep-toe heels. So when he saw her, he hoped it wasn't her. Then he was shocked that it was her, this woman who was in all black but was sparkling, her outfit shimmering as though woven with cubic zirconia.

She was leaning over a table, talking to a seated man. Both her hands were on the table, and the man was looking up at her. He didn't seem to have any plans to stand, nor did he look like he was paying much attention to what she was saying. Still, she kept standing there. As if she wouldn't budge unless she got what she wanted from him. He downed his water and asked for another. People were crowding around the bar, jockeying for drinks. He was close enough to her that she would see him if she looked his way. He couldn't move. He stared at the man, as though the man was who he was interested in. The man was wearing a jacket and a white button-down over jeans, no tie. On his feet were brown Tod's. He was in his late forties and looked stylish and trim, but he would look more at home in a well-tailored suit. He had a sharp, straight nose that made him look haughty. Like a young Eugene O'Neill. The man was sitting at the press table, which was otherwise unoccupied.

He remembered the first time he had met her. She had been talking to a man then, too. He had to admit that that was of no help now. That time she hadn't leaned forward or made exaggerated gestures with one hand. There hadn't been a secretiveness shared by the two; here it was evident. She hadn't paused like now to look around. They spotted a man with a camera approaching the table. He saw something else as well. As she turned to walk off, the man uncrossed his arms to drop his hand; they briefly held hands and let go, as if they'd planned it. He caught that single second of movement.

She glanced at the entrance as she headed to her seat. He stood in place. There was no need to move. He was no longer present.

He heard an announcement that the event would begin. He dragged himself to the exit. He wasn't certain whether her face, glowing with surprising vitality, was what he had been hoping for all along. Whether he was glad she was alive.

57

Ashamed

She could see the waitress and the cook bustling about in the kitchen as she entered the restaurant. The waitress told her that her aunt would return in about an hour. It was five thirty in the evening. Early for dinner but the best time to visit with her aunt. She picked a table from which she could see the entrance and settled in, leaning against the wall. The restaurant wasn't even fifteen yards away from the woodworking shop, but the street looked different from this vantage point. The overpass was taller and curved on the east side, and if it weren't for the people walking on the broken sidewalk pavers among the zelkova trees and past the worn signs on the stores across the way, the area would look like a film set. It felt inorganic, as if everyone had stopped breathing. She must have forgotten about spring. She'd left Tokyo just before the beginning of spring, before she got to see the cherry blossoms in full bloom. That was supposed to have been her last spring on earth. She had assumed she would never again see winter. But she was back here after a long detour. From time to time, she wondered which artist from which country might be living in number 605 in Negishi. She imagined Abe-san's shop packed with people searching for a taste of winter blowfish; Abe-san, who'd taught her to handle fish like they were jewels. When she had said her final goodbyes, Abe-san had said one thing and one thing only, his face inscrutable: "Sayonara!" He had bellowed it, as if asking a customer how he could help; it hadn't sounded like a goodbye. It had sounded like a concise, simple greeting. She had said simply, "Sayonara," to Abe-san, to all the things she'd seen in Tokyo, to almost all the things that had fought her, and left.

The waitress brought out a dish of deodeok jeon and small dishes of mul kimchi and vinegary soy sauce. Food her aunt had made herself. Food that tasted clean and simple, with hardly any seasoning, any taste. The waitress, an ethnic Korean woman from China whose Korean wasn't fluent, said her aunt was at the Gu Office, then smiled, as if to say, *You know what I mean, right?* For about a month, her aunt had been attending a class for expectant grandmothers at the Gu Office. Last spring her cousin had announced her pregnancy, and she was due in about a month. Her cousin would have to return to work after two months of maternity leave, and her aunt would be watching the baby during the day. Her aunt had confessed that she was worried, saying, "It's been such a long time since I took care of a baby." She thought her aunt had seemed almost panicked. It was strange that her aunt would be a grandmother helping to raise a baby. She wanted to know if her aunt would continue running the restaurant next to the woodworking shop, even after becoming a grandmother.

Her father's estate had been meager. She remembered the death cleaner telling her that the more planned the death, the simpler the estate.

On her third or fourth meeting with the death cleaner, he'd received a phone call and picked up his bag, saying he had to go. She'd asked him where he was going. The death cleaner had hesitated, then told her he'd received a call from a funeral director. She'd tagged along without asking. When the train had arrived, he'd turned to look at her. She hadn't said anything. She hadn't wanted to go, not to where a person had died. The funeral director and the deceased's family and the police had been gathered outside a crumbling rental apartment building. Without looking at her, the death cleaner had told her that the body had been there for more than two weeks before being discovered. It had sounded like he was telling her to leave. She'd settled on a bench in front of the building. A room that had contained a dead body for more than two weeks. A room crawling with maggots and pungent with the stench of death. How could anyone possibly walk into a room like that? She'd pushed her anger down. She hadn't known who or what she was angry at or why. She'd watched the death cleaner speak with the police and the funeral director and the family. She could hear bits and pieces of their conversations. The family member, who looked to be in his midthirties, appeared to be the deceased's son. He lived in the building right next door. "I should have . . ." the son kept saying, weeping. "I should have . . ." She couldn't hear what else he'd said. The death cleaner had glanced at her as he'd gone into the building with the others. She'd nodded and gotten up from the bench, then walked away, not looking back. That had been the last time she had seen the death cleaner. For a long time, she thought about the words *I should have*. She found herself back in Seoul as she repeated to herself, "I should have, I should have." Sometimes she wondered whether she'd really met a death cleaner. The way she wondered whether she had really decided to kill herself.

A visitor. That was how she thought of the death cleaner. Someone who had visited her briefly, observed her life, and left.

The woodworking shop was the one thing she and her aunt couldn't agree on. Her aunt wanted to keep the woodworking shop as it was. But she was the one with the authority to decide what to do with it. She gave up her inheritance rights and entrusted her aunt with the problem of what to do with the shop, the inheritance, and the Hongeun-dong house. It felt right that her aunt would legally own the things her father had left behind. It did surprise her that her aunt hadn't refused, not even once. Mr. Song ran the woodworking shop. In the summer her aunt had sold the house and handed her a bankbook in her name. "Why don't you move out of your place?" her aunt had said as she mopped without looking at her, her tone suggesting that she knew all about her relationship with Baek. When she got back from Tokyo, she'd quickly sold three works at auction against her gallery's advice. It hadn't been enough for the deposit on her Naesu-dong studio. She had taken the bankbook. Baek hadn't picked up the phone. She could always leave Naesu-dong and find another place. But if Baek took the deposit, she wouldn't need to. Baek no longer had keys to the house and hadn't even wanted to talk to her on the phone.

She finally managed to get an answer out of Baek when she saw him at the charity event. Nine months. That was how long it had taken to solve that issue. She'd held his hand briefly as she'd brushed past his table. Baek's hand, which she'd probably touched for the final time, hadn't been sensual like it had been when he'd first come to her studio, nor had it been burning with regret. His hand had been incredibly cold. Cold and uncaring and dry. She couldn't help but think it was indicative of Baek's pride, a farewell. A man who turned cold if things got too heated. She'd let go and turned away from him. In the short moment they'd held hands, she'd realized she was thinking about someone else's hands. Baek's bank account number came in via fax. Now that all that was left was sending

Baek money, she felt nothing. Kind of like how she'd felt when she'd first met Baek, after she'd lost all her innocence. It wasn't freeing or joyful, but it was something she absolutely had to do.

She wrapped her hands around the mul kimchi dish. Her aunt spent all day in the restaurant kitchen, not using unnecessary ingredients and cutting out superfluous steps. Her aunt sat in class, learning how to be a grandmother. Her aunt had had to hear the news of her eldest brother's death and her daughter's pregnancy at almost the same time. She didn't know which version was closer to who her aunt really was. But the most significant truth in her aunt's life was that she was now all alone. She thought she knew a few things about her aunt. Maybe her aunt was also feeling relieved, finally freed from the constant worry that her eldest brother would kill himself, a worry that had gradually closed in on the people who'd remained by him. Her aunt had been exceptionally close to him. Perhaps the relief her aunt felt now was less than the weight she herself had shouldered. The siblings had been entwined for so long, just like how, in Tokyo, he had described his relationship with his brother. Death was coldhearted. When someone died, there was no emissary who informed the family that the deceased was now in a peaceful state. Those left behind began to gradually forget the deceased; time flowed on. The pain of being separated, the guilt of being still alive, the longing for the dead—they would all eventually pass. She was watching her aunt reclaim her life.

He had told her that this process took a very long time. Something that couldn't be achieved through training, something that required willpower and willpower alone.

She thought of her aunt and, at the same time, thought about him losing his brother. She wanted to confess to them—or to anyone, really—that she hadn't felt such a great loss when her father had died. She hadn't been able to admit that to anyone. That would mean she had lived her life having never been close to anyone. When she told herself that in the mirror, it had made her feel even more ashamed than when she had been obsessed with dying.

He had told her about his childhood, the way he and his brother had grown up like twins. About the lonely evenings during which they'd relied on each other, waiting for their parents to come home, in a foreign country whose language they couldn't speak, in the undulating loneliness of nighttime. And how it felt to be left behind, on his own. He'd said it had felt like they had been rowing a small two-person boat down a river the best they could, sensing each other's body heat, back to chest, when the person in front, the one who had been steering, had suddenly jumped into the water. And how the wide river and the roiling current had unfurled before his eyes and how he couldn't have gone forward even as he'd tried desperately to steer the boat away from the whirling waters, away from the same fate. About how empty and betrayed he'd felt when the body heat and heartbeat he had been so used to all his life had vanished in the blink of an eye, without any explanation.

He had told her once that her aunt probably felt that way, too.

She could hear his voice in her ears. She put her chopsticks down.

Memories didn't pop up chronologically. Some memories got tangled with others. Some inflated, some flowed backward, and some emerged instantly, out of nowhere, and settled next to her, like this.

She accepted the drink her aunt poured her. "What did you learn today?"

"Infant first aid," her aunt said, and smiled.

"What's next?"
"Tips on preventing infant ADHD."
"That sounds like a lot."
"It is."
"How do you learn all that?"
"There's a six-pound baby doll. Today we learned to hold it over our shoulders so the baby's facing the back. You hold the head and neck securely, then clench one hand like you're holding an egg to tap the baby's back five times."
"When are you supposed to do that?"
"When they can't breathe."
"When they can't breathe?"
"Right."
"What does the doll look like?"
"Soft and round."
"Light, like a baby?"
"Well, no. It gets heavy when you keep picking it up."
"Gomo."
"Yeah?"
"What do I smell like?"
"What are you talking about?"
"I'm just curious."
"Why?"
"In case I smell bad." She downed her glass and ducked her head, sniffing herself. She could still smell the blowfish's blood and bones and guts from that early morning in number 605, that heavy fishy smell that had dogged her all summer long. The woman who had spoken to her at the Mori Art Museum, the woman with the perfectly symmetrical face, had smelled like lavender. The woman who had been a terrible liar. There hadn't been an artist photo in the exhibition catalogue or pamphlet. She had realized that as

she'd paged through the catalogue on the plane, on her way back to Seoul.

She was certain he would remember her like that. As the woman who'd smelled of fish and wanted to kill herself. That he would remember her that way made her feel worse than when she had thought solely about dying.

58

IF THERE'S A SINGULAR TRUTH IN THIS WORLD

He drank everything he was offered at dinner with his colleagues. Eventually he found himself standing alone in front of Seoul Station. Colorful lights illuminated the facade of the Seoul Square building. Pop artist Julian Opie's *Crowd* was on view. The huge LED canvas was close to a hundred yards long and a hundred yards wide. A man in a sky blue shirt, a woman in a red skirt, and people wearing black clothing walked across it continuously, their arms swinging lightly. Their strides were lively and huge, too wide for anyone to catch up to them. Seven giants walked on the huge screen along the exterior of the building. On the ground, tipsy travelers grasped their coats by the lapels against the cold and rushed to catch the last buses. Nobody was standing still. He wanted to walk along the river. Maybe he'd feel better if he could be out in the cold air until he froze. He could get to the Han River if he went from Seoul Station to Namyeong-dong and then past Yongsan. It was already seven degrees below freezing. Or he could cross the street, grab a taxi, and be home in fifteen minutes.

He thought he spotted a familiar face in the crowd. A man had walked past him; he turned to look again. Familiar glasses and a dark purple birthmark beneath, an old leather bag. It had to be that man. The death cleaner. He almost shouted, *Hey!* People who looked like that man were interspersed throughout the crowd, walking toward him in endless rows. One person came up to him and asked to borrow some money for a taxi. He grabbed all the cash he had and handed it over. Another came up and confided that he had forgotten how to get home. Yet another suggested they head off together. Some other person was crying, saying they'd found their child dead when they'd woken up. They all looked like people he knew. But he didn't actually know any of them. The streets grew cacophonous with honking horns, arguments over taxis, music trickling out of bars. He was watching life brush past before his eyes.

His fingers touched something flat in his coat pocket. A business card or a note or the invitation with her name printed on it. After she left Tokyo, he had met up with the death cleaner a few times. Each time they had drunk themselves into stupor. Once the death cleaner had told him to take out the contents of his pocket. It had sounded like the setup of some joke. Without much hesitation, he'd begun emptying his pockets onto the table. His wristwatch, coins, his cellphone, a piece of folded paper. The one thing that had weighed on him was that piece of paper—he had drawn a box, and he'd sketched her face inside it. She had wanted nothing from him, demanded nothing from him. The death cleaner had laughed and said these could end up being his personal effects. "If there's a singular truth in this world, it's that everyone dies," the man had said, giggling. "So"—here the death cleaner had paused—"you have to be careful. Do you know how dangerous every single day is?" The death cleaner had begun getting ready to head out but passed out right on the table. By the time the death cleaner came to, it had been his turn to be drunk out of his mind.

He didn't cross the street or hail a taxi. He walked toward Yongsan. Black plastic bags and flyers tangled underfoot. He turned and looked back. The giant crowd was still glowing vividly, like an enamel painting, lit against the night sky. He had never actually seen her work in person. He could have looked for her work at the charity event. He picked up the pace. If he had, he might not have seen her with the man who resembled Eugene O'Neill. What he had witnessed could have been just one out of ten interactions. One that was easy to misunderstand, one that didn't tell the whole story. Or what he had seen could have been the single instance that encapsulated the full story. No matter how he thought about it, the conclusion seemed to be decidedly unfavorable and tyrannical to him. He remembered how a strange force had pushed him to come to Seoul. The force of a herd of galloping horses. Whatever it was, he'd hoped he would be swept away by it.

This city wasn't safe. He shouldn't be here if he could stand it only by roaming around like this every night. All he could do to shake off these thoughts was to walk, and although he was freezing a mere half-mile into his journey, he couldn't stop. The Han River, far away, was coming closer to him. The blistering cold flash-froze his self-pity and sorrow. He walked on, shivering. He felt like he was hugging a block of ice. He was almost at the river. He might be able to accomplish one thing he'd wanted to do today. He let out a whine: "Why did you tell me to go, Hyeong?"

59

Where light had momentarily left

The cold snap waned. The days grew warmer, and the vicious wind that had howled for three long days calmed. But the weather forecast indicated that this was a mere reprieve. It was Sunday afternoon. A quiet time, without phone calls or faxes, when all noise vanished from the side streets. The clear western light lengthened across the studio walls and the floor. She hadn't turned on the lights, but it was still bright in the studio. Despite being in a half-basement, the window was big, sixty-four by fifty-one inches, and light came in over the low brick wall and across the open space beside it until right before sunset. It was a gem of a space. On clear afternoons like these, she felt embraced by the flow of air that was normally steely and made her feel defeated. She probably spent more time sitting in the corner, gazing into the darkness, or leaning on her worktable until her legs ached than she did actually working. Many things bobbed up, then disappeared, and many things stood before her before vanishing, one by one, as the sun began to rise. She learned about certain things this way. Like the interplay of light and shadow and the qualities of light.

She always thought of this place as not having a ceiling. If she imagined that, she could stand living anywhere, no matter how tight, how dark, how closed off the space. Like the man she'd heard about who had voluntarily crawled into a cardboard box and lived his entire life inside.

There were four kinds of light. Direct light, which illuminated what was straight ahead; a glow; a partial shade; and a complete lack of light. Now the studio was cast in a partial shade, as though sunlight were filtering through lace curtains. Soon it would end up entirely in the shade. Depending on the season and how the sun moved, there were sunny spots and shaded areas, shadows cast by the objects filling her studio. In brief moments the four types of light even came together. When that happened, you couldn't discern between light and darkness. You would not feel it without observing it for a long period of time. In the winter darkness pounced quickly, suddenly, the way misfortune swept in. As soon as she sensed the shadows growing faint, darkness was already rushing in. She glanced around the studio.

A plastic chair, broken planters, an easel, various tools, paint, frames, dried flower bundles, pieces of wood, a small fridge, cardboard boxes, pencils, brushes, shelves, a saw, books, a warm air circulator, tissues, hangers, a padded jacket, an apron, plastic gloves, rubber gloves, sheets of drawing paper hanging from the ceiling, a phone, a trash can, giraffe and crocodile sculptures, a lump of sandstone that looked like a cactus, a snake plant, a trowel, a broom, a dustpan, scissors, a tin basin, a spray bottle, Styrofoam, artificial flowers, a towel, skeins of colorful yarn, a clock, mismatched shoes and sneakers, balls, curtains, a drill, chains, a desk and a chair, a globe, plastic cups and plates, piles of paper, a full-length mirror, a worktable.

She approached her worktable. She turned on the overhead lamp. Its large conical light illuminated the table. She had done a preparatory sketch but had stared at it for over half a year, thinking it impossible to finish. What would be the result of agonizing over one single thing over a long period of time? She wanted to give shape to the conclusion of that process. She began clearing the things strewn about on the floor. She must have grazed her palm against the saw blade, though she hadn't felt any pain. She moved a volleyball, and blood smeared on the white ball. She dropped the ball and looked at her hands. A few drops of blood fell onto the floor. "I didn't do it on purpose," she murmured.

Her father had done this very thing every time the urge to kill himself had tugged at him. She didn't know if that was the right thing to do, if it really worked. He would cut himself a little and bleed, just a little. It had happened only in the deepest silence, in the deepest darkness. Cutting the back of a hand or an arm seemed similar to cutting paper or cloth, and she had been the one—not her aunt, who'd always wanted to be near her eldest brother—who'd watched him through a gap in the door without screaming or making any noise. She'd stayed behind him like that until he'd regained his equilibrium, until he drew in a big breath and let it out, until he fell asleep and then began weeping, calling for his mother as a nine-year-old boy. His scarred arms had looked like tree stumps that had been sanded smooth. Only now did she wonder if those scars had been evidence of his struggles to live, not his attempts to die. "I didn't do it on purpose," she said again, addressing her father.

Someone turned her around by the shoulders. A precipice-like darkness was gazing quietly at her from across the way. She didn't budge. She didn't sit down. She couldn't tell how much time passed. She felt hungry; she couldn't remember if she'd eaten. She couldn't recall if she'd come to the studio yesterday or today. One thing was clear. She was once again facing the darkness, the terror that entrapped her, body and soul.

She thought about the life her grandmother had led.

She thought about the life her father had led, the life she had been leading.

She thought about the life she would lead in the future.

It wasn't always true that heavy things plummeted faster than light things.

She thought about a life that wasn't artificial in any way.

She reached out and touched the darkness. With a gentle touch, a caressing touch. Death was something she would experience at some point. Something she wouldn't experience while alive, something that wouldn't allow her to do anything as long as it was embedded in her like this, like shrapnel. She stroked that precipice-like darkness again and again.

As she mixed water with plaster, she remembered a hand touching her. Her face and chest. Her shoulders and back. It hadn't fumbled. It hadn't been hesitant. It had gently caressed her. It had reassured and calmed her. A hand seemingly made of regret and hot breath.

As she looked down at where darkness had been, where light had momentarily left, she was remembering clearly that it had been his touch she'd felt on the night she'd collapsed.

60

Every story about life was about beginnings, not failure

He was running a high fever, but the doctor told him he was otherwise fine. He had taken three days off from work. He had planned to take the high-speed train to the southern coast. But he had been burning up when he'd awoken in the morning; it had felt impossible to get out of bed, and everything ached, as if he were being torn apart. He drifted off to sleep. Park's housekeeper had brought down some juk for him. He heard his phone ringing. He managed to wake from time to time to take his medicine. It was dark every time he opened his eyes. Though cozy, the studio wasn't well-lit or heated. He cranked up the heating pad and pulled several blankets over himself. Despite the fever and his breath feeling hot, he shivered in the brutal cold. It had been a long time since he'd slept so soundly without the aid of sleeping pills. He knew he would feel better on the other side. But he didn't want to wake up. He wanted to stay in this pit of deep, endless sleep.

He was standing on the furthest edge of time as it circled. He was on the outside, watching. So many people appeared. Most were angry, interrogating him. He must have done something terribly wrong. His brother was sitting quietly on a windowsill. The cold March wind rustled his brother's wavy dark brown hair and the jersey curtains behind him. What he had actually witnessed had been his brother's face after everything had played out, doused in dark red blood and who knows what else from the force of his head striking the ground, but now he was seeing it from the beginning. His brother pulled his legs up, hugged his knees, and looked his way, as if wanting to say something, then leaned to the left, shifting his weight. That small movement pulled his 165-pound brother down five stories in less than a second. *None of it matters*, the law of gravity seemed to be jeering. When he had seen his brother on the ground, limbs twisted at odd angles, he had been numb, as if all his sorrow had evaporated in an instant. He hadn't even cried. But in his dreams, he felt a searing pain as he screamed and wailed for someone to save his brother. It was always the same. In his dreams he could fully give himself over to unbearable sorrow. He gently moved his brother's head. It wasn't his brother's face; it was hers. She was sleeping deeply. She was breathing evenly, not having a bad dream. Everything stank of fish. He cleaned the entire apartment with care. He scraped the blowfish meat and guts, skin, and blood from the table into a huge plastic bag, and he even threw away the knife and the chopping board. He opened the living room windows to air out the place. The thing he had been afraid of had happened, and it was a little less terrible than he had feared. It felt like fate that he was there. He had become someone who knew something that nobody else would ever know, someone who had seen something nobody else would ever see. All that was left was for her to wake up. In the meantime he wanted to clean everything, as if nothing had happened. He wanted to tell her that every story about life was about beginnings, not failure. The apartment felt warmer, heating up little by little from her breath, from the sound of her breathing. He closed the windows and looked to the southeast, at the steel structure glowing white under the moonlight like animal bones. The construction site of the new tower was close by, its boundaries faint. In the fall she could stand here and gaze at the new tower, containing his long-ago passions and vigor. If she was still living there. He recalled how he had worked on designing a tower that could create harmony between humans and the environment. Back when he had wanted it to appear like a huge artificial tree that could be one with the night. Back when he could draw, focusing only on things like that. He had forgotten that he'd once lived a life balancing function with beauty. He was proud that he could look back on something like that. He could tell her not to leave. He could tell her about the things they shared. Like how they both drew lines and left those lines on paper, how each line contained individuality and vitality. He stretched his arms above his head. He swiveled them in a circle and extended them in front of him. He wanted to touch the farthest point he could reach. "What are you doing?" he heard her say. He startled awake.

He drank a glass of water. It tasted fishy. He leaned back against a cushion. What did it mean that the most painful experience in his life became bigger and more vivid in his dreams? Was pain pulling him toward a deformed life through his subconscious? He drank another glass of water and flipped open his cellphone.

His mother answered and said his father was asleep. She said it was too windy for her walk today. At the beginning of the summer, his father had started accompanying his mother on her walks. Right before he'd left Tokyo, Dr. Suzuki had suggested to his father, who had wanted to check himself into the hospital for sleep therapy, to try walking on a dirt path. The smell created by microorganisms in the dirt was supposed to have a calming effect. He had been surprised that his father had taken up the suggestion, but perhaps it had been his ailing father's latest attempt to try to survive his illness. Every weekend before his departure, he had driven his parents to a nearby park or forest. His parents had drifted along the dirt paths without speaking. Hoping to lessen their anxiety and depression like the other people walking there. If his father hadn't begun taking those walks, he wouldn't have been able to come to Seoul. Sometimes he wished he hadn't confided in Dr. Suzuki. For a while after arriving in Seoul, he couldn't shake the thought that he had left home not on his own accord but because his father had sent him away from their deadened house. Regardless, he was glad that his father was continuing to walk, whether in the botanical garden or the indoor walking path at the hospital.

"Did you see . . . ?" his mother asked.

"Who?"

"Who you wanted to see."

He didn't answer. His mother might not be asking what he thought she was asking. She might be referring to his brother.

"You're living so close to there," his mother whispered, as if sharing a secret.

He told her he'd had a high fever but was feeling better.

She didn't reply.

He left the door open a crack. Cold air whooshed in from the parking lot. It smelled like sweat. *Who you wanted to see.* It had never occurred to him that someone else could be with her. It was impossible, unbearable to imagine. He stuffed his feet into his sneakers and stumbled out. It was dark outside. He couldn't tell if it was late at night or early in the morning. He couldn't tell if his sweat was cooling or his fever was breaking. The cold wind was awakening his sensations. He remembered how he had been standing like this, his legs braced, on that afternoon last January as he'd waited for her at Sensō-ji. Waiting for her. The woman who'd looked like she had been sinking into dark waters. Back when he had only vaguely begun to feel the force of the emotions that would drag him forward.

Emotions that weren't love or despair or hope but something that had felt like his own from the very beginning.

He coughed. He wanted to go to a forest. He wanted to walk barefoot.

61

Two People

The year-end party was hosted at the KAC office. She'd been invited to several of Park's dinner parties there. She would often slip out early. Because of that, she didn't really know much about Park. All she knew was that he ran a large architectural firm and was a renowned art collector. His gatherings were populated by the young artists he supported, curators, doctors, corporate executives, chief prosecutors and judges, architects, photographers, actors, and film directors. She would see many of the same people at exhibitions or auctions. Park seemed to derive huge satisfaction from introducing people to one another. He had big, thick fingers and the largest, longest ears of anyone she'd ever met. Though he had a dynamic and outgoing personality, he would be lonelier than anyone else when the parties ended.

She'd accepted the invitation because she'd wanted to see a picture hanging in the KAC office. Works from Park's personal collection adorned every level of the five-story building.

It was the second week of December. About fifteen people sat around the dining table. She glanced at the bottles of wine, the small porcelain dishes of black olives, the handblown Riedel wineglasses. She knew some of those in attendance, and there were also sculptors and painters she didn't know; they were so young, as though still in college. The female anchor for the nine o'clock news and a few others were helping Park cook. She could smell seafood and garlic from the kitchen. Every time someone entered the room, people got up and shook hands, greeting one another. She stayed sitting in her seat, her head bowed. She wanted to get up when the others did, stick her hand out when the others did, but she couldn't get herself to do it, and she was sure people would misread her intentions. Whenever she left her studio, it felt impossible to fall into a different set of rhythms. There were times like these when she couldn't manage to get up along with the rest of the group or even head to the bathroom when she had to pee. When she was working, she felt like a new and incomplete creation, one that could be improved on before becoming a fully formed person. She could only think about one thing at a time. She couldn't tell if she was happy or sad or hot or cold. And then, whenever she thought, *How long can I live like this?*, she would feel a shattering ache.

She'd come straight from the studio. She'd taken her apron off, washed her hands, and run a comb through her hair before shrugging on her coat. She hadn't thought to bring cake or wine like the others had. Her mind was clearly still at the studio. She murmured to herself that she shouldn't make people feel uncomfortable, but there seemed nothing she could do at this lively party that was going so well, that was brimming with goodwill. She kept thinking about the figure she'd left on her worktable. What was it like to believe in herself, to do something that had meaning? She was still taken aback anytime someone called her an artist. She didn't think she would be worrying if she were an artist who deserved to be recognized as such. For quite some time, whenever she was making art, she felt that she had skipped over a section of music but had just kept playing. She felt this way even though she was often invited to exhibit, even though her works were selling. Maybe she had to start from the beginning. Maybe she had to go back to drawing lines on paper again. An important question resulted in an important decision—she had to question what it meant for an artist to believe in herself.

The man sitting beside her poured her some wine. Before her was a dish of baked shrimp and potatoes in a pale green sauce the color of pureed cauliflower. The clinking of forks and knives on square white plates sounded like a signal of sorts. They were all on a small stage, everyone acting in roles perfect for them. She got up, saying she needed to wash her hands, even though nobody asked.

Each level was monitored by CCTV. As she walked down the stairs, she heard a mechanical whirring above her head. She glanced out the windows. Snow was piled on both sides of the path leading to the entrance. The traces of someone's careful sweeping had frozen solid. She'd heard that offices were on the first to the fourth floors. She tiptoed past the door to the offices. Closed doors always gave her the feeling that they would be impossible to open.

The undated picture looked different every single time. That was why she'd wanted to see it again. It was a charcoal drawing of two people by the late artist Park Kosuk, who had usually painted landscapes. It was evident that he had drawn many lines before erasing them. What remained were the outlines of two people. One large, the other a little smaller. On the left was the larger figure, whose arm was raised above their head, and the smaller one had a hand on the larger figure's shoulder. Their genders were unclear; the artist must have wanted to simplify sexual characteristics with his thick charcoal lines. Mother and son, brothers, brother and sister, sisters. They could be any of those combinations and more. There was no background, no shadow. She stared at the two nude figures made of a thin line, a thicker line, and a very thick line. Their strong calves and their short arms and their necks, all similar to one another. They didn't look glum or happy or as though they were anticipating or waiting for something. They stood there, just *Two People*, with the most minimal of physical contact. They were less two people than two trees. They looked like two people emerging from a single, shared root.

62

The scene

Once he had met his brother's girlfriend. She had been shy and soft-spoken and given the impression of being slightly off-kilter, her neck disproportionately long. She'd worked in the administrative offices of the university that had employed his brother. He had been surprised that his brother had been with someone so different from his purported ideal. It wasn't long after his brother had begun working at the university, not long after moving to Seoul. His brother had liked short, opinionated girls in flats who didn't hide what they wanted. Girls who were direct about being happy or sad. But this inscrutable girlfriend had deep-set black eyes that seemed liable to sink into their own world at any time, at the flick of a switch. She hadn't laughed easily and she had been quiet, which was the opposite of what his brother had liked. Most notable had been her limp. He had been rude and forced alcohol on her, but that might not have been his gravest mistake; he should have realized that his brother hadn't been the right person for her.

At dinner the girlfriend had gotten drunk off five small cups of jeongjong. She'd become more talkative, and he'd kept goading her. His brother had sat there quietly, his annoyance simmering near the surface. Malice had rocketed in him like drunkenness. He had wanted to make fun of her in front of his brother. He had wanted his brother to learn things he hadn't known about his own girlfriend. It was unbelievable even now how cruel he had been, but at the time he hadn't been in a state to make rational decisions. He hadn't been able to believe a girl was why he had been disappointed in his brother for the first time in his life. She had gotten drunker and talked more and more. He'd egged her on every time she spoke. Then he'd asked her if she loved his brother.

"Stop it," his brother had snapped, his jaw clenching.

The girlfriend had now realized she was drunk and begun drinking water instead of talking.

He had been the only one in the mood for jokes. He'd said, "Our mother once said that love is like a weather forecast."

"How so?" she'd asked, her voice cracking.

"You only know what it is by checking it constantly, and you have to be prepared for a storm."

Nobody had laughed.

The girlfriend had shifted in her seat, uncomfortable. She'd downed another cup of jeongjong before suddenly looking straight at him. "You asked about my parents earlier. Why don't I tell you? My father drives a taxi, and my mother's a homemaker. My mother doesn't do any housework because she listens to music all day long. You want to hear about the music she listens to? You want to know what love is?" The girl had enunciated clearly and slowly so he wouldn't miss a word: "The love I witnessed was a food tray. You must know what a food tray is?"

His brother had shot her a look and told her to stop.

"No." She'd met his brother's gaze coldly. "My mother didn't clean or cook or do the dishes. Ever since I was really young, we ate all our meals on food trays. It was my father's idea. Maybe it's crazy, but I don't remember ever eating on a plate or out of a normal dish. Even though it was just the three of us. My mother would manage to make a week's worth of food and put them into plastic containers, and my father and I would scoop them out onto our trays. Then we washed our own trays and went into our own rooms. That was how my father loved my mother. Me? I'm someone who ate off a food tray for twenty years until I moved out. I can still hear the aluminum spoon and chopsticks scraping that aluminum tray. It sounded like a knife fight."

With that the girlfriend had sprung up, grabbed her things, and left.

When he'd recovered from his shock, he'd found himself alone in the private room of the restaurant. That had been their first and only encounter. At some point she'd left for somewhere in southern India. He didn't know if she'd played a part in his brother's decision to die. His brother hadn't left behind a letter or any other clue. He thought about that girlfriend who had gone to India. The girl he'd met only once but had strangely made him question love, even now. Nobody knew what his brother had done or felt in the year after his girlfriend had left him. His brother hadn't said anything, not even to him, and it had seemed like his brother had been keeping the world, not just him, at arm's length. His brother had quit his job, returned to Tokyo, and decided he needed treatment, and everyone had wanted to believe his brother could still recover. It remained hard to talk about what his brother had been like at that time. He thought it would have been better for his brother to hide inside a cardboard box, the way he had when they were young. At least then he could have followed his brother in.

Sinae called. He was in a taxi going home. They had just managed to pass city hall when traffic became clogged in front of

Koreana Hotel. The driver informed him there was a festival at Gwanghwamun Square. He got out of the taxi, his phone glued to his ear. It was early evening. He could tell from her voice that this would be a long conversation. The call would last while he went from Gwanghwamun to Anguk Station and then along the Changgyeonggung walls until he got to Daehak-ro.

He hadn't spoken to Sinae in a long time. For a while he had thought of Sinae day and night. He knew she must have thought about him, too, but he didn't think she felt the same as he did. At least not anymore. He asked how she was doing. He crossed the street toward the Kyobo Building. The square was crowded. Sinae asked him where he was. He told her Gwanghwamun, and Sinae told him she hadn't been there in such a long time. And that she was at Mun's bar.

He looked up, dazed. A huge snowboard jump chute that appeared to be taller than ninety feet and longer than a hundred yards had been erected in the middle of the plaza. Pedestrians lined Sejong-ro all the way to Gwanghwamun, and pojang macha were selling ramen and fish cakes along the street. Dance music blared. He cried, "Hello? Hello?" Sinae told him to stop yelling, that she could hear him well. He explained that a snowboarder was hurtling down at high speed. Then the snowboarder launched himself into the air. He described the scene, telling her everything he was witnessing. Sinae listened quietly. At the peak of the jump, the snowboarder attempted a flip, holding his board with one hand, and stuck the landing. *Sinae might be able to hear the roar of the crowd*, he thought.

"It couldn't have been more than a hundredth of a second," Sinae said.

"What couldn't have been more than a hundredth of a second?"

"How long the snowboarder was in the air."

Deflated, he murmured that Seoul had changed a lot.

"How so?" Sinae asked.

"I don't know, in good ways and bad."

"That's the way cities are," Sinae said.

He felt alienated by the athletes and the cheering crowd. He didn't know how else to explain this artificial scene. He was thinking about snow-covered Baegaksan hidden behind the jump chute. The mountain was more beautiful and constant than the humans racing down the slope. "I'm sorry," he said to the love of his irresponsible self, the woman who had been safe and familiar, who hadn't needed him to be responsible, who had let him experience love that had not been passionate or desirous or wondrous or filled with jealousy or melancholy or painful or hellish, love that had been neither faithful nor aggressive nor holy nor ethical nor fateful. He apologized for his future love, of a different someone, someone more similar to him.

"For what?" she asked.

"For not being able to love you enough."

"And?"

"And for not being able to love you even that much anymore."

63

HER FATHER'S NOTEBOOK

Her phone rang. She normally kept the ringer on low, making it hard to hear during the day. She glanced at the clock, then picked up the phone. It was Saim, sounding tired, asking her what she was doing. She told her friend she was parboiling spinach and was about to take sliced ham and cheese out of the fridge to make herself a sandwich. Saim listened quietly. She told Saim that a baguette didn't seem like bread but like a tool, like a pencil or a spoon. Though she was the one who'd called, Saim stayed silent. She turned off the stove. Spinach bobbed up to the surface, having turned muddy green; she had missed her chance to drain it. "Turn on the news," Saim said, and hung up. She wondered if she should drain the spinach first but went ahead and turned the TV on.

Hyangiram Hermitage was on fire.

She looked up at the clock again. They were reporting that Hyangiram had begun burning just past midnight. Now it was two in the morning. Hyangiram looked like a pile of ash, the flames not fully under control because of strong winds. This temple was on a steep spot halfway up Geumosan, about five hundred feet above sea level. Yullim-ri, Dolsan-eup, Yeosu-si, Jeollanam-do. Ever since she'd learned about how her grandmother had really died, she had never forgotten this address. Her father had been born not far from Hyangiram, in Yullim-ri, where his stepmother, now more than ninety years old, lived alone in the empty house. She had scattered his ashes behind Daeungjeon Hall at Hyangiram, where you could look down upon the South Sea. She had scattered his ashes there, thinking, *Now the earth and the wind and the trees will have Abeoji.* She'd gone there with Saim last fall. Now the temple was burning, tearing through the night of December twentieth. The darkness vomited flames. Her grandmother had sent her father to that temple to be a boy monk. It must have been around the time she had been planning her death. Her grandmother's death hadn't been spontaneous or accidental. When her grandfather had returned home from the seas, her grandmother's plan had been put into motion as though following fate. Her father had decided to leave the temple on his own. Her aunt had told her that, from time to time, her father would wonder what would have happened if he'd just stayed at the temple.

She'd watched all night long when Sungnyemun had burned down. This was different. This was more personal—nobody else could understand Hyangiram's importance to her—and it felt like a memory was being sealed shut. An untrammeled sorrow overwhelmed her. She was more used to pushing sorrow down than feeling it. She looked around. She was alone, and she was at home, and she could not hear a thing. She wanted to choose not to suppress her sadness but to feel it, at least tonight. That was possible only if nobody was watching. Saim must not have been tired when she'd called; her voice must have been muted with sympathy for her. The TV screen was dark red. Firefighters sprayed water on Gwaneumjeon and Samseonggak, and huge pillars of white smoke billowed above the flames. It was unclear when the fire would be extinguished. Everything could turn into ash in a second, or the wind might settle and tame the fire. She was witnessing time that was uncertain, suspended. Yet another condition of life, like death or extreme hunger in the middle of the night. Fitful regret and emotions that couldn't exactly be called sorrow or frustration stabbed her in the heart.

It had taken her some time after her father's death to open his notebook, even though she had thumbed through it now and again when he had been alive. If she opened the notebook, she knew she would end up reading the whole thing. *If I live.* That was the title of his journal, a title that couldn't have been written by an idealist or a mystic. His entries were disappointingly pedestrian and ordinary. They were failures that could not possibly move or influence anyone. He had wanted such mundane and insignificant things. He had wanted to use his saw in a more laid-back manner, and to know all the names of the trees in the forests, and to develop a more discerning eye. Merely what any average carpenter might say once in his life. Dreams that could have been achieved—that would have been achieved—if he'd just lived longer. At least that was what she thought. They were nothing special or extraordinary. But his writings brought up an important question. And now this question was different from what she'd asked herself last spring in number 605 in Negishi.

That night in March, as she'd pried her sweaty hair off her cheek, he had told her, "You're an artist. You can give voice to what's overpowering you, what's weighing you down." He would have been trying to console her, but to her, his had voice sounded strained, like he had desperately been squeezing out all his optimism. He'd turned toward the window and told her about towers. He'd said that wind was the most formidable foe for high-rises and towers. He'd said designing a tower was like designing wind, not a structure. He'd said his dream was to build something that didn't move in the face of wind and earthquakes. That none of that was possible without understanding and controlling for wind. She'd slipped back into sleep while he had been talking, but she remembered what he'd said. Should she be glad that this was all she remembered? She wanted to avoid questions about her true nature, even now.

If I live.

That question had stayed in her head. It was the first time that a single question—an incomplete phrase, really—had expanded like this in her mind, continuously and multilaterally.

After destroying Daeungjeon, Jonggak, and Jongmusil, the fire was finally extinguished. It was nearly four in the morning. She remembered Daeungjeon, now a pile of ash, the roof tiles on which people had carefully inscribed their wishes, the thousand lotus lanterns that had been lit four hours before the fire. She remembered the first sunrise of the new year, which could only be described as majestic, which she'd seen as a child accompanying her father. And Odongdo and the path that led from the island to Jasan Park and the breakwater and the observation deck and Dolsan Park and the harbor filled with container ships. Yeosu, where her father had been born and where he'd struggled his entire life to stay away from, though he'd yearned to return.

I should have . . . She thought about the dozens of ways she wanted to end that sentence.

She would go back to Yullim-ri.

64

SAFE NEST

The E University Library project that had begun in the late fall was now facing challenges. The school had requested an interior renovation of the building, leaving the exterior intact, and that the construction be completed before the start of the new semester. The university had decided to renovate not because the building was old and needed repairs, but because of the library's inefficient flow. The library wasn't being used effectively, with a lot of wasted space. It was also dark and claustrophobic, as if nobody had considered the importance of light. The first and second floors were wide-open, without any partitions or dividers, and held rows of large tables. At each site visit, he and the design team or the interior team tried to figure out what needed to be removed, what was lacking.

On weekend afternoons he headed back to the library. A renovation was impossible without a deep understanding of the space. Students seemed to struggle to focus in the vast room. The small act of someone putting their bag down or flipping a page was louder than it should be, the sound waves hitting the farthest ends of the huge room. The library had been built more than a hundred years earlier. It might have been an innovative and unconventional design at the time, but what was needed now was more partitioned spaces to project stability. Every space, every object, had to be an appropriate size. What E University Library needed most was division. It was worth thinking about Herman Hertzberger's realization about a Montessori school. The Dutch architect, upon observing children playing in a nursery school, discovered that they didn't need a single large play area but several smaller play areas. Children preferred to play in small groups and in more confined spaces, perhaps feeling more secure in those homey environments. When the play area was large, the children distracted one another and didn't seem to be as cohesive.

With other members of his team, he toyed with creating four large rooms centered around the pillars and then dividing each of those large rooms in half. He drew a floor plan, deciding on plaster and wood for the entrances and walls, and glass for the smaller rooms so students could see inside. Someone pointed out that this design would result in a bloated budget and a delayed timeline. He tried to reduce those possibilities in the floor plan and come up with something practical that would also resolve any issues of two-dimensional flatness in the design. After all, architecture was an amalgamation of small, organic decisions, and the architect's role was to reduce useless spaces and expand practical ones. As more challenges cropped up, the team couldn't agree on a way forward. He kept thinking about the library. As if thinking about it would help him survive the long winter.

Daily meetings continued. At every chance he had, he visited other university libraries. In his head he had a blueprint perfect for a library, but that was merely a plan made of lines, an unfinished blueprint that failed to garner support. As the project became more delayed, he felt more and more relaxed about it, though a part of him did feel responsible. Having drawn a blueprint, an architect had to have the ability to turn it into reality. The library closed at eleven on weeknights. By mid-December he was staying so late at the library that he didn't have time to go back to the office before heading home. Sometimes he sat by a window and watched the sun set. He believed that the most beautiful time in a city was when the sun went down behind high-rises. The fading light that briefly outlined the buildings highlighted the majesty of the night, and it made him feel a vague anticipation about what had not yet transpired.

Three subway stops separated E University and Hyehwa-dong. He walked home, weaving through the city. As the days edged closer to Christmas, the streets grew more crowded. He didn't know what was drawing people out. He wanted to go home. Every architectural project pursued the idea of a safe nest. A safe nest made of red brick had been his ideal when he'd first entered the world of architecture. He wondered where he could find a comfortable, amiable place that would be a safe nest for him at night in this city. The kind of place everyone needed but not everyone had. He wondered about the possibilities and the impossibilities of having a place like that.

65

A WOMAN TURNED INTO ANOTHER WOMAN

The woman was one person and, at the same time, two.
She was looking down at the figure on her worktable. She had been working on this piece for two months. She had sketched it out much earlier, drawing a naked woman seen from behind. A woman lying on her side, knees partly folded. She had sketched it on brown newsprint at her worktable, not even on a proper sheet of paper. The newsprint had been a piece of trash, something that might have been wrapped around a cup or a hunk of bread. Her pencil had moved automatically. She hadn't decided to draw a nude woman from behind; her hand had followed a line, and soon a woman had appeared. Her spine had centered the drawing, and her ribs had been prominent, her bottom and shoulders narrow. It wasn't clear who the woman was. She hadn't referenced an image of a model. You couldn't tell if the woman was sleeping, curled up, lying there unconscious, or dead. Or whether she was crying, her back turned; or laughing quietly to herself; or clamping a hand over her mouth in terror. There were so many things you would not know from behind. It was a drawing of just a few simple lines, but it automatically evoked the various emotions a

woman could reveal while lying down. She had tacked the drawing up on the wall. She'd looked at it from time to time. Eventually she had forgotten about it. Until Saim had asked her about it.

It had been a quiet night. It was early fall but cold enough to turn on the electric heater. She had told Saim about her grandmother. She had never told Saim the story, and uttering the word *Halmeoni* had made her feel deeply uncomfortable. She had been nervous, as if she had been getting ready to talk about herself in front of an audience. She'd told Saim how she had gone to Tokyo to learn to handle blowfish. It was the kind of story you couldn't tell in daylight. Saim had been staying with her for three days. Whenever Saim felt blocked, she stayed away from her own studio. Saim had stayed awake for three days and three nights straight. She couldn't tell what Saim had been thinking. Her friend's eyes had been bloodshot. When morning came, Saim would drink a huge glass of milk. Saim had curled up in a long chair at the opposite end of the studio and pulled a blanket over herself. That was when she'd began to talk. She'd hoped Saim would fall asleep and not remember a thing once she woke up. Saim hadn't asked any questions or even moved, so she had been able to tell the story in full, this thing she hadn't been able to share. Saim's leg had even twitched, the way her legs did in sleep. She had relaxed. She'd wanted to say more about her grandmother, about blowfish, about what it had felt like when her body had begun absorbing the toxin. And how she had no longer been able to look straight up at her grandmother, sitting on top of the tree.

"Why? In case she disappeared?" Saim had murmured, as if speaking in her sleep.

"No." She had shaken her head.

At the time the only thing she could have done was turn away from her grandmother. Evening had been rushing in, and though there were small branches everywhere, when she'd looked up, her grandmother's face had been bathed in a strange light. It had been shining, rippling. She'd had to look away. She'd dropped her head. She had confided to Saim that it was like averting your eyes from the sun.

Saim had been quiet.

She had told Saim that she still remembered how her grandmother's face had glowed between the glossy black branches, and what had been behind it. She'd wanted to say that her grandmother's face had looked like a stain, the faint mark of a regret-filled world.

Her grandmother had failed to stop her. That wasn't the role of nature. Nature didn't speak. Death was nature. Her grandmother was nature. Bells had rung from the church, announcing evening prayers. She'd held her face in her hands so she wouldn't be swept away by an even stronger urge.

Near the beginning of fall, Saim had pointed at the drawing hanging on the wall. "Looks like you'll need a model for that piece," Saim had said offhandedly, as if that were the reason why she hadn't started work on the nude.

Saim had layered two blankets on the floor and taken off her clothes. She had watched Saim. The body before her had resembled Saim's but had an anonymous, singular quality to it that made it not exactly Saim's. Maybe because of the silence or the heaviness in the air, it had felt as though her studio had been submerged three thousand feet below a deep ocean. She had bent and straightened her fingers. She'd begun to move slowly. She wouldn't take photographs.

She'd begun casting. She'd applied lotion all over Saim and then Vaseline on her friend's pubic hair, the hair on her head, and eyebrows. She had posed Saim's arms and legs. Saim would have to lie in this position for at least two hours. She had dipped plaster strips into the mixture. But then she'd suddenly sat down in a chair. Saim's knobby spine had looked like a line of pebbles.

"It's freezing. Aren't you going to start?" Saim had asked.

She had pasted the plaster strips on Saim's body one by one. To eliminate air bubbles, she'd rubbed the cloth against Saim. No matter what she did, she couldn't stop the chill from clinging to Saim's skin. The exposed parts of Saim's body had taken on the color of unripe plums, purple and blue. The cloth had adhered snugly to her skin.

She'd brushed Saim's body with the side of her hand. "You don't know what I was going to do with the blowfish," she had said. "I got so close. I got something from it that you can't get without touching it, without eating it. I've never experienced that before. I realized that death wasn't the thing dragging me down, but the desire to live. That night the blowfish bones spoke to me. They said that sometimes life is something you have to work at with your whole being. The blowfish eyes spoke to me, too. They said that you have to look at and understand certain things before what matters to you ends up disappearing. And then I opened my eyes. What I saw when I opened my eyes—that's what I'm waiting for right now."

Saim had appeared asleep, frozen.

She had felt she was in a dream. As though she had put the plaster strips on her own body, as though she were stroking her own body with her own hand. It was damp and hot and soft and felt like her skin would be torn away.

The final step had been the face. She had rolled two small pieces of paper into tubes and stuck them in Saim's nostrils so she could breathe. Saim had not smiled or frowned.

"Are you okay?" she had asked.

"How could I be?" Saim had replied cynically.

She had laughed. "Anything else you want to say?" Saim wouldn't be able to speak until the plaster set.

"Just put the plaster directly on my face," Saim had said.

She'd hesitated. Saim had known that putting plaster directly on her face would bring out minute details. She had begun feeling anxious, a different emotion than excitement or expectation about her work. She'd breathed out evenly so she wouldn't rush. And then she'd said to Saim, "Hang on just a little longer." She'd begun to put plaster directly on her friend's face. It couldn't be too thick; the face might turn out drooping from the weight of the plaster. Thoughts had bubbled in her head; some had remained, while others had evaporated. More had remained than not. She could not tell if she wanted to laugh or cry, if she was hot or cold, if she was sweaty or shivering.

Two hours had passed. Saim had emerged from the plaster mold. She had applied the plaster and worked as quickly as she could, but it was impossible to speed up time. The mold looked like white armor, like hard, cast-off skin. It would need to dry in this state for about a day. As moisture evaporated, the plaster would harden. Wrapped in a blanket, Saim had looked down at the two plaster pieces she had emerged from. She had known that, at least in that moment, she couldn't say anything to Saim.

Saim had started walking up the stairs before pausing. "You should know something," Saim had said to her. "You're always thinking about yourself."

Two months had passed as she'd worked on the plaster pieces.

She had lined the pieces with release agent and molded a mound of plaster. That would become the second woman, the old woman within, who would be revealed when the sculpture deflated. With a chisel she'd carved wrinkles and other details of an aging body. She hadn't known much about an old woman's body; she hadn't ever looked at an old woman closely. The photos and images she'd referenced were gone from her mind. But her hand holding the chisel hadn't hesitated. Or paused. As though she were sculpting a body she knew well. Her hand had moved; she'd followed her hand. She'd thought about her grandmother's body, which she'd never seen. She'd imagined what her grandmother's body must have looked like. That seemed to be the only thing she could do at that moment. But when she'd finally put the chisel down, she couldn't say if what was before her was her body or her grandmother's or someone else's. It was one person's body and, at the same time, that of so many people she'd seen. She'd thought about the person who'd said to her, "Maybe what you're holding on to isn't your grandmother but all the people you read about and met and imagined, who each ended their lives in different ways."

Now she connected a hose to the air compressor below the short wooden pedestal. She set the timer to seven minutes and plugged it in. She pressed the button for the vacuum pump. Then she waited.

She stood behind the figure, putting herself back to when she'd sketched it. The woman breathed. Seven minutes. It didn't feel too long or too short. You would need at least that amount of time to see someone for the first time. The woman appeared to be deflating from somewhere invisible. She aged slowly. From a young woman to an old woman, from an old woman to an even older woman. Or from a girl to a woman, from a woman to an old woman. The woman slowly recovered. The distinctions among the different ages weren't altogether clear. A woman turned into another woman, which was like a woman becoming the same woman. It wasn't clear if she was the same woman or a different one. Seven minutes. The time it took for the woman to shrink and then recover. During those seven minutes, one viewer might see a young woman, and yet another might see an old woman. The only difference was time.

Some might see just one moment in time, skipping the entire process. That might be all they saw.

For a long time, she hadn't wanted to believe that her grandmother's love for her grandfather had been unrequited. Just as she hadn't wanted to acknowledge that fact as the reason for her grandmother's death. Without complaining her grandmother had sorted the fish her husband had caught, then gutted, salted, and stored them with hands that had wanted to make clothes. Then she had made blowfish soup. Only her grandmother had known that she had made it with karasu, its toxic parts intact. She had made the soup with utmost care. The last meal of her life. In everyone else's bowls she'd ladled out seaweed soup. The family had gathered around the table for her birthday. Her grandmother had downed the bowl in front of her grandfather. Her father would remember how blood gushed from her nose, like it had been fake. How his mother, gripping the edge of the table, had shuddered like fish that had been tossed on a boat, and keeled over.

She had already left home when it had occurred to her that her father's life had been shaped by memories like that. Her father himself had claimed that he hadn't remembered a thing. In his sleep, he'd insisted that that hadn't been his mother.

Her grandfather had continued to live in the house he'd shared with his wife. The house her grandmother had died in, the house with the yard and the well that her step-grandmother had jumped into but had managed to survive. What she remembered of her grandfather was a man who crouched by the well, smoking cigarettes, looking small in spite of the stories about how tall he had been. Nobody told her how her grandfather had died. Her father had never gone back to his hometown. At least not with her. Only her now-ninety-year-old step-grandmother, who combed her long hair every morning and wound it into a traditional bun, remained in that house, with that well. She had even heard that her step-grandmother's hair was starting to turn black again. That was the last thing she'd heard about her step-grandmother.

She didn't know much about her grandmother. The only thing she knew was this: Her grandmother had expressed herself in the end, before dying.

The figure lay on the floor of her studio, completed.

She watched the woman gradually shrink, then recover. It looked like deterioration. It looked like change. It looked like the moment of revival. She inhaled deeply. The woman was breathing. Her own breathing reverberated in the room. She could speak with silence. A title came to mind. *Breath of Being*.

The title of a work that could only be described as the crystallization of who she was.

66

The sound of a cherrywood cane rapping on the ground

The narrow spiral staircase glowed silver-blue in the morning light. The stairs, simple and utilitarian, resembled an airplane's stairs. Thanks to that staircase, the studio gave the impression of being organically connected to other spaces. Every morning, when he woke up, he found himself looking not at the clock but at the staircase. As though just looking at it would propel him outside to a vast, open world. The sturdy, gleaming staircase sometimes looked like a narrow passageway leading even deeper underground, but he tried not to let his mind go there. He gauged the brightness of light coming from the first floor. It was still a hazy gray all around him. The air smelled familiar, and he realized it was time to get up and begin his day. Perhaps it would be like any other day, or maybe it would be entirely different. He always felt a slight anxiety and a sense of anticipation in the mornings. Unlike every other day, he turned to his left to get out of bed. Bones cracked along his spine. He drank a cold glass of milk and washed up. He put on a dark gray suit and a black lined jacket, picked up his bag, and went out. The parking lot was empty. He looked back toward the entrance, which was obscured. Maybe he would feel like this when he returned from work and opened this door again.

After they presented their plans for the new H motor company office building, he and the rest of the design team went to lunch at a nearby restaurant. Long benches made of something hard, maybe birch, lined the entrance. He rapped the bench on his way in, and it let out a heavy but clear sound. It must have been birch. The only tree that sank in water. This Italian restaurant was known for its décor, the interior walls and tables covered with wallpaper by the English artist Richard Wright. Nanae and the others debated whether it was really art or just wallpaper and furniture. He ordered a simple pasta with garlic and olive oil. He knew a little about this British artist. Once his brother had said about Wright's work that it didn't look like art but like a Rorschach blot. The images covering the walls and tables would fade away at some point. But Nanae explained that Wright wasn't afraid of that; apparently he didn't want his art to last forever because he wanted to show that art, like life, was ephemeral. Others argued that this went against the fundamental point of art, insisting that its eternal nature was what was most important about it. As they argued, he thought about the presentation they'd just given. He'd wanted to explain and demonstrate something else, but he hadn't had the chance. People tended to turn their attention to the back of the building once the building was completed. He unfolded a napkin and began to doodle. Who was the architect who said an architect could make a work of art but an artist couldn't make a work of architecture? During a lull in the conversation, Nanae asked him what he was drawing. He said it was nothing and folded the napkin, sliding it into his pocket. Their food arrived. He picked up his fork and looked around at the walls as he ate, at the geometric pattern in primary colors. He wanted to ruminate on why he had turned to his left as he got out of bed this morning.

It looked like it would start snowing at any second. Posters and plastic bags and pigeon feathers skittered around. He walked past Hyehwa Station, holding a plastic bag of water and other beverages. He passed Samtoh and headed toward ARKO Art Center. The brick buildings glowed red as the sun set, light and shadow wrapping around them in an intricate pattern. Many things were visible in that pattern. He could see a shadow of some kind, too. He hoped the shadow was permanent, one that appeared in all situations of life. He thought back to his blueprint. It was a small space, but he'd poured everything into it, a home he would build in the future. A safe space wasn't one without earthquakes but where someone he longed for lived. He placed two bricks on that site. Now he could begin to build. A two-dimensional plane morphing into a three-dimensional building. He stood rooted there for a long time, facing ARKO Art Center. He wouldn't understand the essence of brick by looking at it. He wanted to understand brick. He wanted to hear what the brick was saying.

He turned in early. He thought he heard something booming in his sleep. Maybe it was an earthquake. But then he remembered he was in Seoul, not Tokyo. When he heard it again, he realized it was the sound of a hard birch—no, cherrywood—cane rapping on the ground, the exact thing he had been searching for ever since he'd heard the story. He didn't want to open his eyes. He didn't want to wake up from this dream. He hadn't had this dream in a long time. He wanted to go where the cherrywood cane was headed. He would go fearlessly where the cane led him, its *boom boom boom* reverberating through the ground.

67

THAT MIGHT BE A LITTLE BRIGHTER THAN THE PRESENT

She got out of the taxi. A banner announcing the opening caught her eye. It was four in the afternoon. Still an hour to go before the opening. She didn't go into the gallery. She remained standing on the sidewalk. A westerly wind blew over her; it was cold but not enough to make her want to go inside. She'd been running a slight fever since last night. The wind tousled her hair. Her ears, always hidden under her hair, felt exposed. She thought about the shapes of her ears. They might be paler than her face, her earlobes pointy or maybe even hanging lower than the average person's. She'd never examined her ears in a mirror. Why was she thinking about her ears on the day of her opening? She wanted to laugh, but it got stuck in her throat. She felt tense. Though that was better than being nervous. Cars moved sluggishly toward Samcheong-dong and the Blue House. Maybe it was because of the old stone wall around Gyeongbokgung Palace, but everything on this street seemed to flow at a snail's pace. The sun illuminated the stone wall at an angle, bathing the protruding stones in light. All light and shadow seemed condensed in the stones. The wall stretched on until it gently curved to an end. The world seemed not round but wavy to her. Pale pink clouds feathered the sky. The five-story pagoda of Gyeongbokgung Palace was standing to the right of the wall, while on the left was a haughty bramblebush, tall and bony, revealing its pointy spikes. She turned around. A tiny sign for Jatnamu-gil indicated the street that led up to the gallery, Space2. She wished that the street sign were bigger and in a more noticeable color. The winter sun would slowly but then quickly set, and then you wouldn't be able to spot the sign even if you were looking for it. And the backlight. She thought about that light. She had never been afraid of sunset or of darkness rushing in. She headed down Jatnamu-gil. Her new shoes pinched her feet.

Breath of Being was installed in the middle of the gallery.

Spotlights illuminated the work. People surrounded it. Everyone stood in place, waiting for one woman lying on the floor to grow old, breathe, gobble up time, then vomit it up, sleep and dream, then turn back into a young woman. She stood in the crowd. There seemed to be more members of the public than invited guests. She couldn't hear anyone talking or whispering. In this all-white gallery, only two things existed: a thick layer of silence and a woman lying on the floor. She listened intently to that silence. Other people's breathing layered over hers, faint and peaceful, like evening light and shadow. She felt tension draining out of her body. She balled her fists tighter by her side, wanting to maintain her balance. She wanted to feel this shining silence for a little longer.

The woman looked to be at peace, not as though she had collapsed or died. The silicone gently puffed her up and shrank her down at regular intervals, returning her to her original state. She appeared to be lying in the most appropriate place, the coziest, most ideal spot. Visitors were streaming up to the second floor as well. She thought she saw Saim. She thought she saw others—her grandmother, her father—heading upstairs, hunched over. She turned to head out, but the curator took her by the arm, smiling, and said it was almost time. She told the curator she had something to do, that she was waiting for someone. The curator nodded and turned toward the people coming through the entrance. For a moment she stood against a wall. If she stood there in her white shirt a little longer, she might be able to get sucked into the white wall. Although a new work was before her, and visitors were walking around, and she could hear talking and breathing and footsteps and the door opening and cameras clicking. She was separated from all that. She thought about all the things residing in this gap, about all she had lived through to be back here. She was the same person, but she also wasn't. Many things had changed, but some things would be even more different in the future. Maybe her transformation wasn't only because she had the strength to overcome her experiences and her pain. Maybe the times she'd struggled to stay afloat had turned her into someone else. Now she would be happy even if she came to understand only one single thing, even if that was all. Now death was something that would be determined by her. And the same was true of life. It was hers and only hers.

She pushed open the glass doors and left.

Outside, the parking lot led to a small street that linked up to the big road. Old hanok were on either side of the street. There was a vintage store and a small florist. She'd forgotten her coat in the gallery. Wind burrowed into the nape of her neck. Shivering, she gathered her arms at her chest. She turned left, down the street. The sun hadn't set yet; shadows lengthened along the ground. She could still see the sign at the bottom of the street that said Jatnamu-gil.

He was standing at the end of the street.

She stopped. He did, too. As if they had promised to stand still for a moment. They weren't yet in speaking distance. But they were close enough that, even backlit, they recognized each other. She dropped her arms. He was holding a bouquet. Blindingly white, the stems too long to hold comfortably in one hand. Calla lilies. She remembered the name of those flowers. Holding calla lilies and wearing a suit, he looked like a young man about to enter a wedding hall. He looked like a bride. He looked like a frightened boy adept at hiding, or a very sad boy. He was the person she had been waiting for, the person she had been afraid she would never see again. She wanted to ask him if he was giving her these flowers' beauty or their tears. She wanted to remember this moment forever. She did not walk toward him. He, too, stood there without moving, staring at her. She couldn't tell if he was smiling or frowning. She would recall this moment again a long time later, though she did not yet know that. She thought about what she had wanted, what she had been waiting for. A future that might be a little brighter than the present. The remaining days of her life, which might become more passionate and more desperate. No one else was out. Only he and she were standing there, their shadows elongated, unable to figure out how to approach each other. She wasn't ashamed anymore. She wanted to start over. She stuck her head forward, slicing through the air, the way she had when she'd come into the world many years ago. Hoping it would look like a greeting, like she was dancing. Leaning forward, she walked toward him.

Author's Note

Sadness and beauty and fear and death—I write about what overwhelms me. About what possesses me, about what doesn't let me go. I began writing this book last fall and only finished it in the spring. It has never taken me this long to write a novel. I wasn't reluctant or hesitant or seeking something else. I would think about the act of writing, the meaning of it. The blank screen of my laptop, my small room, and me gripping the edges of my desk—we spent a long time propped up by one another.

I don't want to be closer or kinder to someone else, to anything else. I don't want to be more upbeat or happier. Because now that writing has become a calling for me, I don't think I should wish for anything more than that. What I want is a simple life, one in which I can think and read and write. While writing this book, I realized what a lofty dream that is. I realized how impossible it is to achieve that dream, how much solitude it requires. There is no need for a long explanation. I want to see how much more I can think, how much more I can read, and how much more I can struggle to write.

I have been waiting to write this novel from the moment I put pen to paper. I didn't want to tell this story too soon, this story I knew I could write just once.

My deepest thanks and friendship to S and K, who were the first to read this manuscript. And to sculptor ByungHo Lee, who graciously let me use his works in the book; to my partner, who has long been and continues to be quietly supportive; to my readers, who are always interested in what I am doing. I will make the biggest promise possible here, in these pages: that for as long as I write, I will remain earnest and true to the very end.

SEPTEMBER 2010
KYUNG-RAN JO

Photo courtesy Kyung-Ran Jo

ABOUT THE AUTHOR

Kyung-Ran Jo made her literary debut in 1996 when her short story "The French Optical shop" won the Dong-a Ilbo New Writer's Contest. She is the author of eight short story collections and five novels. Her novel *Tongue* was published in English by Bloomsbury in 2009. She is also the recipient of Today's Young Artist Award, the Dong-In Literary Award, and the Yi Sang Literary Award, among others.

About the Translator

Chi-Young Kim is a literary translator based in Los Angeles. A recipient of the Man Asian Literary Prize for her work on *Please Look After Mom* by Kyung-sook Shin, she has translated more than twenty books. Her translation of Cheon Myeong-kwan's *Whale* was shortlisted for the 2023 International Booker Prize.